BREATHS OF DESIRE

A SEYTON MATES NOVEL

OCTAVIA KORE

Editor: LY Publishing

Cover Artist: Jesh Nimz

DISCLAIMER

This is a work of fiction. Names, characters, places, and incidents either are the product of the author's imagination or are used fictitiously. This work of fiction is intended for adult audiences only and may be triggering for some. Strong language is used. Proceed at your own discretion. This book is an MMF romance novel. It contains adult situations, graphic sex, sexual assault, and violence

**A forbidden attraction, an unexpected love, and a madman
willing to risk it all to keep humanity pure.**

Life in space didn't prepare Samantha for all the things she would
find after her mysterious crash landing on planet X9: forests filled
with massive red trees, plants that drip a liquid eerily similar to
blood, and let's not forget the demonic aliens who snatch her up
the very first time she leaves the wreckage of her pod. The
intrepid scientist is kidnapped by one alien and gifted to another
the moment she enters the village. She never expected to become
a captive bride, and she certainly never expected to find herself
falling for two males who can't seem to stand each other.

Hunters don't get happily ever afters. Zuran is no stranger to loss,
but when Samantha is ripped away from him and given to Olan,
he feels the last threads of his sanity begin to fray. The breeding
heat is taking over, pulling him into the inky darkness of madness
he will never come back from. The spark of hope Samantha
ignites in him is the only thing keeping him sane, but will he have
the strength to pull himself out of the shadow of his past?

As a breeder, Olan has been preparing for his mating since the
moment he stepped out of the agmari bloom, but the fiery human
female his chieftess presents to him is not the bride he envisioned.
She's stubborn, mouthy, refuses to do as she is asked, and even
has the gall to escape his hut while he sleeps. Samantha may have
been bound to him by the All Mother, but Olan soon realizes his
bride is going to make him earn the right to call her his.

*Thank you to our alpha readers **Caitlin**, **Amanda (Seebs)**, **Jessica**, **Julie**, **Diamond**, and **Dona**. You guys are awesome!*

*To **Samantha**, we hope you enjoy the story!*

*And to our significant others **Michael** and **Aaron**, thank you for supporting our dreams, giving us inspiration, and loving us no matter how weird we are. We love you*

A NOTE TO OUR READERS:

This book contains dark themes that may not be suitable for all readers. As survivors of rape and sexual assault, Hayley and Amanda understand that these subjects are difficult to read about. Breaths of Desire contains an instance of sexual assault against the heroine, as well as the rape (not described/non-specific) of a secondary character. For those who may be sensitive to the subject matter, or who simply do not wish to read it, please avoid the ending of chapter 27 and the beginning of chapter 28.

PREFACE

For those of you familiar with our Venium Mates and Dauur Mates series, the Seyton Mates series is set within the same world, after the world has ended.

In this time, the war with the Grutex is over, and the Venium have "saved" humanity. While some may find this to be a spoiler, if you read the original short story for Ecstasy from the Deep, then you know these events had already happened by the end of the book and the world had started to die.

This book is a standalone, and you do not need to read any of the Venium Mates or Dauur Mates novels to understand and enjoy it. One thing to keep in mind is that this is not our heroine's first contact with aliens. Humans have lived with the Venium for some time now and have had both positive and negative experiences.

We will attempt to keep most spoilers from the other series at a minimum.

PROLOGUE

SAMANTHA

*S*amantha's fingers flew across the smooth surface of the keyscreen as she searched through the data displayed on the main computer. The information that scrolled by was nowhere near her area of expertise, and she was pretty certain she'd be in hot water if she were found sticking her nose where it didn't belong.

After the conversation she had overheard, she was willing to take a risk.

Marsel had something planned, something that was going to affect everyone on board, and she was going to find out what that man was up to. *Where are you...?* A projection of the solar system they were currently traveling through opened up when she clicked on the navigation menu. The star maps the Venium had provided them with were incredibly detailed, going so far as to catalog exactly what minerals and natural resources were present on each planet. The information had been critical to their mission many times over the last few years.

Samantha spun the projection, looking through the trail of planetary bodies they had previously orbited. None of these had come close to being inhabitable. Not by a long shot. In fact, the only one that had been promising was X9. Her brows knit together when she reached the planet's projected icon. Whereas the other bodies they had visited were lit, X9 was shaded. When Samantha attempted to select the icon, large red letters flashed in front of her.

"Banned?" she murmured, trying to swipe the glaring message away. Since when were entire planets banned?

She stilled when voices sounded outside, but they faded just as quickly as they had come. The breath she had been holding released slowly. There was no way she could afford to get caught. She needed to get the information and get the hell out of there. Tempted as she was to linger and explore more in depth, Samantha turned her attention back to the data logs. If they were within range of a planet, there would be evidence. The crew would be checking the atmospheric conditions, compatibility with human life, and whether or not the body was currently inhabited by another sentient race of beings.

Samantha huffed in frustration. "What the hell?" Lip caught between her teeth, she considered her options. The smartest thing she could do would be to just forget what she had heard, head back to her quarters, and lose herself in a book.

Nope. Not gonna happen.

Okay, that left only one other option. She had never been much for hacking or really anything overly techy, so she couldn't even rely on those skills to aid her in this situation. Her rank was the only tool at her disposal. With that, she shouldn't have any problem gaining access to any of the encrypted files, but identifying herself meant that anyone with more pull than her would be able to see that she was the one accessing the information.

Making sure everyone on board is safe is worth the risk, she reminded herself.

With her pulse pounding out a beat in her ears, Samantha entered her clearance code. The icon that had been shaded a moment before lit up, opening a new log. Samantha's shoulders sagged when she read the one data entry available to her. *Planet Inhabited.*

"Seriously?" she grumbled, her head falling back against the chair. "Who do they have inputting information these days?" If she had done this little when she had been starting out, she definitely would not have made it as far as she had. Even as a child, she had taken better notes than the person in charge of logging X9's information. Minutes ticked by as she sifted through other files, praying against the odds that she would find something misplaced.

As she logged out of the server, the whoosh of the automatic doors behind her made her blood run cold.

Fuck.

With as much courage as she could muster, Samantha spun the chair around. A very unhappy Marsel stood in the open doorway. His arms were crossed over his broad chest, and his blue eyes were narrowed on her.

Yup. She swallowed around the lump of fear in her throat. *I'm in deep shit.*

"Hey, Marsel. Did you need something?" she put on what she hoped was her most convincing *haven't been in here spying on you* smile and laced her fingers together in her lap.

His eyes darted over to the screen before returning to her face. "What have you been up to in here?"

"The usual," she shrugged, rising from the chair. "Getting all the information I need for the field op, making sure we're ready to go when we stop."

She nearly cringed when his brows arched and the small smirk that tugged at his lips made her stomach drop. *Stupid lie.* Samantha had never in her life been considered for one of the field teams. Fieldwork, much like hacking, was not something she excelled in, and Marsel knew that very well.

"I see."

She watched as he stepped toward her, his hands moving down to rest on his hips. There must have been some sort of trigger placed on the file that had alerted him to her snooping. How else would he have known to come?

He still hadn't answered her question. "Did you need something, Marsel?"

"It's time for the briefing." He jerked his head toward the door in a silent command for her to follow.

Samantha swallowed her fear and stepped through the doors after him. If they didn't already suspect she had been up to something, the way she trembled was bound to give her away. She had attended briefings before, but all of those times she had been at the front of the room giving the team details about the planet they were about to be sent down to explore. Her area of expertise was not in retrieving the samples, but studying them after they were brought back to her lab by the field team.

It looked like she was going to be getting up close and personal with X9. With the possibility of what they were planning, she didn't have the luxury of staying on the ship this time while others did the legwork.

The viewing room was filled to the brim when they arrived. Essential personnel pressed in on one another, trying to wiggle their way into a spot where they could hear what was being said inside. Even though this room was the same as it had been when she had transferred to this ship years ago, Samantha was always awed by the advanced level of technology they had been gifted. The metal walls were materials naturally found on Earth, but the electronics built into them and scattered around the ship in general were completely alien. Gifts from the Venium.

In the center of the room was a large holograph of X9. The planet spun slowly on its axis as clouds drifted, concealing sections of the surface. The water was the prettiest shade of pink Samantha had ever seen. Whether this was due to some sort of plant life, like seaweed or algae, or something far more alien, she wasn't sure yet.

There had been instances on old Earth when salt lakes would be pink due to the green alga *Dunaliella salina* and the archaea *Halobacterium cutirubrum*, but this didn't seem like that; only testing the water would tell. Whatever it was, it only added to the beauty, and *everything* about the planet so far was beautiful.

After years of being stuck on this tin can of a spaceship, Samantha looked at this planet and saw freedom. A vacation destination like nothing she had ever seen in her life. She hadn't ever lived on Earth, but she had watched every video she could get her hands on. What would it be like to touch honest to gods real soil? What would it be like to walk on the planet that her ancestors had been birthed on?

She sighed as she squeezed through the crowd behind Marsel.

That was a dream for another day.

As Marsel ascended the steps to the small platform, the crowd began to murmur louder, some calling out to him for answers. He raised his hands, smiling as he hushed them.

"My friends, as most of you may know, we are currently orbiting what seems to be a habitable planet." Excited murmurs rippled through those collected. "After spending our lives in space, on this ship or the station orbiting Earth, finding a planet with the potential for colonization has been one of our main goals. We want nothing more than to be able to raise our families on solid ground, to establish roots. This planet," he motioned to the hologram of

9

X9, "could be our chance at that dream. We have a chance to start over without the threat of the Venium taking our women away from us. They will be here, with us, where they belong. No longer will we have to watch them being sold like cattle."

A few shouts of agreement went up through the crowd as people applauded politely. Marsel was a natural charmer, a confident speaker. People paid attention to him, they believed the lies he spoke, and it made Samantha's skin crawl to see the adoration in their eyes. Human women had never been sold to the Venium, but these people seemed to have forgotten their own history. He had also conveniently left out that this planet was off limits, banned by someone with far more power than they had.

"Is it safe for us?" Lucy, one of the women near the front of the crowd, asked.

"We will be sending a team down to run all of the necessary tests."

Samantha couldn't let her friends die because Marsel seemed to have a death wish. "What about the fact that X9 comes up as banned?" she asked.

"Kitten," Marsel tsked as if she were in trouble just for asking, but he smiled indulgently as if he found her silly. "We were able to open the files. The planet looks perfect for us. That's most likely the reason why they marked it as 'banned.' They don't want us to have our own home, to be self-sufficient again. The Venium want us to keep relying on them for everything."

Samantha was the head of the Scientific Studies Department and, as far as she knew, had one of the highest clearances on the ship. She needed it to gather all the information to properly run the lab on board. How in the universe had he managed to acquire information that she wasn't even privy to, especially when it concerned something as important as an inhabitable planet?

He could be lying. Maybe X9 wasn't as perfect as he was leading them to believe. She didn't necessarily hate Marsel, but she didn't trust him. Samantha wanted to believe he wouldn't lie to the people he was meant to lead, wouldn't take them somewhere that could mean the destruction of their species, but something in the back of her mind warned her that he might be desperate enough to do so.

One thing she knew for sure was that he was hiding something.

"Will you do it, kitten?" Samantha was pulled out of her thoughts by his question.

"Do what?" she asked, frowning up at him.

Marsel turned to face her slowly, his lips twitching as if he was fighting to keep up his smile. He was calculating, formulating his thoughts before he spoke again. It was a look she recognized from all the times he had whispered sweet lies in her ears before he'd gotten into her pants.

"Will you lead the field mission? Perhaps getting out into some real fresh air will be good for you. You're always cooped up in that lab of yours."

She blinked rapidly, trying to decide if he was joking, but something in his eyes told her he was dead serious. "Well, I—"

"The data indicates X9 is inhabited by a sentient species. Who better to send in to forge an alliance than our top scientist?" He reached a hand out toward her, running the backs of his fingers down the side of her face.

She knew he wasn't lying about that. In fact, it had been the only thing in the logs that she had been able to find. Was it possible that she was just overthinking this? Maybe her opinion of him was just clouded by their shared history. Maybe she wasn't giving him a fair chance.

"Go into the field solo?"

Marsel laughed, tucking a strand of purple hair behind her ear. "Of course not, kitten. You would have a team behind you, guards to protect you in the event that the locals turn hostile. It's entirely possible that the Venium are lying, that they want us to avoid this place. Perhaps the data is out of date and there are no longer native inhabitants at all." He shrugged. "I would hate to think you wasted all that time researching just to miss the opportunity to get in the field time you seemed so eager for."

Damn. She was caught. "Right," she stammered. "I just… This field mission felt important to me and I'd—I'd love to be included."

"Who knows, kitten? Maybe this will be the vacation you didn't know you needed." Marsel winked at her before turning back to the rest of the crew.

She spent the next few hours discussing the mission—going over the training she had received years ago before she transferred here, selecting her team—and she was exhausted. All she wanted to do was to fall face first into her bed and sleep until it was time to launch, but her growling stomach had her turning around and heading for the dining facility. The last time she had eaten was at breakfast, and with the ongoing rationing, it had only been a half meal at that.

"Sam!" Lucy called out as she ran up from behind. She was wearing the standard black uniform, and her dirty blonde hair was pulled back into a tight bun; the tiny baby hairs gelled flat to prevent flyways. "Are you okay? You seemed a little spacy at the meeting."

Lucy was a childhood acquaintance, but they hadn't really become close until they were transferred to the *S.S. Constellation* in preparation to explore the universe. The woman was a badass as far as Samantha was concerned. She had fought her way to Head of Security, proving herself to be a force no one wanted to go up against. On the side, Lucy wrote some of the steamiest romance novels Samantha had ever read.

"Yeah, I'm fine. Just a little surprised that we found something so perfect this soon."

"I mean, there was—"

"That was different." Samantha hurried. "It didn't turn out the way it should have, but this one... Hopefully this is the one."

"Right." Her lips turned up in a soft smile. "I'm sorry. I shouldn't have brought that up."

"Don't worry about it." Samantha sighed, shaking her head.

They stood in silence while they waited in line for their rations. How did she always manage to make things awkward? Samantha held her tray beneath the dispenser and grimaced when she pulled it back. A film-covered square containing the recommended amount of water for the meal and a protein bar the size of her palm rested in the center.

Ah, the joys of space food.

"So, you gonna tell me what you're really up to, or are you going to make me withhold the next chapter of *Sweet Seduction* until you fess up?" Lucy asked as they took a seat at one of the circular dining tables, breaking off a piece of her bar before popping it into her mouth.

Samantha grinned. Lucy didn't miss anything. "I'm not sure if we can trust Marsel. Something about this whole thing just seems shady to me." She leaned forward, lowering her voice so no one around them would hear her before she disclosed the potentially damning evidence. If this were anyone else, she wouldn't risk telling them what she knew, but she trusted Lucy with her life. "When I looked into the file on X9, the only information it gave was that it was inhabited and, more importantly, banned from exploration."

"I thought it was strange he didn't really acknowledge your comment on that in the meeting." She whispered. "So what are we gonna do, boss?"

"*We* do nothing. I'm going to go down there and get as much evidence as possible, and then I'm going to tell everyone what he's been hiding. Marsel can't make this decision for us. The people here deserve to decide for themselves." Samantha bit her lip. "You can't tell anyone."

Lucy's hazel eyes grew wide, and she nodded before clearing her throat. Her eyes followed the person who passed behind Samantha before she spoke up again. "I won't. Be careful, Sam. You know Marsel could ruin your career if he wanted."

"I know." She sighed.

Three dings sounded in the hall, signaling that it was time to turn in for the night, and they pushed back from the table. She wrapped Lucy in a hug and bid farewell to her friend before heading to her small but comfortable room aboard the ship. Marsel's had been huge, but she preferred the cozy feel of hers. Samantha was so tired she didn't even bother taking off her lab coat before falling into a heap on top of her blanket.

CHAPTER 1

SAMANTHA

*C*ool metal pressed against her cheek was the first indicator that she wasn't in bed anymore. Her brain felt foggy, and her whole body ached as she stiffened. Had she had one of her old night terrors? Maybe she had taken up sleepwalking. The last thing she could remember was falling into bed and closing her eyes. Something didn't feel right, and the nagging in her stomach had her forcing her eyes open.

Her vision was blurry, and she blinked rapidly in an effort to clear it. Even then, everything looked as if she were trying to peer into a thick fog. Samantha had been on the receiving end of a few pranks back on the space station, but those were childhood antics. No one on board the S.S. *Constellation* would dare to do anything like that. She squeezed her eyes shut once more, taking a deep, calming breath before she pried them open again.

The scene before her was not at all what she had been expecting. Instead of the walls of the cabin that had become her home over the years, she was met with painted metal panels of one of the rescue pods. In the middle of the white wall to her right was a single tiny window. To her left was a seat and some secured storage, but for the most part, the pod was empty to ensure whoever used it wasn't going to be injured by stuff flying around the small cabin.

Samantha frowned, pushing herself up on shaky arms. Maybe she had some sort of temporary amnesia and couldn't remember the events that had led up to her needing to escape? She lifted a hand to her head and neck, gingerly searching for any lumps or abrasions, but found nothing to indicate she had been knocked unconscious.

Had she been kidnapped? Samantha nearly chuckled at the absurdity of the thought. Of course she hadn't. What would be the point in that?

"Computer, what is my location?" she asked with a shaky breath. She was met with something garbled and unintelligible. "Computer. What is my location?" The AI started to speak, but it broke into a series of strange squawks and clicks before going silent.

Damn it.

With a grunt, Samantha climbed to her feet, leaning heavily against the metal wall as she peered through the window. Foliage blocked most of her view, but from what she was able to see, she assumed she had landed on X9 somehow. This couldn't be how they conducted field missions. Admittedly, she had never been on one, but this was far from professional and she was alone. Marsel had told her that she would be with a team, and they had even gone over who would be here to ensure her safety.

Everything is fine, she told herself. *I'll just wait here for the rest of the team.* Her mother had told her when she was a child that if she ever found herself lost, that she should stay exactly where she was and wait for someone to come for her—so that's what she would do now.

Someone will *come for me. They have to.*

Right? Gods, she hoped they would. The fact that they wouldn't have come down in the escape pod had occurred to her, but she chose to ignore that detail for the time being. There had to have been some kind of mistake.

The first few days Samantha spent within the pod were nerve wracking. A massive storm had moved in sometime on the second day, bringing sheets of rain and lightning far brighter than anything she had ever recalled seeing in the video archives.

She had studied Earth's weather as a child, and had been fascinated by hurricanes and tornadoes. Ten-year-old Samantha would have given anything to have been able to set foot on a planet and experience this first hand. Thunder rumbled so loud outside that it shook the pod, causing the rations within the shelving to vibrate violently.

There were thirty days' worth of prepackaged rations in each of the escape pods on the *S.S. Constellation*. Surely that was more than enough to see her through until someone came for her.

On the fourth night, the storm finally subsided, and she watched the fog roll in through the small window. The sounds of the forest around her were muffled by the thick padding within the pod, but what she could hear at night made her wonder if the planet supported life similar to Earth's Mesozoic Era. The thought of giant lizard-like animals stomping around somewhere outside sent a shiver down her spine. *Cenozoic Era creatures wouldn't be much better*, she thought, remembering the picture books filled with things like Terror Birds and Wooly Rhinos.

Would she even be able to survive outside of the pod? It seemed as if the air filtration system the Venium had installed was still working, so she didn't have to worry about suffocating just yet. None of the instruments she could have used to analyze the conditions outside were currently functional, and she wasn't willing to risk opening the doors to find out for herself.

As long as she had food and shelter, she could focus all of her efforts on fixing the failing systems. She wasn't anything even close to an engineer, but if she could manage this, she stood an even better chance at surviving X9.

CHAPTER 2

ZURAN

*Z*uran had watched the rock plummeting through the sky, flames trailing behind it as it drew closer. The light from the fiery object had made him squint as he followed it with his eyes. When Ama gave him and Zyar the task of trekking through the misted forest to find the object, they hadn't hesitated.

It was their duty as the hunters of the tribe to protect and provide. The safety of the tribe was priority.

It had taken the rest of the night and most of the next day to travel to the site of the crash, but he welcomed the task. Fire licked low in his belly, an unavoidable consequence of going into the village. He would never be free of the heat... he would never be able to quench the ache that was his constant companion. Eventually, it would consume him as it had all of the hunters who had come before.

Zuran was made to be a hunter. He would live and die as the All Mother wished. Death, he knew, was coming for him far faster than he had anticipated, and Zyar had taken notice.

"Again?" the other male asked. "It is getting worse."

"It doesn't matter," Zuran replied. "I am no different than the many before us."

"It is not fair."

"Many things the All Mother demands are not fair, brother." Although they were not bound by blood, they had both been given the title of Hunter from the All Mother and had found refuge with one another over the years. "Be on guard," Zuran reminded him, nudging the other male with his elbow.

They moved in tandem, getting closer to the silver rock. Its smooth surface glinted in the dim light of the moon that broke through the trees. There was no movement from within, and nothing moved around the outside, but Zuran knew better than to believe that meant they were safe. Under the cloak of night, he crept closer, peeking into the tiny window on the side of the rock. There, lying on the floor within, was a lone form. *A Star Born.*

He motioned Zyar forward. The other male growled low in his throat before spitting on the ground with a soft curse. They worked together, using the blades at the tips of their tails in an attempt to pry the strange rock open, but as was the case with the others they had found, this one did not give up its occupant.

"This is useless." The other male grumbled, kicking at the churned-up earth.

"We will wait here until the Star Born reveals itself." They always did.

Zyar nodded, following Zuran into the trees. This was nothing new to him. In fact, he had done this type of stakeout many times before, waiting patiently for the alien within to emerge. Each Star Born had been different, no two quite looking the same. He didn't question what he was told to do. If the All Mother had wished for them to know the reasons for such things, she would have given them the knowledge. Zuran settled into the lower branches of a tree near the rock and curled his tail up into his lap.

"Why didn't you tell me it was getting worse?"

Zuran sighed, rolling his eyes at the probing. "What good would it do?"

Zyar scaled the tree, his claws digging into the deep red bark as he swung up onto the branch above him. "Zuran, you know I would normally offer to help ease it, but..." He rubbed the back of his neck with a grimace.

"I would not ask you to break Vurso's trust for me."

Zyar frowned, but inclined his head. Vurso was a breeder living within the unmated male's village. Recently, the two of them had developed a relationship, and while male companionship was not unheard of among hunters, it was not something seen as favorable for the unmated breeders. If they were discovered, Zuran wasn't sure how Ama would react to such a thing.

"I might not be volunteering to help ease it as I once did, but that doesn't mean I am not your friend or that I don't wish to help in other ways."

"You and I both know there is nothing more to be done." Zuran stared up through the treetops as the clouds rushed past. A storm was approaching, and they would need to find shelter soon or risk getting caught in the downpour. The weather wasn't their only concern. It was nearly time for Seytonna's suns to merge, and that meant the festival was fast approaching. "Will Vurso be traveling to the Festival of Light?"

"Not this time, but we know Ama may choose to send him at any time."

"And if she asks him to go and he is mated to one of the females? What then?"

Zyar let out a long, sad sigh. "Then he will follow the will of the All Mother. We knew the risks when we started our relationship, and I will spend every moment I'm given with Vurso showing him how much I care for him."

The storm raged for days, sweeping through the forest, and

pummeling the silver rock. Zuran and Zyar kept watch from within a small cave, watching as lightning illuminated the shadows. By the time the fog had rolled in, small rustling sounds could be heard coming from within the rock.

At night, under the cover of darkness, Zuran climbed one of the nearby trees, peering into the single window. Even with the enhanced vision he had been gifted with during his transition, he couldn't make out the details of the Star Born lurking inside. The shadowy figure moved around the small space, touching the walls and causing lights to flash sporadically. When the Star Born placed its hand on one of the other flashing lights, a spark, similar to his own lightning, shot out, causing the being to stumble backward. It tripped over something and fell out of sight within the rock.

All Mother, have mercy. He may not even get the chance to kill the thing if it kept this up. Zuran chuckled to himself as he watched the thing climb to its feet, swaying as it got back to work. Perhaps it was attempting to find a way out.

He would watch and wait.

CHAPTER 3

SAMANTHA

*S*amantha inhaled deeply, drawing precious oxygen into her lungs as if it were the last time. To be fair, that was absolutely a possibility. This was the moment of truth, the first time she would step outside of the pod and onto an alien planet without a suit. She had been born on the space station orbiting the healing Earth, and had never ever set foot on real, solid soil. Sure, they had greenhouses and indoor parks with turf, but that could never be a substitute for the real deal.

This was the ultimate gamble, a leap of faith.

The air on X9 could very well kill her if it were anything like Mars, or any of the other planets that orbited Earth's sun. It could be too thin, containing too much carbon dioxide for her to breathe, but if she didn't take the chance, she was going to starve to death inside the pod. Even splitting up the rations, she had run out of food the day before, and her stomach was rumbling.

She was out of options and time, and had already fried the motherboard on the pod's computer. If she tried again, she ran the risk of taking out the air filtration system next. *Now or never.* Samantha clutched the small knife in the pocket of her lab coat and shoved open the hatch. That first hesitant breath had her heart racing, but as the clean fresh air of the forest filled her, Samantha nearly collapsed in relief.

The bright stream of light that filtered into her vision had her squinting against the twin suns high in the sky. The scientist in her couldn't help but marvel at the atmospheric conditions on the surface of X9. From the data collected over decades of humanity's travels in space before the fall of Earth, she expected to find X9 to be cold, but this place was far from frosty. Today was the hottest day she had experienced so far, and from the information she had studied in her time on the ship, this seemed to be similar to what Earth's climate had been before the war.

The regular partial eclipses had become her way of logging the weeks as they passed. Samantha checked her watch again, wishing that it actually told the time on X9, but the numbers on the face were constantly scrambling. Assuming her calculations were correct, forty days had passed since she lost contact with the *S.S. Constellation.* Forty days of her stuck on the surface alone with nothing but the supplies that she had been sent down with. She was never meant to be here for longer than a month—she couldn't recall any of the previous missions even coming close to that—and all of her rations were gone at this point. Hungry, tired, and frustrated, Samantha stomped through the misty woods, searching for something safe to eat.

Another oversized mosquito bit into her arm, and she swatted at it frantically, vowing once again that she would never sign up for another first exploration as long as she lived. Sure, it had sounded like a great excuse when she had lied after getting caught trying to find out what Marsel and his men were up to, but now, as she fought off bloodthirsty insects and struggled to breathe in the constant humidity, Samantha was having reservations.

With any luck, a rescue team would come down and whisk her away soon, taking her back to the comfort of her own lab where she could read about the planets rather than being the one sent down to explore them.

"Who knows, kitten? Maybe this will be the vacation you didn't know you needed." She could hear Marsel's snide comment in her mind and sneered.

"Vacation my ass," she grumbled. This wasn't a vacation; it was a nightmare. She was beginning to doubt that there would ever be a rescue team.

Without thinking, she rested her sweaty palm against the fleshy leaf of the plant at her side, yanking it back when she felt something slimy run across her skin. She shook her hand. The red liquid that dripped from the stem onto her palm could be easily mistaken for blood, and the sight of it made her stomach clench in disgust. If she hadn't been so focused on trying to stay alive, she might have wished she had a vial to collect a sample of the liquid.

Calling her decision to come out here a mistake was a serious understatement.

Fieldwork was obviously not her strong point. No matter how interesting the world around her looked, it was clear she wasn't cut out for this. Flowers the size of trees towered over her, wrapping around the hard red bark of the trunks. Screams from beasts she knew nothing about pierced the air, and she bemoaned the fact that her only defense against whatever resided in the forest around her was a soiled lab coat and a small pocketknife she had found shortly after waking up. It was something Lucy had given her a few months ago, but she hadn't remembered slipping it in her coat the last day on the ship.

While being back on the ship would mean she was safe, walking around down here afforded her the opportunity to breathe in actual fresh air. Finding humanity a new home while Earth healed itself meant that she spent a lot of time in a ship filled with stale recycled air. Honestly, she would do almost anything to smell that again.

It wasn't that she wanted to be stuck behind the confining walls, but it would be better than ending up as lunch for the next mutated animal that crossed her path. The beasts here were incredibly territorial, and they defended their areas with blood-curdling cries and claws the size of daggers. Getting by the last one had nearly cost her an arm, and she wasn't in a hurry to repeat that encounter anytime soon.

"If Marsel doesn't see my worth after this fiasco, then I'll offer him up as a sacrifice to the mosquitoes of death on this damn planet." He had lost faith in her and talked about replacing her after what happened on F2, the planet they thought would be their home.

Samantha wiped her hand across her lab coat, remembering how white it had once been, before slicking back her sweat-drenched purple hair from her face. What she wouldn't give for a hair tie. *Or another bottle of sunblock.* She grimaced, remembering she had used up the rest of her last bottle earlier in the day. It wouldn't be long at all before she would be worrying about exposure to the harmful rays of the suns.

Getting in shape for an assignment like this hadn't been very high up on her list of priorities before she was dropped here on the planet of doom, but it obviously should have been. Instead of focusing on physical fitness, Samantha had preferred to read through all the research that had been compiled on the planets or to immerse herself in a good book. Maybe making use of the gym and the glass pool in the ship would have been better than reading one of her coveted romance novels, but it was a little late for that.

Well, she couldn't imagine being a boring old scientist—and how does a girl even explore the stars without a little romance and fantasy to fuel her along the way? Though she hadn't lacked offers, Samantha didn't have anyone warming her bed every night.

Although the flight was long, she'd found that her one sexual experience with Marsel, misguided as it was and fueled by the celebration of finding a planet that humans could survive on, was more than enough contact with the men on board the ship. Especially after what happened after that. The deaths of those people she had sent to the surface of that godsforsaken planet would be burned into her heart and soul for the rest of her life. The pain of Marsel's punishment when he had found out had been nothing compared to the pain she had inflicted on herself.

Something far too close to her made a sharp hiss, and her head swung left and right as the sound echoed around her. There was no way to pinpoint which direction it had come from as it bounced off the trees. She shivered as the image of an old-world anaconda dangled at the forefront of her mind.

Maybe it was more like one of the big cats from Earth getting ready to pounce on her when she turned her back to it, or so the old vids said. She should have spent more time over the last forty days getting a feel for the planet's native flora and fauna and less time attempting to repair her malfunctioning console.

"Fuck, fuck, fuck, fuck, *fuck!*" The curse had become her new mantra since coming here.

Samantha crept over the deep purple terrain, careful not to make any sudden movements that might draw attention to herself. Her flight response was definitely being triggered, but she knew better than to give the predator something to chase. Just like cattle, she felt like she was being led to slaughter. The hiss transformed into menacing growls that seemed to be closing in from all sides, surrounding her. Shadows lurked in the fog before her, creeping around the trunks of the trees and engulfing the smaller plants. The further in she walked, the denser the gloom became.

Even if she turned around now, she doubted she would be able to find her way back to her ship.

A sharp pang pierced her gut, a reminder that it had been two days since she last ate. Two days since her supplies ran dry. Turning back now was not an option. Three-headed creatures similar to Earth salamanders with wings atop their back rushed across the forest floor, slithering over her leather boots. Under different circumstances, those guys might have been cute, but she was already spooked by everything going on.

Little silvery glowing bulbs shot up from the ground, static seeming to emanate from them as they sparked. An arachnid with a ruby-colored rock for an abdomen crawled up the nearest tree, its fangs nearly the size of its long spindly legs.

"Nope! Nope, nope, nope." She stumbled back.

Another shiver rolled through her as a large shadow loomed overhead, craning her neck uncomfortably in an attempt to take in the whole thing. That was another nope. The name of every living nightmare she could think of came to mind just as her feet began to fly over the uneven ground.

They'd had no information on the inhabitants of this world, which was probably why she had to sign that pesky waiver at the end of the meeting before she was allowed to come. Uncontrollable, intense fear sped through her like the raging winds that brought in a storm.

Get away! Need to hide somewhere. The faster, the better.

A cluster of rocks had tumbled into each other and created a perfect nook for her to duck into. She needed to get between the stone walls before whoever, or whatever, was pursuing her caught up. If the mounting screams and cries behind her were any indication, that would be sooner than she liked.

Diving into the tight, damp space, she sent up a silent prayer that there were no venomous creatures crawling around the corners as she curled her legs up to her chest. Samantha's heart pounded behind her ribcage, threatening to break free as the air fled her lungs in her terror.

Maybe if she hadn't been so sleep-deprived and distracted by hunger, she probably could have thought more clearly.

A shadow slithered across the ground, drawing her gaze and making her press back harder against the rocky wall. Its movements were almost snake-like, making her earlier fears seem a lot less imaginative and far too real.

She waited with bated breath for several moments before the shadow waved as if it were watching her movements. After a few drawn-out seconds, she released her pent up breath. Nothing had attacked her yet.

Had she just been paranoid?

The black form of the body curled in on itself suddenly. Like a house cat playing with a mouse, the shadow figure seemed to toy with her emotions. It crept closer, causing her stomach to drop just as the silky tip of something curled around her ankle and pulled her across the ground a few inches. Her gasp seemed to stop it for a second before it tried again.

It wasn't a snake—she was almost positive—but none of the pictures she conjured in her mind were much better.

Her shirt rode up her torso as she was dragged from the shadows of the hole she hid in, branches and rocks scraping and scuffing her soft skin as she struggled. Samantha's fingers clawed frantically at the ground, but it was nearly as hard as the rocks she had sheltered in, and she only succeeded in fracturing her already short nails.

The creature who held her was too strong, and despite her efforts, she felt her body twist around so that she slid on her back across the debris-strewn forest floor before being lifted into the air.

A shriek left her mouth as she swung for a moment, spinning slightly. Before she even had time to renew her struggle, she found herself face to dick with an unknown alien. The length hung between his legs, covered only by a loincloth tied at his waist.

It was honestly pretty impressive and oddly arousing—*No, I'm not going there right now.*

There were more important things to focus on. Like the fact that a rather primitive-looking alien had captured her and was dangling her upside-down like an animal caught in a trap while her shirt dropped down to obscure her face, leaving her stomach and cleavage exposed. Samantha did her best to tug the material over her body, blood rushing to her cheeks.

He pulled her a little higher as if he were trying to figure out what he had snagged, and she wiggled in his grasp. This only made her swing closer, her nose nearly brushing the area above the cloth.

"Whoa!" She clenched her hands to keep from reaching out to steady herself. "If you could put me down that would be great," a huff fell from her lips as she looked up the length of his body to his chiseled face. "This isn't even a flattering angle," she muttered to herself.

His skin was the color of the darkest onyx stone; the little silvery-blue dots scattered across his face and down the sides of his body seemed to spark with electricity. His white eyes glowed softly and were bisected by a black pupil, much like a feline's.

Two large, curved horns crowned his head, shaped like a shotel blade but slightly twisted at the top; they were the same shimmery black as the braided hair spilling over his shoulders. The small beads woven into his hair caught the light from the sparks, sending tiny prisms scattering across his face. Two of his braids were so long that they reached down all the way to his four-toed feet, nearly brushing the ground.

When he spoke, it was in a language she didn't know. It was melodic, beautiful in that *"I'm going to die because he thinks I'm the enemy"* sort of way. He didn't look at her like he was afraid of what she might be or what she might do. He looked at her like he had come to dominate, and he wasn't going to suffer any disobedience.

The thought sent a shiver down her spine, and she gulped down the urge to moan at the image it brought to mind.

What the fuck is wrong with me? Nothing like being turned on by the strange alien that looks dead set on killing you.

CHAPTER 4

ZURAN

*Z*uran pulled the little alien higher in the air, inspecting her. It wasn't very often that one of their kind fell from the sky and lived. None of them had ever looked like her when they managed to break free from the flying rocks. He tilted his head as he gave her another cursory glance, wondering how she was not uncomfortable in the restricting garments she wore. Most days, the heat here was too much even on Seyton skin.

He could feel his lightning building alongside his agitation. What was stopping him from killing this alien, like all of the ones who had come before? Maybe it was the fact that he had been able to identify her as female. All of the other aliens that had fallen here had been males as far as he could recall. Her species must not care too much for their females if they stowed one in a flying rock and flung her from wherever it was these creatures came.

Unthinkable.

The sharp retractable blade that hid deep in his tail jutted up out of its sheath so that the tip shined under the twin suns. They were the only things visible through the thick fog.

He knew he should dispatch her with haste, unsheathe his blade fully and end her as quickly and painlessly as possible, but he couldn't bring himself to do it. Perhaps he would keep her. She wiggled in his grip, muttering in what he assumed was her native tongue. Surely Ama wouldn't care if he kept a female from the stars for himself.

"Zuran! You have made a catch? What is our reward?" Zyar called, his tail curling with anticipation as he appeared, stepping through the thick fog.

"I have caught a female."

Zyar bent down, twisting so that he was nearly turned upside-down next to the alien, his face scrunching as he sniffed her. "She smells. You have caught a smelly alien female."

"A female all the same." Zuran narrowed his gaze on the alien as she spoke again, this time a little louder and more insistently. "I think I will keep her. I cannot imagine one of the Star Born could ever be a coveted one."

Nodding in agreement, Zyar straightened, his hands coming to rest on his lean hips as he scowled. "Surely not. Will you share her?"

Zuran looked down at the female as her face turned a deep red, her hands covering her mouth in the most peculiar way, causing the clothing she wore to reveal the mounds of her breasts as they spilled from the top of the sling she wore.

"I do not know. She is strange, is she not?"

"Should she be turning that color?" Zyar reached out as if to remove the female from Zuran's hold.

Swinging his tail toward his body, Zuran pressed her close. "Do not touch!"

Zyar curled his lip over his fangs, pupils dilating as he huffed in annoyance. "Then you will have the honor of explaining to Ama how you killed the female."

With a sneer, Zuran reached out, grabbing the little thing around her waist and flipping her around so that her strange feet were on the ground. Satisfaction surged through him when the red began to drain from her face, returning her to the pale color she had been when he found her hiding between the rocks.

"There." He steadied her as she swayed, his tail still wrapped possessively around one of her legs. "I fixed her. She is fine now."

Zyar pinned him with a droll stare and sighed. "Simply amazing. They will name you the next village healer for this miracle. I am sure of it."

Ignoring the teasing remark, Zuran looked down into her strange blue alien eyes. She was magnificent, even if she was tiny. The top of her colorful head barely reached the bottom of his chest.

Yes, he thought. *I will keep this female.*

"*Y*ou will *not* keep the female," Ama declared in a harsh whisper as she stared down at the pulsating red glow of the vilebloom that the Star Born cradled in her palm.

The vilebloom was a sacred and ancient tool his kind used to determine whether a female was fertile or not for as long as the Seyton had existed. By the way the crystal glowed, it was obvious that the alien he had captured was fertile and ready to be bred.

"With the greatest of honors, Ama, surely you have no need of an alien female." Zuran's tail snapped with sparks as he tried to retain his control.

"She is in her prime for breeding, and you are far from fit to see to her needs in that respect." She looked around at the gathered members of the tribe. "Olan is looking for a bride. He was set to cross the misted forest the day after tomorrow, but you have kindly saved him the journey."

Zuran was aware he hadn't known the female long, that he shouldn't even care where she went, but his head snapped to the side in irritation at Ama's words. "There are plenty of Seyton females for Olan to breed."

"*All* fertile females are coveted, *hunter.*" She cut her gaze to his. "You forget your place."

His eyes narrowed on the head of his tribe as he tried not to hold her words against her; it was their way, after all. Hunters were not permitted to marry since their responsibilities were considered too dangerous, and they were infertile. Even if that weren't the case, the dark pigment of their skin was not considered desirable despite the fact that it aided them with their hunts.

Colored with reds and aquas and lacking the dangerous blades on the tips of their tails, breeder males were seen as perfect partners and exemplary specimens of Seyton masculinity. Their eyes were as colorful as their skin, and their horns contained their own electrical current that attracted the female eye. Everything about them was designed to draw in a potential bride.

Ama crossed white-clawed arms over her chest as electricity ran up her biceps and bounced between her straight horns. Her long white braids created a curtain around her, concealing her partial nudity. Zuran watched as her brows drew down over closed eyes.

"I will pretend we did not have this conversation," she murmured as her black wings unfurled behind her back. "I would hate to lose our best hunter."

Tingles ran along his skin where the tip of one feathered appendage brushed across his bare chest. It was more contact than he had in a long time from any among his tribe. Though he was allowed to seek out pleasure among willing females, his body's demand for procreation was nearly unbearable. Some days it felt like the All Mother was being cruel, making them infertile but still putting them through a yearly heat that drove them mad with the desire to procreate.

Most hunters lost their sanity when the breeding heat seared through their blood, and soon he would be at the All Mother's mercy. Staying away from the village, avoiding the females, was the only way to keep them from finding out how close he was to succumbing to the heat. Ama was an exception as she was the only female safe for the unmated males. She was too close to the All Mother's grace to push at a male's breeding heat.

Zyar rested his tail over Zuran's shoulder. "It was just not meant to be."

Zuran looked down at the little female, who stared around their village with wide, curious eyes, muttering to herself in her soft language. He reached out to caress the violet strands of her hair, making her flinch in surprise.

The thought of handing her over to a breeder, even with the knowledge that she would be cherished and provided for, made his stomach twist. He had always known he would spend his life alone, with only his fellow hunters as company, but this was doing something inside of him that he hadn't been prepared for.

"I apologize that I cannot keep you, little one," he whispered as his fingers trailed over her chin. A white hand reached out to grab the alien's arm, pulling a hiss from between his lips. "Do not touch her!"

Electricity raced up his arm, causing him to stumble backward from the force of the shock as Asa, the female who had attempted to lead the alien away, snarled at him angrily.

"Watch yourself, hunter," she spat, looking down on him with disgust.

The alien female yanked at her arm in Asa's grip and made

the most pitiful growl he had ever heard. His eyes widened when she lifted a small foot and slammed it down on the bare one of the larger female. Her fiery blue eyes narrowed on Asa as she tugged at her arm again, a triumphant look crossing her face when she was released.

The little one nearly knocked him over in her attempt to attach herself to his side. A grin pulled at his lips, and he just barely managed to suppress it as the alien clung to his hip. He stroked a careful hand down her side, pressing her body more firmly to his; he didn't mind that she wanted to hold him.

Actually, he rather enjoyed that the female was determined to stay by his side, that she touched him so openly. It was as if she was convinced that he was the male for her. The dagger in his tail peeked out, shooting a spark of warning at Asa's feet.

"I do believe it is *you* who should watch yourself."

Zyar's tail fell from Zuran's shoulder as he took several steps back, clearing his throat softly. "I will see you on the hunt, brother," he turned quickly, nearly running from the village in his attempt to avoid the confrontation.

When Zuran looked up, he saw the reason for Zyar's hasty retreat. *Olan.* The breeder male approached where they stood, the female still pressed tightly to his side. "You would dare to withhold a female from her chosen?"

Zuran slowly raised his hands, casting his eyes to the ground, knowing what such an accusation could lead to. His tail ran delicately along the side of the alien female to show that she refused to release him.

"I do not," he barely held back a snarl as Olan stepped closer.

"Very well."

The scale-spattered aqua stripes that ran along the male's skin began to glow bright, making the red that ran alongside them look more like the sap from the fuzzara leaf as lightning began to bounce between his horns. His tail curled this way and that, moving so fast it was hard to keep track of as he began to dance in dizzying motions.

This was the mating dance, a display the breeders put on for their chosen females to entice them. The little alien female's eyes widened, seeming to gloss ever as comprehension left her gaze. She slowly pulled away from Zuran's side, drifting toward Olan.

Each sparkling bolt that shot between his horns drew her further from Zuran, and she nearly fell over herself in her attempt to get to the colorful male. Zuran should have known she had been too good to be his, even though she seemed to choose him.

She obviously hadn't realized she had better options.

CHAPTER 5

OLAN

A FEW HOURS BEFORE...

*H*is feet moved across the ground, each step precise and carefully thought out. Olan's arms stretched high above his head, and he swayed his hips in the manner he had been taught. If his dance wasn't perfect, he would never attract a female.

The mating dance required precision and dedication. Each fluid motion was done to the rhythmic beat of his heart. If his pulse sped up, so did his dance. Electricity sparked between his horns as he moved, another trait of the breeder male that was needed to enthrall a female.

Olan pushed himself harder and harder, the twin suns beating down on his sweat-slicked skin. This would all be worth it when he made his journey through the forest; when he performed this for a female and she accepted him as her breeder. Soon, he would have kits and a female to provide for. His dreams would be fulfilled soon, whether he believed he deserved that honor or not.

As a kit, Olan had lived with his family in the unmated females' village. His youth had been filled with joy and unrealistic expectations of what his future would be. After he matured, he had moved here, to the main village. Although families had the choice of living in either village, the unmated males and females were required to live separately after their ceremony. The only females allowed within the main village were the mated ones.

Once he had found his chosen, none of this would matter. She would decide where they made their home, and everything else would be in the past. This part of his life would join the rest of the memories he no longer thought about.

"Olan." Asa's voice was soft as she placed her hand on his shoulder, tugging gently.

Olan turned to her as he panted in exertion. "Yes?"

"Ama requires your presence. It seems she has found you a mate."

He frowned at her, wiping his hair from his face. "Before the ceremony?"

Asa shrugged her shoulders. "Apparently."

"I have not even proven myself yet. My journey through the misted forest is still two days away."

"That no longer matters. A Star Born has been brought into the village, and Ama wishes her to be your mate."

"A Star Born?" Olan felt his jaw drop open in disbelief. *As a mate?* Completely unheard of, but if Ama had seen fit to match him, then who was he to argue with the will of the All Mother? "Will you go to her while I bathe? I do not wish to be filthy for our first meeting."

"Of course, my friend. It would be my honor."

Asa and her mate Vane had become the closest thing to friends he had here. None of the other males had gone unmated as long as he had and he often wondered if their pity for his situation was what had driven them to extend their friendship.

"Thank you," he said with a deep nod before hurrying away.

The second female to the chieftess taking care of his mate? It was the greatest honor. Olan wasted no time getting to the bathing pools, cleaning the sweat from his skin and hair as quickly as he could.

He wouldn't give his Star Born mate a moment longer than was necessary to doubt his commitment. She would have no reason to regret being chosen for him.

If the tension in the air wasn't enough to alert him, the crowd of onlookers would have been a clear indication that he had reached his destination. Pushing his way through the gathering crowd, Olan came to a stop at the front, taking in the scene.

Standing before him was one of the most intriguing—and admittedly odd—beings he had ever seen in his life. Surely this had to be the Star Born female. She was a tiny thing, her head barely reaching his chest. Light violet hair had been shorn just above her shoulders, and she had the most brilliant blue eyes. Where Seyton females were slender and built for flight, this female had soft, lush curves.

He was so enthralled by her appearance that he nearly over-looked the fact that *his* bride was wrapped around Zuran's body. Rage filled him as he watched the hunter's hand slide down her side. The last time they had interacted, things hadn't gone well. Olan shook off the thoughts before they could even form.

He couldn't change what the All Mother had decided, but he was not going to let this continue.

CHAPTER 6

SAMANTHA

PRESENT TIME...

*T*here was no doubt in Samantha's mind that the black demon alien was incredibly dangerous. She had seen the dagger that popped out of the tip of his tail more than once, even in the short amount of time since he'd captured her. Electricity sparked from between the colorful alien's horns, even though she knew he was just as dangerous as the dagger-tailed demon, she couldn't seem to look elsewhere.

Only vaguely aware of her body pulling away from the dark male who had captured her, she felt herself lean forward, her eyes locked on the other alien as he swayed to a rhythm he created. It was like being in a trance, her muscles moving without her commands. Every spark that leaped from his horns enticed her a little more than the last, and she became lost in the tempo, in the dizzying blur of colors that seemed to swirl around him.

This wasn't right. None of this was. She was helpless to sever whatever it was that was attaching itself to her and luring her in.

"That's it," the voice that came through her translator purred. It had started picking up words here and there during whatever confrontation she had found herself in the middle of, but it still wasn't proficient enough to give her a clear picture. Still, it was obvious that this male was pleased by her reaction, delighted even. Someone behind her, most likely the dark male, growled softly. "Fanahala," the one in front of her whispered, curling his bladeless tail under her chin as he leaned forward to press his brow to hers.

Was this some sort of greeting? It seemed far too intimate to her, but she knew nothing about this culture. Hell, a few hours ago she had no idea these aliens even existed. What *did* she actually know?

One thing she knew for sure was that these guys weren't Grutex, nor were they Venium. Although this was all new to her, it seemed like her body had decided for itself. She was being dragged further and further away from the only being here who she had felt she could trust, despite the level of danger he represented. A part of her protested. She didn't want to be separated from him, even though he'd essentially snatched her from the forest and brought her here.

"Wait…" The protest was weak, but the colorful male's electric show intensified, snapping all around her head. "I—I don't wanna leave him…" Samantha managed to choke out through the haze.

What had she understood during the argument? *Think. Think, damn it!* It hadn't been much, since the translator was still working out the language. Why hadn't she wanted to be removed from her captor? Bride? "Hunter" was something she had recognized when they referred to the dark male, but she wasn't sure if it was his name or a title.

This fog in her mind was driving her insane, and she was pretty certain it was being caused by the male who had his forehead pressed to hers.

"Enough." Samantha pushed against him, but he was huge, and she hardly even managed to sway him.

Well, fine then. This wasn't the first time she had fought off unwanted attention.

Reaching down slowly, she slipped the small pocketknife from the clip on her hip, pressing the release so that the blade sprung out. "I said *enough*, Sparky!" Swinging her hand up, she felt the sharp steel sink into something soft and heard a hiss as the male in front of her jumped back, clutching a small wound high up on his chest.

The group of aliens who had gathered around them gasped, a couple of them rushing to the colorful male's side as he stood motionless, staring at her like he was in shock. Samantha stumbled away from him. Her lungs felt like they were burning as she struggled to draw air into them.

All around her, there was noise, shouting, and growling. The air felt supercharged, and the hairs on her body stood at attention. Two of the light-colored females stepped toward her, and she brandished the pocketknife at them. "Back off! All of you!"

The females glanced in confusion at the one who still held the red crystal in her hands. That female watched her with curious eyes, her head tilted to the side as she seemed to ponder what action she was going to take.

A soft growl at her back had her spinning around and coming face to face with the dark male, her breath catching as she stared up into his white eyes. *Survive a crash landing on an alien planet? Check. Spend forty days alone on said alien planet? Check. Get kidnapped and not do something to get myself killed during first contact? Not going so well.*

Her whole body clenched at the thought that she might have

just signed her own death warrant. *Real smooth.* Just as the male stepped toward her, a growl rumbled loudly through her stomach, and heat blossomed on her cheeks as embarrassment flowed through her. The ghost of a smile played over the male's lips, and she prayed that the translator had learned enough that she could at least request a last meal before they disposed of her.

"So, uh, would anyone be willing to spare some food?" she asked, turning to give the group an awkward smile.

pparently, a growling stomach was universal for *"I'm hungry"* because the table she was led to was nearly overflowing with all sorts of delicious-smelling dishes. It wasn't food she was familiar with, but she couldn't have cared any less. A few of the dishes were vegetables she had spotted on her trek through the forest while others looked to be types of meat.

While most of the spread before her seemed edible, the sight of the creature still in its exoskeleton had her nose scrunching up in disgust. *Not going near that one.* If she ever made it back to the ship, she was going to suggest they start a class teaching all of the crew how to politely tell aliens you've just met that you want nothing to do with their giant roasted bugs. Something akin to sprouts was on the left of the bugs, and next to that was a steaming pile of gray roots that reminded her of a radish. She wouldn't have called these her favorite foods based on looks alone, but beggars couldn't be choosers. When on an alien world, eat alien food, right?

"Is there something I can get for you to try, Fanahala?" the red guy, Sparky, asked her.

Lips pursing, she glanced around before pointing to a green, meaty looking substance. "Maybe that?" Fingers crossed it wasn't that color from sitting out too long. "What was your name? I

45

don't think I caught it." Her tongue felt stiff as it formed the words. The first couple hours after her translator "taught" her a brand new language was always a little odd, but in situations such as this, she was grateful to have the little bug inside her. She tried not to think about the fact that it had burrowed into her brain and had the ability to change and teach her things.

"Olan," his smile, although a tad toothier than she normally found appealing, seemed genuine and warm. Their species as a whole seemed to have considerably sharper teeth than humans, and the fact that she had attacked this guy without that knowledge made her queasy. Samantha's eyes drifted over to the darker male, the thorn in her side, the entire reason she was here in the first place. "That is Zuran. A hunter for our tribe," Olan spoke, following her gaze.

"Olan and Zuran. Great. I'm Samantha. Nice to meet you both." She snorted at the absurdity of the introductions, as if this was some run of the mill business lunch. "Which one of you is going to tell me why I'm here?"

"The rumbling of your stomach indicated that you were hungry, so you were brought here for the evening meal," Olan explained.

Not helpful. "Yeah, I got that part. I want to know why I was brought here to this—" She gestured at everything around her, struggling to find the words. "Village?"

Zuran watched her as if she was going to pop out of existence if he blinked. It was clear he was agitated by the fact that he'd been seated on the opposite side of the large table instead of near her like Olan was.

"It is not safe outside the village," Olan growled, his eyes narrowing on the other male in warning.

"That's not much of an explanation. I was doing fine before Zuran found me. Why can't I just go back to my ship?"

"You were tested against the vilebloom." He must have

guessed she was confused by the look on her face because he clarified, "Ama used the vilebloom, and it was determined that you are a fertile female. You, like the rest of the fertile females, belong in the safety of the village. The forest is fit for no one but hunters and beasts."

This was obviously a point of contention because Zuran cut his gaze to Olan and sneered. "Well, as nice as it is that you're all offering to keep me safe, I'm not one of your people." She gestured down to herself, as if their differences weren't glaringly obvious.

"You are not Seyton. This is correct." Olan inclined his head. "You are from the stars. Star Born." The smile he gave her seemed strained, like he wasn't exactly thrilled by that information. "However, you have been selected for me as my bride, and you will remain in the safety of the village."

Samantha inhaled quickly, nearly choking on the food she had frantically shoved into her mouth, her eyes wide as she coughed in an attempt to dislodge the meat. Olan patted her back while Zuran nudged a cup full of liquid into her hands. She took a deep gulp and wiped her teary eyes. "I'm sorry. Wow. Umm, I don't think that translated right. Could you do me a favor and repeat that last little bit?"

"You are to remain in the safety of the village because you are to be my bride, my Fanahala. You are the female who will bear my young, who I will create a home with."

A strangled, hysterical laugh burst from her throat as she stared at him incredulously. "You aren't serious, right?"

"He is," Zuran interrupted.

Her fiery gaze shot to him. "And who exactly got to decide this?" Anger began to boil her blood. Olan hadn't even known her name before he tried to manipulate her into following him. He had used whatever magic pull he possessed to lure her into his arms, and she wasn't about to accept that this was something she should just go along with.

If she had to choose, she would honestly much rather be with Zuran. The worst he had done at their first meeting was hold her upside-down with her face nearly pressed into his dick. Big deal.

"I decided," the white female at the end of the table answered.

"And what in the hell gives you the right to choose who I marry and have kids with?"

"Ama is the chieftess of this tribe, Fanahala. All matings are presented to her for approval." Olan practically vibrated with electricity as he inclined his head toward their chieftess. "Her decisions are guided by the will of the All Mother."

"Olan is correct. The All Mother has spoken, and it has been decided you will be his," the regal-looking woman spoke, her words traveling easily over the space between them.

These people were crazy. There was no way she was sticking around to be a delivery machine for some alien because their deity willed it.

"I hate to break it to you, but I will not fucking—" Her words were drowned out by a massive crack of thunder. No, that wasn't exactly right. Samantha squinted up at the sky and nearly toppled over backward when she leaped from her seat at the sight of the drop ship breaching the planet's atmosphere.

They were coming for her!

The excitement of seeing the ship faded when she realized the trajectory was insanely off. Something wasn't right. If they didn't slow down, they were going to crash. Samantha pushed past Olan as he stood and raced through the open field that the table was set up next to, trying her best not to lose sight of the craft, but it disappeared behind a towering grove of trees. Only seconds later, a loud, echoing boom filled the air around her, and she knew without a doubt that the drop ship had made contact with the rough, unforgiving terrain of X9.

CHAPTER 7

OLAN

*T*he fact that his bride was already vehemently denying that she belonged with him within moments of being told about the blessing was not at all lost on Olan. With time, and perhaps some coaxing from him, she would learn that this was just the way things were done here.

No one had a right to argue with the All Mother, not even an alien from the stars.

Every time Zuran's eyes fell on Samantha, Olan wanted to wrap his tail around his throat and choke the life from him. The bond between them had once been so strong, but now... it no longer mattered. That was all in the past, and he refused to dredge up those memories right now. There had been no agreement to take the hunter on as a pleasurer, and Olan wasn't too keen on doing anything that would allow the other male access to *his* mate.

His attention snapped back to the conversation going on at the table. Samantha was having a disagreement with Ama, something he wasn't sure he had ever witnessed before, when the sound of a star rock colliding with Seytonna reverberated through the village.

"Whatever was that?" Ama looked curiously in the direction the noise had come from.

"*That* was our drop ship falling from the sky. It was filled with my team." Samantha breathed, anxious eyes cast toward where the star rock had landed.

"Why have they come here?" Ama's eyes narrowed on his bride, and he felt himself puff up some in her defense, his tail wrapping protectively around her waist.

"They're most likely a backup team. They've probably figured out something was wrong by now…" Her hands ran nervously through her violet hair. "We're scouting planets, looking for a new home."

"A new home?" Ama questioned. "Are your people running from conflict?"

"Our home planet, Earth, is in a stage of rebirth. It was nearly destroyed during the last war and is completely uninhabitable at the moment."

"Your people have devastated your world and now you wish to settle on Seytonna?" Ama's laugh was anything but humorous.

"My ship is in orbit above the planet to observe. There's nothing set in stone. My team and I were supposed to come to the surface to investigate the possibility of settling here. That's all."

Samantha flexed her grip on the small knife she carried, and he gently placed his hand over hers, shaking his head softly. Olan didn't want his new bride's actions to be seen as a threat to the chieftess. It would win her no favors in the long run.

"There are women and children on board. They've never known anything but life on that ship. We're only looking for a chance to live—a chance to be free from our ancestors' debt to the Venium."

Olan watched Ama as she studied Samantha, her face impassive, but he knew her mind was working. He released a pent-up breath when the chieftess nodded.

"I will consult with the All Mother," she finally said.

"I'd like to go find my team and make sure they aren't injured."

Ama shook her head. "I understand your concern for your people, but my responsibility to mine is my priority. Zyar and Niva will be sent out." When Samantha let out a frustrated growl, Ama narrowed her eyes on his bride's face. "I will not waver in this, little one. You have shared things here that make me hesitant to trust your people. You will remain in the village under our care until we have properly investigated."

"We don't want to hurt you." Samantha insisted.

"You are asking me to entrust the safety of my people to the word of a stranger. You said there are women and children on this thing you call your ship? There are children here as well, Samantha, and they are my responsibility. Certainly, my apprehension is something you can understand?"

Olan could tell his bride wanted to argue, but she clenched her jaw and gave a stiff nod, sticking her hands into the pockets of the dirty rags she wore.

"My presence is required at the Festival of Light, but I am confident that Olan and Zuran can be trusted to watch over you in my absence."

"What's the Festival of Light?" Samantha asked, her brows drawing down.

"A celebration," Olan answered. "Breeder males and fertile females gather in hopes of finding a partner. I was meant to join them this solar, but that was before the All Mother saw fit to gift me such a lovely bride."

Samantha snorted, a sneer taking over her pretty features.

"I've yet to agree to being *gifted* to you, or anyone else in this place."

This defiant streak should have put him off. It should hurt him that the female he was to be mated to for a lifetime was so adamantly denying him, but the truth was that it excited him. When he had first laid eyes on her, this tiny creature with blunt teeth and no claws or wings to speak of, Olan had been worried. How would a female with no natural defenses be capable of guarding their young?

His fingers ran absentmindedly over the wound she had inflicted. She was a fierce little thing.

"Is there somewhere I can clean up?" His female tugged at her tattered clothing, grimacing at the dirt that was smudged on her skin. "I haven't bathed in weeks."

"Of course." Ama looked slightly aghast, as if she were only just noticing how filthy Samantha was.

"I could escort her to the pools and stand guard," Zuran offered, electricity running along his tail as he frowned at the hand Olan kept on his bride's back.

"*You* will go nowhere near *my* bride." A growl tore up through Olan's chest as he positioned Samantha behind him, sparks bouncing between his horns at the mere thought of Zuran being alone with her.

This male, this *hunter*, thought himself worthy to attend to the needs of his female, to see her in such a state of undress before he even had the opportunity to lay claim. It was Olan's right and his honor to care for her. He would watch Zuran eat fire before he allowed this.

"Wow. This little light show the two of you are putting on is fascinating, honestly, but I'm perfectly capable of washing myself. Just point me in the direction of the water." Samantha pushed at his tail as she attempted to wiggle free.

"I would prefer you go nowhere within the village without a

guard. Zuran," Ama turned her attention to the hunter. "You will accompany her."

Olan's eyes jerked to his chieftess' face in surprise. "Ama—"

"Your bride will be safe with Zuran. He knows his place and would not dare overstep... again." She raised a delicate brow as if daring the hunter to object. "I would have a moment of your time, Olan."

"Yes, Ama." He bowed his head, uncurling his tail from around Samantha and hating how empty he already felt without her heat. Samantha glanced back at him before she turned to follow Zuran through the trees.

"Come, Olan." With a sigh, he turned and took the seat the chieftess indicated. "I do not wish to see the death of our world at the hands of these people. I would ask for your help in determining if aiding Samantha's people is something we can risk."

"How would you have me do this?"

"Keep a close eye on her. Try to learn more about her people and how many of them we will potentially be dealing with."

The fact that he was being asked to spy on his new bride didn't sit well with Olan. He couldn't ignore the possibility that they would need to wage war to keep Seytonna and her people safe from outsiders, but could Samantha's people really pose such a threat?

The Seyton had killed every other male alien that had come before her, and he knew without a doubt that they wouldn't hesitate to do so again. If Samantha spoke the truth, there would be females and young among those seeking refuge.

"You are asking me to spy on my bride, Ama. This is the female I will be tied to for the rest of my life."

"Do not look at it in that light, Olan." Ama sighed, looking wearier than he had ever seen her. "Doing this will help ensure we can protect our people and the family, All Mother willing, that you and Samantha will create. If Seytonna falls to these Star Born, we all fall."

"And the females and young my bride spoke of?"

"We can offer them protection should the males prove to be a threat. The only way for us to know if they will be is through her." His eyes followed Ama's gaze as she turned to look over the trees toward the plume of smoke that was rising high above them. "If Samantha breeds well with you, then their females would be a welcome gift to our people."

Having an abundance of new females would certainly put them at an advantage over the other tribes. The fact that the younger males of the village wouldn't have to fight so hard just to win a bride was something he knew they would find appealing. Something they would be willing to fight for. The truth had been looking them in the face for a very long time, but they had staunchly carried on, ignoring it. More females were ending up infertile, becoming hunters when they blossomed from the agmari bloom at maturity.

They were losing more than they gained.

Olan stepped up beside the chieftess, drawing a deep breath into his lungs as he looked around. He could not imagine this world dying in the same way his bride's had. If her people had been the cause of that destruction, how could he knowingly give them the opportunity to repeat their mistakes? His young would be born into this world, and he was going to make sure it was as safe as possible for them.

"If it does not put my bride at risk, I will do my best to gather any information that might help us."

Ama's black wings rustled near his shoulder, and he heard the soft sigh that left her lips. "It is all I ask."

CHAPTER 8

ZURAN

*S*he was the embodiment of everything he had ever desired. That she would never be his made it that much harder to look at her. Zuran's tail twitched in agitation as they neared the bathing pools. *You are only to guard her.* The pools were naturally heated and contained at least ten different levels of rocked-off bathing pods. It was a natural formation that his people took full advantage of.

Samantha looked up at him, her head tilting a little. "Do you guys have soap?"

"What is *soap*?"

Her face scrunched up, brows furrowing above her eyes. "What's soap? The stuff you use to clean your skin." She looked horrified. "Do you guys not clean your bodies?"

"We do." If he hadn't found it so funny that this dirty, smelly little alien was accusing him of being unclean, he might have been offended. "We use our electrical currents."

"That sounds a bit deadly. Like throwing a toaster into a tub to get clean."

"What is a toaster?"

A sweet, melodic giggle echoed through the pools. "I just meant that normally, electricity and water don't make a great combination. Not for humans, at least." The smile that lifted her lips was infectious and warmed his entire body.

"It is not a very strong charge, only enough to kill off anything clinging to our skin." He fought back the smile that threatened to blossom over his face.

"Sort of like those little fish that pick off all of the dead skin and eat it."

"Your kind allows water dwellers to eat dead skin from your bodies?" The thought was so foreign that he had a hard time imagining what that would be like. She balked at the idea of his electricity being used for cleaning and then spoke of how they let creatures within the water pick at them? The water dwellers on Seytonna were equipped with multiple sets of sharp teeth, and he couldn't imagine letting any of them nibble on him.

The face he made must have been amusing because she started laughing even harder. "Some people really do! Well, did."

"I suppose it is not dissimilar." His blood ran cold, and he shivered as he looked down at her exposed skin, trying not to imagine it being torn open by the fangs of some alien water crea-ture all for the sake of being clean.

"Well, I'm not so sure how I feel about you zapping me, weak current or not." She chewed her lip. "I very much like staying alive."

Rubbing his hand nervously across the back of his neck, Zuran glanced over at Samantha. "If you would like, I could show you?" She looked like she was about to refuse, so he rushed to continue. "It will not harm you. I swear it." Her blunt teeth pressed into her bottom lip, and she sighed.

The heat that crawled along his skin when she nodded made him grateful for possibly the first time ever that he was so dark. Unlike Samantha, who seemed to change color with her emotions, Zuran's rush of pleasure was hidden. The slight twitch of his ears was the only indication of how he felt, and he preferred to keep it that way.

A puff of air left her mouth, causing a few strands of her violet hair to fly away from her face. "Okay, but turn away." She twirled a finger at him.

"Of course!" He turned his back on her quickly, tail twitching with anxiety.

Zuran could hear her moving around behind him, most likely shedding the filthy garments. A splash of water had his ears twitching with interest and his tail whipping back and forth as he tried to dispel the images his mind wanted to conjure of her without her coverings.

"Oh my gods, this feels so good!" A soft moan fell from her lips, the erotic sound causing sparks to jump over his skin. "All right, I'm ready to be electrocuted."

The words had him shaking his head, the humor of them dispelling some of the tension from his muscles. His tail moved slowly into the water, and she yelped softly when the tip brushed against her body. A spark, the smallest he could muster, zigzagged down his appendage, flowing and spreading through the water at his feet. He kept his eyes trained on the tree line in front of him, ignoring the overwhelming need to turn around and check on her.

Sweet All Mother, what if I was wrong?

When the water rippled around his skin, he let out a sigh of relief. "That was…" Her voice was relaxed and airy. "So strange. I'm pleasantly surprised to still be alive."

Zuran's sensitive ears tracked her movements as she began to tread through the warm waters of the pool. He closed his eyes, enjoying the close proximity to the female as she soaked. She may not have wanted him, but he wanted her with an urgency that surprised him.

He'd been trying to deny the tug of attraction since the moment he found her wandering through the misted forest alone. She had been brave, courageous, a little naïve. Most importantly, she had known nothing about their society. Perhaps it was unfair of him to have considered taking her without her having any knowledge of the differences between hunters and breeders, but was it really so bad to want something for himself?

Traditionally, the All Mother, through the chieftess of a tribe, paired off fertile couples or approved pairings requested by individuals who sought a union. His people weren't known to instantly fall in love, but he had.

He was lost to her no matter what happened in the future.

"Ooh, so, so soft." He heard her mutter in quiet fascination as water splashed up onto the stone he stood on. What was it about the soft little alien that called to him? It could have been the allure of her abundant curves or the feisty way she had fought off Asa. Watching her stab Olan had been the highlight of his life thus far. Or maybe it was that she hadn't immediately turned her back and shut him out just because he was a hunter. She hadn't seen him as unfit to marry; she had merely seen *him* in a way no other female ever had.

He was ignorant about the mating customs of her species, but surely they had to be different than his own. Perhaps he could show her his worth, prove to her and her people that hunters were more than just their profession. Her very existence could open up a world of possibilities for him and his brothers.

Zuran turned his head to the side, keeping his eyes averted. "Could I ask you something?"

"Mmhmm. Ask away."

"When a male of your kind wishes to mate with a female, does he first seek approval of the All Mother?"

"Nope."

"Your chieftess, then?"

"Nuh-uh."

Zuran frowned down at his feet. "Then what must he do in order to mate?"

"He needs the approval of the woman, the female he wants to be with."

He nearly turned around to make sure she wasn't joking, that this was the honest truth. "And if this male is a hunter?"

"I don't follow." He heard her draw closer to the edge of the pool. "Why would that matter?"

"On Seytonna, being a hunter means you are not permitted to mate."

"Huh? Why not?"

"Our profession is dangerous." He shrugged his shoulders, trying to shake the mounting tension from them. "We are gone for long stretches of time. Who would care for our families while we were away or if we were killed while on a hunt? That is the reason, some say, the All Mother made us infertile."

"Zuran, I mean this in the nicest way possible, but that's one of the most ridiculous things I've ever heard in my life. And I've worked with people who thought the Earth was flat, so that's saying something." There was a moment of silence as Samantha seemed to think. "Humans don't dictate who's allowed to marry and who isn't. We're allowed to be with whoever we wish to be with for however long we choose."

"That sounds like a dream."

"Zuran?" Her voice was barely a whisper, and it sent a chill throughout his body.

"Yes, Samantha?" The alien name felt foreign on his tongue.

"You're a hunter, right?"

"I am." He nodded.

"Have *you* ever been with a woman?"

"I have pleasured a female once," he answered truthfully.

"Only pleasured her?" She sounded surprised. "You've never actually had sex with one?"

"I have not." He didn't want to have to explain to her why he hadn't.

"Hunter?" Hearing the derogatory term from her lips stung. He didn't want her to think of him as his profession. Only as Zuran.

"Yes?" His tone was sharp.

A warm, wet hand touched his back, water dripping down his skin from her palm. He had been so caught up in his thoughts that he hadn't even heard her leave the pool. "Turn around," she whispered. "Please."

His heart hammered against the inside of his chest, a bottomless pit opening up beneath his stomach as it dropped. Turning around slowly, Zuran fixed his gaze on a spot just above her head, clenching his fists to keep himself in control. Her small hands curled around his braids as she tugged him down to her level. He went willingly, knowing that his punishment for being harsh with her would be severe. Surprise stirred inside of him as she pressed her lips to his in a hard kiss, holding him close to her like she could keep him from escaping. The pleasure that surged through him tore a rumbling moan from his throat.

The sound was enough to jolt sense into him and yanked himself back, stumbling away as if she had burned him. Why would she have kissed him? He shouldn't have allowed that, shouldn't have let himself be pulled in like that. Zuran closed his eyes, drawing in a deep breath.

"You should dress." He grabbed the clothing he had acquired for her, holding it out, and refused to meet her gaze.

"Zuran…"

"Please."

He heard the gentle ripple of the water, but refused to turn around, and didn't even open his eyes in case the temptation was too great. The sound of her wet feet padding up to him made his body tingle. Samantha slipped the cloth from his fingers and murmured her thanks.

"I'm finished," she said, placing her tiny hand on his arm.

Without uttering a word, Zuran ushered her from the pools, keeping his hand light on her back as they returned to the village. Once they reached Olan's hut, he fisted his hands at his sides and nodded toward the entrance.

"You will stay here." It was all he trusted himself to say before turning on his heels.

"Zuran!"

He heard her call him, but he didn't dare to turn back. With the way the mating heat was coursing through his body, making him feel as if he were going to burn from the inside out, Zuran couldn't trust himself not to touch her again.

She had told him that her people chose their mates, that they were not judged based on their positions, and this gave him more hope than she could have known.

CHAPTER 9

SAMANTHA

*O*riginally, Samantha intended the kiss to be sweet, playful, and light. Something to show him she didn't think like the members of his tribe. He had shocked her when he pulled away as if she'd branded him.

Honestly, she hadn't ever been the girl to kiss on a first date, or first *day* in this case, but the fact that Zuran had shared with her that he had never been given something as simple as a kiss touched something deep inside of her. She sighed as she watched him disappear among the other huts, wishing she could understand how his people could treat him so poorly.

Samantha eyed the circular hut he had brought her to, biting her lip as she considered her options. She could try to run now and hope no one caught her, but she scrapped that idea quickly. There were far too many people milling about the streets. She was bound to be seen and stopped before she could reach the trees on the edges. Maybe she could wait until nightfall and slip out while everyone slept.

She needed answers, needed to know why she had been sent here alone and left to fend for herself for so damn long.

With the beginnings of her plan set, Samantha turned her attention back to the hut. The outside was made from the dark red bark of the trees she had seen in the forest and reminded her of the simple homes that had once made up some of the smaller villages on Earth. There were two colorful windows on either side of the door, and she reached out, running her fingers over the beautifully crafted glass.

She had seen designs like these in the old Earth vids. *Stained glass*, that's what it had been called. Delicate things such as these weren't made for life on the spaceship she called home, but she knew a few samples resided in the museum on the space station.

Pressing down on the metal lever that served as the handle, Samantha stepped inside. "Hello?" When no one answered her, she pushed the wooden door open and took in her surroundings. The inside was much larger than she had imagined. The thatched roof spiraled up to a point, making the single room feel open and airy. Light from the suns shown through the windows, scattering prisms along the floors and the freestanding wall in the middle of the room.

To her left was a curved wooden table, piled high with bolts of gorgeous fabric and sewing instruments. Cubbies with even more fabric shoved inside of them lined the wall, and she marveled at the selection.

This wasn't a guest hut. The space was far too lived in to be anything except someone's residence. Samantha felt like an intruder when she stepped around the freestanding wall to see the soft pile of furs thrown haphazardly against the wall and the shelves lined with intricately carved wooden figures and other little trinkets.

One of the carvings, a small figurine of what seemed to be a child, caught her eye. It was painted white, with its features painstakingly depicted. A smile curved her lips as she took it down from the shelf, running her fingers gingerly along the side of its small face.

"Please don't touch that."

Samantha jumped, snatching the pocketknife from her cleavage where she had stuck it after her bath and spun toward the voice. Olan stood on the right side of the wall, his eyes fixed on the figurine she held clutched to her chest.

"What the hell are you doing here?"

Olan arched a haughty brow, his eyes sweeping over the weapon. "Is that necessary?"

"It is when you come into a home unannounced."

"I wasn't aware I needed to announce myself in my own home," he retorted.

His home? Oh, gods, the organized chaos of the room made sense now. "Zuran told me this was where I was staying. If I had known it was your home, I wouldn't have let him leave me here." Samantha placed the figure back on the shelf and turned to leave.

"Fanahala."

Something in his voice made her halt, and she glanced back to see him adjusting the placement of the little wooden child.

"This is my home and you are my bride, which means," he turned toward her slowly, "that this is your home now as well."

"I'm not sure how many times I have to tell you that I'm not your bride. I'm not staying here with you." She jerked her chin toward the pile of furs. "I'm not getting into bed with you."

"There is nowhere else in the village for you to stay tonight. I don't know what males on your Earth are like, but Seyton males do not force females to mate."

"No, they just force them into marriages they don't want any part of." She gave him a droll stare.

"Take the furs then. I will sleep at my table."

An annoying sense of guilt ate at her. *Damn me.* "Wait. That's ridiculous. This is your house." Samantha sighed. "I'll stay on one side of the furs, and you will stay on the other. Deal?"

Olan nodded. "If that's what you wish." He plucked the pocket knife from her hand, hushing her protests with a shake of his head. "Your weapon will be there when you wake. I don't need you stabbing me in your sleep." She watched as he placed it on the shelf next to the figure.

"Did you carve that?" she asked.

"No."

"Oh. Your father?"

"No."

"Was it passed down to you?"

"No, Fanahala."

Real forthcoming. "Who made it?"

His jaw clenched for a moment before bent to pull down the top layer of the furs. "Someone I knew a long time ago."

"So, a friend—"

"Fanahala, please." He sighed. "I don't wish to talk about it."

She smoothed her hand over the soft red dress Zuran had given her before slipping past Olan and crawling into the warm, plush bedding. She turned her back to him, facing the wall, and took a deep breath.

She could do this. In a couple of hours, she would sneak out and she wouldn't have to worry about sharing a bed with Olan anymore.

The furs shifted a hair when Olan climbed in beside her, and she barely stifled the gasp when his tail snaked around her ankle as he got comfortable.

It's one night, she reminded herself. *You've got this.* Samantha glanced over her shoulder, glaring at the back of Olan's head.

Sneaking out with him here was going to be tricky, but if she could wait for him to fall asleep, she was sure she could make it work. Cocooned within the warmth of the furs, Samantha fought her exhaustion. It had been weeks since she last slept on anything close to a real bed, and her body was begging for just a moment of rest.

No. No sleeping. You can sleep when you've found the team.

The harder she fought, the harder it became to open her eyes whenever she blinked. When she managed to pry them open again, she was startled to see that she had her cheek pressed up against a colorful muscular chest. Gods, she must have fallen asleep and cuddled up to him. Cuddling was a weakness of hers and was just one of the reasons she hadn't intended to fall asleep. Olan was snoring softly, his face relaxed and his mouth hanging open just the slightest bit.

With extra care, Samantha peeled herself away from his chest, slowly slipping her foot from the loosened hold of his tail. His arm was draped over her hip, and she slid out from beneath it, carefully lowering it to the bedding.

When she finally sat up, she realized she shouldn't have taken the side near the wall. She couldn't crawl off at the top or bottom without having to jump over stacks of books and small boxes. The only way out of the furs was to climb Mt. Olan. Samantha grimaced as she threw her leg over his. What the hell were they feeding the men in this village? She felt so tiny in comparison, and Zuran had been even bigger.

She cleared his legs, stepping down onto the floor as quietly as she could before turning back to make sure Olan still slept. One hurdle down. Creeping over to the shelving, Samantha snatched her knife up and headed for the door. The wood barely made a noise as she secured the door and turned her back on the little hut.

She wasn't naïve enough to think she could navigate the forest on her own. The first time she had tried that, she ended up being captured, but if she could convince Zuran to come with her, she could eliminate a lot of stumbling around blindly, hoping she was going in the right direction.

If I were Zuran, where would I be?

Samantha zigzagged through the huts, stopping at each one to peer through the small windows. She felt like a peeping Tom, but Zuran didn't occupy any of the homes located around Olan. If she couldn't find him soon, she was going to have to suck it up and head out on her own. The people Ama had sent to search for the drop ship might already be there, and she was here wasting precious time.

Eventually, she found her way to the large entrance to the village, the one Zuran and the other male had brought her in through. She hesitated as she approached the massive wooden pillars, each one carved with intricate details.

Her people were out there, but was she really going to leave the safety of the village to go looking for them? The forest had been terrifying during the daylight hours, but now, shrouded in shadows, it was even more ominous. She stepped around one of the pillars and directly into the hard, dark body of one of the Seyton.

"Ouch!" she hissed, rubbing her hand over her nose as she looked up into the familiar face of her demon alien.

"Where do you think you're going?" His voice was a soft grumble, sparking arousal inside of her. She honestly needed to stop lusting after these aliens and focus on her goal.

"I was actually looking for you."

Zuran frowned down at her. "Me?"

"Yes. I need you."

"Why?"

"I need to bust out of here, and you're going to help me." She grinned up at him. "I need you to take me to the crash site so I can make sure everyone's okay."

"Niva has been sent to aid them. She is the second-in-command within the unmated female's village. Zyar, who is a very good friend of mine, has been asked to accompany her." Zuran's lips tilted up slightly, showing the tiniest hint of the fangs. "You, on the other hand, are going to be returned to your mate."

He spun her around before she could even comprehend the fact that he had turned her down. She wiggled against the hand he pressed against her lower back, trying to dig her heels into the dirt. "He's not my mate. I don't want to be given to anyone! What I want is to find my—" The words died on her tongue when she saw Olan standing just inside the entrance. For a split second, she watched the raw emotion flash across his face before a wall went up.

Zuran nudged her forward, until the three of them were standing no more than a foot apart. "I'll release her into your care." He murmured, his hand skimming over her hip before he stepped back.

"Traitor," Samantha mumbled, as she watched the sparks of electricity bounce between the colorful male's horns.

Olan said nothing to either of them, merely scooping her up into his arms and spun around. She wanted to demand he put her down, to pound her fists against his body until he released her, but she kept seeing the pain in his face. A strange sense of guilt nagged at her.

When they reached his hut, Olan pushed the door open, slamming it shut with his foot before setting her on her feet. She watched in silence as he dug through a pile of scrap fabric before he pulled out a long, braided length. He wrapped one end around her waist, securing it with a knot, before attaching the other end around his torso. Olan gave the knot on her end a tug, causing her to stumble into him.

"What's this about? Olan?" She could feel the anger rolling

off of him in waves. It, like his electricity, made the air around her crackle.

He didn't respond to her questions, but took her by the arm, guiding her behind the wall and back into the area where they had slept. With a huff, he extinguished the candle on the shelves and nudged her until she climbed back into the furs. She felt him move up behind her, his arms moving around her body until she was locked against him.

"Are you mad?" she asked. "Okay, that's stupid, of course you are, but honestly, you shouldn't be mad at me." Samantha sighed, trying to turn in his arms so that she could glare at him properly, but he only pressed his big hand to her cheek, turning her away. "Look, humans don't *do* this. We don't get assigned a partner. We choose."

She hated his silence. She would have preferred to hash this out, put everything on the table, but he staunchly ignored her.

"Are you seriously going to give me the silent treatment?"

Fine. She had survived forty days alone, shut in that damn rescue pod with no one but herself and a glitchy AI to talk to. This was nothing.

And she would bite her tongue off before she admitted that she was already missing the sound of his voice and Zuran's traitorous face.

CHAPTER 10

OLAN

"*I* am not going with this damn rope tying us together!" his bride insisted, her little foot stomping the ground.

Olan narrowed his eyes and pushed her into the outhouse. There was a door separating them. He wasn't sure why she insisted on throwing a fit about it when he knew she must need to go. To his shame, he hadn't taken this particular aspect into consideration the day before.

"Still not talking to me, huh?"

Again, he nudged her forward without a reply, shutting the door as she spun around to argue. He heard her grumbling, cursing him as she went about her business. As she stepped out, Olan blocked her exit, using his body to force her back into the small facility.

"Oh no, you can go to the bathroom on your own. You're a big boy. I believe in you."

He couldn't trust her to stand outside for him. Knowing his little mate, she would take off before he even realized she'd loosened the knot. He merely shook his head and locked the door. Samantha's cheeks turned a pretty shade of pink before she huffed and turned her back on him, tapping one of her feet as he relieved himself.

When he had finished, he brought her outside to the pools so she could clean her hands and wash her face. The small stream that ran beneath the outhouse carried the waste downhill, away from the bathing areas. He squatted down beside her, dipping his cupped hands into the warm waters so he could splash his face.

"So we've used the bathroom and washed up. What now, Sparky?"

If she thought this nickname was going to get a rise from him, she was mistaken. Olan didn't trust himself to speak to her when he was feeling so many emotions. No matter what he said, his bride refused her title, refused him and everything he was offering.

Instead of using words, he would show her how a mating should be.

Never had he heard of a mate sneaking off into the night like a damned thief. When she had wrapped herself around him in her sleep, Olan had foolishly believed she was beginning to trust him, to see that he was only trying to do his best by her and follow the All Mother's wishes. That illusion had been shattered upon waking to find his furs empty and his mate not within the hut. He had questioned everything he had done. Had he been an inadequate male or was his human bride merely trying to lower his guard so that she could escape him?

He would not make that same mistake twice.

Samantha's growl of frustration as she tugged at the material binding them nearly made him grin. The heat of the day had yet to reach its peak. Just above the treetops in the distance, the twin suns were rising, nearly connected at this point in the cycle, signaling that tomorrow's eclipse would be on time for the festival.

Olan led Samantha into the heart of the village for the morning meal. His bride needed more time, needed to see that all he wanted for her was happiness. If he pushed her too hard, he was going to lose her before he ever even got a chance.

He would win her over. He had no choice.

He lifted her easily onto the bench beside him. She was tiny in comparison to his people. Her legs didn't quite reach the ground, and he fought off the grin that tugged at his lips as he tugged a stray strand of her hair behind her ear before turning to fill her plate. He selected some fruit she had liked at the evening meal, as well as one of the winged samara eggs. The creatures were practically flightless, which made them easy to keep on the small farms that dotted the west side of the village.

He briefly considered taking Samantha to visit them, but he looked down at her delicate hand where it rested on the table and reconsidered. Samaras were cranky on their best days and downright evil on their worst. Even the most practiced farmers had been known to lose a toe or even the tip of a finger to the little beasts.

Olan placed her plate in front her, grunting in satisfaction as she dug into her meal. Some of the younger hunters joined them, sitting at the opposite end of the table, but Zuran was absent. He glanced at her as they ate in silence, admiring the flush that crept into her cheeks every time she tried something new and found it to her liking.

When they finished, Olan lifted her from the bench and collected their plates. The washbasin to the side already had a neat stack of dishes, and he placed theirs on top. Whoever was in the rotation would come by soon to clean them and set them back out for the afternoon meal.

"So are we still playing the quiet game?" she asked as she picked up her pace, trying her best to keep up with his long stride.

Olan only grunted, stepping out into the main road and heading back to his home. She grumbled under her breath, crossing her arms over her chest as she followed.

With the festival taking place tomorrow night, he had many last-minute adjustments to see to. A few of the younger males were already waiting outside his hut by the time they arrived; the fabric Ama had chosen for them in hand.

He couldn't ever recall being as hopeful as these males on the eve of the festival. From the moment he stepped out of the bloom, Olan had felt a sense of guilt, as if he didn't deserve to have been selected as a breeder. He shook away the memories as he opened the door, welcoming the young breeders inside.

Samantha huffed as he spoke to them, taking their garments for their final alterations and promising they would have them in time for Ama's inspection. He worked quickly, expertly stitching together the material in the way Ama had instructed. How she managed to know what color and pattern each pair would need had always been a mystery. She had told him once, when he was still in his apprenticeship, that the All Mother guided her, whispering the matches.

All Mother forgive him, but he wasn't at all sure what she had been thinking when she paired him with his little human.

"Is this what you do all day?"

He inclined his head in response, still not sure if he possessed the patience to speak to her. *She ran from you.* The thought still stung him. Olan was in the prime of his breeding and exhibited exemplary control over his lightning. By all accounts, he was a perfect breeder. The fact that he was unmated at his age was due only to his own reservations, and that Ama had never pushed him. Until now.

Samantha sighed, standing from the stool he had brought out

for her. She wandered around the wall that separated his work space from his living quarters, pulling the fabric that tied them together taut. When she came back around, she propped her side against the edge of his table. In her hands was the wooden figure Zuran had carved for him when they were young. It had been part of a pair.

"I'll keep yours, and you can keep mine," he could still hear Zuran saying. *"This way, we'll never be apart."*

He watched her fingers trace over the face before she carefully cradled it in her palm as if it were a kit. To Olan, the figurine was a priceless, yet painful, representation of his youth. Even after their fallout, the figure took pride of place on his shelves, along with the animal carvings Zuran had painstakingly made for him.

Why Samantha felt so drawn to this one in particular was something that nagged at his mind.

Shaking his head to disperse his thoughts, Olan gathered the finished dresses and tugged at the material around his waist, pulling Samantha toward the door. She looked up at him with a frown, setting the figurine on the desk before balling her fists on her hips.

"I'm not a dog, Olan. You can't just keep leading me around on a leash like this." She stumbled after him. "Should have stabbed you a few more times when I had the chance."

It took a good deal of his self-control to hold back the laugh at her mumbled words. He greeted his neighbors as they walked down, smiling politely at their questioning glances, but offering no explanation. When they reached Ama's dwelling, he knocked softly and waited.

Her home was the largest in the village, consisting of one large hut and four smaller, circular rooms. When the chieftess swung the door open, Olan grinned at her appearance. Fabrics were draped on both arms and across her shoulders, and a dark blue strip of ribbon hung from one of her horns.

"Ah, Olan, wonderful timing, as always." She held out her hands for the garments he carried. "Is this the last of them?"

"It is. I've just finished them."

Samantha gasped beside him, her hands flying to her mouth in mock shock. "He speaks! It's a miracle!"

Ama arched a curious brow but did not otherwise react. "The day is yours. You have earned it."

"Has there been any word from Niva?"

"Nothing yet. I'm sure we will hear from her soon enough."

"Of course," he said, but a glance at his bride told him she wasn't pleased with this news. Her frown deepened when she turned her gaze on him and sighed. Perhaps he should have been less harsh with her and tried to look at it from her perspective.

These were her people, possibly her friends or family. What if he were in the same position? What if it were Asa or Vane or even Zuran out there? Wouldn't he do anything to assure that they were taken care of? Wouldn't he attempt to leave, to go against Ama for them?

"Come," he commanded softly, ignoring the look of genuine surprise on her face.

The suns had reached their apex, sitting high in the sky together. Asa and Vane would be awake by now. Olan led Samantha down past the small pond and over the wooden bridge that separated the huts. Asa's home, though smaller than Ama's, was far larger than his. Mated pairs required more room, given that many of them started growing their families as soon as possible.

He heard Samantha's gasp of delight as soon as the hut came into view. Unlike the red exterior of the majority of the huts, Asa's was beautifully decorated with painted depictions of the wild flower blooms that grew around the pond. The village's second-in-command painted in her spare time, using anything she could get her hands on as a canvas. Samantha reached out to trace one of the blue blooms.

"Who painted this?"

"I did," Asa said, coming up behind them, a bouquet of wild-flowers in her hands. "It's a pleasure to have visitors. Is this a social call, or do you have business?"

"Social. Merely visiting friends," he replied.

"What sort of pigment do you use for these?" Samantha asked.

Asa shrugged as she eyed her artwork. "Berries and other plants for the most part."

"Do you think it could work on hair?" She reached up to tug at the wild strands. "My purple was fading before I even left the ship, but I hadn't made time to redo it."

Asa smiled. "I'm sure it couldn't hurt to try. There's a berry that grows nearby that stains the skin for days after you use it." She nodded toward the fabric that bound them together, her brow raised humorously as she untied the knot. "You come with me. Olan and Vane can spend some quality time together."

He watched as they disappeared around the side of the hut, Samantha grinning from ear to ear as she spoke excitedly. This would be good for her. Although Asa could be stern and unbending, she was also incredibly empathetic and caring. He would use his time with Vane to mull over his own emotions.

Vane was one of a few tanners working within the village. Olan took the south road back through the center to the area on the outskirts where the tanning huts were located. The smell that accompanied the work meant that most chose to build their dwellings on the opposite side of the village. Hidden amongst a loose circle of trees, Olan spotted the familiar red of the building.

"Vane?"

"Back here," the male's voice came.

Olan stepped around the back of the hut to find his friend cleaning what seemed to be a fresh kill. He worked the sharp blade along the inside of the milory, separating the hide from the underlying muscle. Milory furs were coveted for their warmth during the harsh winter months, and this one was exceptional. With its long neck and fatty body, just one milory could yield two furs and enough meat to create a day's worth of meals for the entire village.

"Quite the bounty."

"One of the hunters brought it to me early this morning. Blessing from the All Mother."

"Indeed." Olan perched himself on one of the stumps the tanners used as stools when they worked. Breeders were not permitted to participate in the hunts. Their work saw them confined to the village.

"Did you need something, brother?"

Olan curled his tail around his right leg, finding himself suddenly self-conscious. "I'm—I fear that I might not be as suited to life as a breeder as I once thought."

Vane looked up from his work with a frown. "What about it has you worried?"

"I'm not sure."

The other male grunted, tossing the beast's entrails into one of the hammered metal basins at his side. He swiped his forearm across his head and gestured for Olan. "Help me get this up."

Olan took one of the milory's long back legs. They had been tied together, and he helped Vane slide the heavy hook beneath the knot so it could be hoisted off of the ground. He watched as Vane continued his work, finding peace in the quiet.

"My mate tried to run from me last night."

Vane's eyes whipped toward him. "Why would she do that?"

"I believe she was going to try and locate her people, the ones who fell yesterday."

Vane seemed to consider this for a moment before turning his attention back to the milory. "This bothers you?"

"Of course it does." Olan frowned. "I was chosen as her mate. We should be preparing for the festival tomorrow, getting ready to promise ourselves and start our family. Instead, I'm having to tie her to my side so that she doesn't slip away again."

"You tied her to your side?"

Olan scrubbed his hands over his face when Vane began to laugh. "I'm so glad my troubles amuse you." He glared, but he couldn't stop the chuckle that bubbled up within him.

"Allow me to share some advice with you?"

"Please do."

"Change is not always as easy as we think it will be. You have prepared for this your whole life, but that may not be the way of it where your female comes from." Vane set his knife aside, wiping his hands on the long leather apron he wore. "Let me show you something I've been working on."

Olan followed his friend into one of the back rooms of the tanning hut. Tucked into the corner, partially covered by a hide, was a small wooden cradle. Long vines and tiny leaves had been carved along the sides and twined down toward the curved bottom.

"One of the hunters has been helping me with the woodwork. It isn't exactly my specialty." Vane ran his hand over the back of his neck as Olan crouched to inspect the craftsmanship.

"Is Asa—you are expecting?"

Vane shook his head. "Not yet." He sighed wearily. "I thought this might lift her spirits. Asa has struggled lately."

Olan let his fingers drift over the wood. He knew about their struggles, had witnessed Asa's tears on more than one occasion after she had gotten her hopes up. They weren't the only mated pair facing this problem. Many seemingly fertile matings were resulting in fewer and fewer young.

"No matter how hard you pray, no matter how hard you fight, some things may never turn out the way you expected."

Olan turned to Vane, watching as the other male blinked back the tears welling up in his eyes. "I think this is a wonderful gift."

"Do yourself and your female both a favor: don't just accept Ama's declaration. Approach this like you would a mating of your choice. Win her affection, give her a reason to wish to remain with you."

He hadn't ever imagined having to persuade a chosen mate to stay with him, had never actually witnessed any of the other males or females resist this much.

"Thank you for your counsel, Vane."

"Of course, brother." Vane tugged the hide back down over the cradle and led the way back outside. "I'll finish up here and then we can retrieve the females for the noon meal. Maybe being around more pairings will warm her to the idea."

Vane was a male of few words, and the ones he did speak were worth taking note. Olan took the advice, thinking it over as he watched his friend work. He shouldn't have expected Samantha to dive head first into this. She had told him herself last night that humans were not accustomed to this way of mating, but he hadn't listened.

When Vane had finished the first stages of fleshing the hide, Olan helped him rinse it in the stream before stretching it over the wooden structure in the small field to the right of the hut. Vane punctured the side and wove string through the small holes, tying each piece off until the hide was pulled taut between the opposing slats. "The farther we can stretch the hide, the easier it will be to divide."

"How much longer will this one take before it is able to be used?"

"A week or so."

He followed Vane back down to the stream so they could rinse off, their electricity ridding them of the lingering grime. They walked in comfortable silence, and by the time they had returned to Asa's hut, Olan was feeling much more confident about his future. The soft sound of laughter from within made his heart race, and he practically ran across the remaining distance, swinging the door open.

Samantha's head was thrown back in pure joy. The fading violet of her locks had been replaced with a rich, shimmering purple. He smiled as he watched her race across the room, her hands and half her cheek stained purple from the berry.

"Come back, you coward! You look like you need a little color!"

The smile fell from his face when she collided with Zuran's dark chest. She wrapped her hands around the long braids at the front of his head, squealing as the hunter gripped her arms.

"I told you it was an accident!" Zuran laughed as he fought her off. "Not the braids, Samantha!"

Sparks of his lightning flickered over his skin, dancing between his horns, but he called on all of his control to rein it in. Samantha stood between them, and he would never forgive himself if he hurt her. Her pretty smile faded when her eyes met his, and he felt the pang of unwanted jealousy that this hunter had the ability to bring her such joy.

"Zuran," Vane greeted him as he stepped into the hut. "Did we have a lesson planned for today?"

"No," Zuran ground out, his gaze never straying from Olan's.

"Ah, well," Vane cleared his throat, no doubt feeling the tension between them. "Perhaps we could speak another day? Today is—today is not a good day."

"Of course. I should be on my way," the hunter murmured.

"Yes, you should." The growl burned the back of Olan's throat as he watched the male set Samantha away from him. She clutched at the braids in her hands, but he gently pried her fingers from the strands.

Olan stepped forward, his shoulder brushing Zuran's as they passed, and he snarled at the sparks that bounced between their bodies. He tugged the length of braided material from the loop on his hip.

"Oh, really, Olan? This is completely unnecessary! I was here the entire time you were gone," Samantha protested, stomping her foot on the floor of the hut.

"Enough," he grumbled.

Zuran's low growl from his back told him the other male wasn't pleased with the way he was treating his bride, but Olan cared little about what the other male felt was appropriate.

"Your message has been received," Asa said coolly, stepping out of one of the back rooms. "We will not take up any more of your time, hunter." The dismissal was unmistakable.

Vane placed a gentle hand on Zuran's shoulder as he passed. "Come find me soon. We will finish up our work."

Olan ignored Samantha's scowl, knotting the fabric and giving it a tug to make sure it was secure. He wanted to tell her she looked beautiful, that the rich purple of her hair made her eyes sparkle, and wanted to bring back the smile that had lit up her face only moments ago. He thanked Asa and Vane for their hospitality and led his seething mate outside.

CHAPTER 11

SAMANTHA

*S*he stared daggers at his back as she followed him through the village. Samantha had hoped that they moved past this, that she'd shown him she wasn't going to take off again. At the first opportunity, she was going to cut this rope into tiny pieces.

This did nothing to convince her that staying here with him was what was best for her.

What was it about Zuran that seemed to flip a switch? Asa had been so kind until the moment he showed up. She had turned cold and dismissive, opting to leave the room instead of staying and speaking with him. Olan's mood was always darker after their interactions, and he seemed to go out of his way to avoid the other male.

The fact that she enjoyed Zuran's company obviously upset him.

Days passed in relative quiet, the excitement of the eclipse that happened during that time fading quickly. They rarely left the hut unless it was to attend a meal, but even those outings stopped after scuffles had begun to break out in her presence. Instead, Ama sent over one of the mated females to deliver fresh fruit and plates of meats and vegetables. She spent her days watching Olan work at his table or pacing back and forth as far as the rope would let her go.

The hut was feeling more and more like a prison with each day that passed.

Today, she sat on the ground at his feet, her legs stretched out in front of her as she rubbed her fingers over the figure. Olan had long since given up trying to take it from her. She glanced up at him from under her lashes, watching as he stitched two halves of a pattern together. The movement of his fingers was hypnotic, but she didn't want to be caught staring, especially when she was so annoyed with him. Her eyes drifted to the opposite side of the room. Something on the leg of the smaller table caught her attention.

Samantha had thought the bugs in the archives and in the display cases on the space station were disturbing, but the thing crawling on the floor was what nightmares were made of. There was an insect her mother told her about, one she remembered her grandmother showing her when she was younger, a moth called *Creatonotos gangis*. The males of the species had four reversible coremata at the tip of the abdomen which emitted pheromones. In all honesty, the moths looked like flying tentacle monsters.

The insect in front of her lacked the wings, and the overall moth-like appearance, but the tentacle looking protrusions were spot on. It crawled around the bottom of the wall on thin black legs, moving back and forth as it weaved a silky web between the wooden feet. Samantha would never claim that entomology had interested her, but she couldn't help but watch in horrified fascination as the creature went about its business. Insects played an important role within ecosystems. That certainly didn't mean she had to like them or want anything to do with the creepy little guys.

When the nightmare bug turned toward her and raised its front legs, Samantha stilled. A shriek of pure terror escaped her as the damn creature shot forward, moving faster than she could have ever expected. Its long legs latched onto her ankle and the tentacles wriggled as it climbed higher. She clutched at the rope, pulling herself up against Olan's hip as she shook her leg wildly in an attempt to dislodge her little hitchhiker.

"Olan! Help!"

"Calm, Fanahala." He grunted as her fists pummeled his thigh.

"It's trying to eat me!"

"It is a kepske. It is not interested in eating you."

Samantha groped around behind her, grabbing the first thing she touched. The fact that it was Olan's tail she used to flick the bug off would have made her laugh if she weren't so freaked out. She wedged herself between his body and the table, climbing into his lap as she watched the bug flail around on its back. Olan glared at her, pulling his tail up to swipe at the tip.

"*It's just a kepske,*" she mocked. Olan lifted her into his arms with a resigned sigh before standing. When he brought his foot up to stomp on it, Samantha grabbed his face. "Wait! Don't just kill it!"

"You just claimed it was going to eat you, and now you are asking me to spare its life?"

"What if it's important to your ecosystem? What if it's one of those good bugs that eats the bad bugs? Just—just throw it outside."

Olan stared down at her for a moment before a wide grin split his face and his booming laughter filled the hut. He shifted her in his arms, cradling her against his left side so he could scoop the little beasty in his other hand. She felt like a child the way she clung to him, her arms clutching his shoulder and neck. Living in space hadn't prepared her for the bugs she was bound to encounter on the surface.

The kepske scurried out of his big hand as he cracked the door, crawling across the path into a small group of shrub-like plants. *Good riddance.* When she turned back to thank him, Olan was grinning down at her.

She hadn't really thought about how close they were, or that she had practically climbed him like he was some sort of colorful tree. His arms tightened around her and she felt her breath quicken when he caressed her cheek, but the sweetness of the moment was soon over. Olan sat her back on her feet, tugging on the rope as he walked back to his stool to continue his work. The odd sense of loss she felt when he moved away left her feeling torn.

"Olan?"

"Yes, Star Born?"

She rolled her eyes at the name. "When are you going to stop being angry with me?"

His hand paused mid-stitch, and she watched his brows draw down. "You think I'm angry?"

"Uh, yeah." She tugged at the rope still tying them together. "Angry."

"I'm not angry with you, Fanahala. I'm hurt."

"Then why keep me here?"

The emotion she had seen flash across his face the night she had tried to escape settled over his features as he stared down at his hands where they rested on the table. "The All Mother judged me worthy of becoming your mate. I've been preparing my whole life for the moment when Ama would make the selection. Imagine my surprise when my female does everything in her power to refuse me, to escape me, when I want nothing more than to keep her safe and make her proud."

"*You* have been preparing your whole life, but *I* haven't."

"I don't know what you want me to do, Fanahala. What can I do that would make you happy?" He turned on the stool, his fingers raking through the strands of his short hair.

"Would you like me to give you the obvious answer?"

Olan huffed. "I cannot let you leave the village to search for your people. The forest is a dangerous place."

"Only fit for beasts and hunters?"

The statement made him wince. "Fanahala…"

She let the silence settle over them for a moment as she studied the figurine in her hands. "What is it about Zuran that makes you hate him so much?"

"Hate?" Olan seemed genuinely taken back by her question. "I could never—I do not hate Zuran, Fanahala."

"Then what is it? Anytime you're around him, you become this overbearing jerk."

"Zuran is a hunter."

Samantha sighed in frustration. "So I've gathered. What does that have to do with anything?"

He looked down at her like he couldn't believe he was having to explain this. "Hunters are not permitted to mate, yet Zuran seems to have decided that this no longer applies to him. He behaves as if he has a right to you."

"No one has a right to me." She was beginning to feel like a broken record. "The way you all treat hunters is barbaric, and, quite honestly, it doesn't help your cause at all. I'm not Seyton, I'm human, and humans choose their own mates."

"We may also choose if the All Mother gives her blessing."

"But the hunters can't?"

"Of course not." Olan frowned.

"You honestly can't see how wrong that is?" Samantha shook her head in disbelief. "So they're just expected to live their whole lives without families and mates of their own?"

Olan's jaw ticked. "Hunters are not safe, Fanahala."

"How so? Because of their profession?"

"Is that what Zuran told you?" He sneered when she nodded. "I'm sure he conveniently left out the fact that all hunters eventually succumb to breeding heat. They gradually become more violent and aggressive as they age until they finally lose their minds. It is why they are kept away from the unmated females. Perhaps you have noticed the chaos your refusal has caused among the males?"

"If *not* breeding is what causes the breeding heat, then why the hell aren't they allowed to *breed*?"

"It isn't that simple," he said, but she could see that he wasn't so sure of himself now.

"You want to talk to me about the dangers of the hunters, about how they can't be trusted around the unmated females, but look at you. You've kept me tied to you and shut in your hut for days now. I've heard nothing about my people, and I'm not allowed to see to their safety myself. If you think this is treating me well, then I'd hate to see what you consider being treated poorly."

Olan stared at her, and for a moment, she thought she might have crossed a line.

"You're right."

Samantha blinked up at him as he reached for her, pulling her close and working the knot around her waist loose.

"I am?"

He dropped the material onto the table at his side and took her hands into his, turning the one that still grasped the figure. She watched as his thumb brushed over the face before drifting over her knuckles. "I will see to it myself that your people are safe."

"I'll come—"

"No. I will send someone before the evening meal to look after you." When she opened her mouth to protest, he leaned down, pressing his forehead to hers. "Please, Fanahala. Let me keep you safe the only way I can. I am trying my best."

She felt the soft brush of his lips across her cheek and shivered. Perhaps this was his idea of a compromise. He didn't want her going out into the forest, so he would do it for her. The thought had to count for something, didn't it?

Olan collected a small pouch, tying it to the loop on his cover, before pausing at the entrance. His gaze met hers for a moment and then he was gone, leaving her in stunned silence as the door slammed behind him.

CHAPTER 12

ZURAN

*V*ane slid the short carving blade along the surface of the wood, shaving down the area around the last of the leaves that sprouted from the vine Zuran had helped him map out months ago. The thin shavings spiraled backward over his hand before falling to the floor of the tanning hut. They sat in comfortable silence most of the time, only speaking to give directions or ask a question.

When Vane had first approached Zuran for help, he had been wary. None of the breeders had ever treated him in such a friendly manner, but he would soon find that Vane wasn't like the rest. He treated Zuran as if he were just... Zuran, not a hunter. The same way Samantha had. He ran the pad of his finger along the body of the figure he was whittling, brushing away the dust that had collected. Since the moment he found her in the forest, he had thought of little else. She consumed his thoughts, filled his mind with her bravery, and infiltrated his dreams.

When he wasn't thinking of her, he was carving her likeness.

The one he held in his hands was nearly finished, but it was different from the others. Pretty, delicate wings were folded behind her; each feather lovingly etched into the red wood. Using the blade at the end of his tail, Zuran shaped and smoothed the curves of her hips.

"I think I've finished." Vane said as he stood, brushing the dust from his hands onto the apron he wore. "Have a look?"

"You did a fine job." Zuran rocked the cradle, watching as it swayed gently from side to side. "Will you paint it?"

The other male ran his hand along his jaw. "I thought I would leave that to Asa. I may have proven myself to be a decent wood worker under your tutelage, but I've spent years with Asa and have yet to absorb any of her creativity."

Zuran grinned, stepping back so that Vane could pull the hide over the gift. While he and Asa had never been fond of one another, Zuran often found himself in awe of her love for her mate. He looked down at the carving in his hand before holding it out to the other male. "A gift for your future kit."

Vane grinned as he took the offering. "Are you sure? It's such a lovely piece to give away."

"I have others." Zuran shrugged, stepping out into the light of the suns.

"He'll come around."

Zuran turned back, his brows furrowing. "Who's that?"

"Olan." The male said, tucking the carving into the pouch at his side. "I know it is none of my business—"

"You're right. It's none of your business what Olan and his mate do, and it is none of mine either."

"Zuran—"

"Let me know when you've finished the milory hide."

Zuran stalked toward the tree line, keeping to the outskirts of the village as he made his way home. His hut was tucked into a small grove of trees just off of the path that led into the village. It was a bit of a trek from the tanning huts, but he could do with some fresh air to help clear away the foul mood hearing about Olan and Samantha left him in.

The breeder had been avoiding bringing his new mate anywhere near the places Zuran frequented ever since he had found him at Asa's. He knew it was better this way, knew that he shouldn't keep pushing the limits, but there was something within him that couldn't let the little female go. Every time he closed his eyes, he imagined her soft lips against his, her fingers curled into his braids, and her body pressed into him.

His cock gave an involuntary jerk beneath the soft leather of his cover, and Zuran groaned, picking up his pace. He would return to the hunt tonight, but before he could leave, he needed to gather supplies. The windows built into his hut were smaller than many of the ones found within the village, but they were circular and dotted the walls, casting their colorful lights around the interior. With the heavy wooden door propped open, the light that filtered down through the branches of the trees brightened the small space.

Zuran lifted the lid of the trunk along the back wall, pushing aside his unfinished carvings. Many of them were depictions of the various animals he hunted or creatures of legend he had heard about in his youth. As he searched for his smaller set of traps, one of the figurines caught his eye. It was the only painted one of the lot, the only one created in his youth that he hadn't tossed into the fire on the day he stepped out of the agmari bloom as a hunter.

"Zuran?"

The unexpected voice had his knees slamming into the trunk as he started, the heavy lid falling onto his hand as he dropped the carving. "All Mother bless it…" He hissed, shaking his injured digits as he turned with a scowl.

Olan stood in the doorway, arms folded over his colorful chest. "Did I startle you?"

"What do you want?"

"May I come in?"

Zuran grunted, jerking his head. This was the first time anyone other than another hunter had been inside his hut, and the sudden sense of inadequacy irritated him. He did *not* care what Olan thought of his home. The way the other male's eyes wandered over his shelves, over the little busts and rough carvings he had whittled of Samantha, only added to the annoyance he felt.

"Did you finally untie her, or has she escaped you again?"

Olan's eyes snapped to his face, and Zuran knew he wanted to bite back, but he shook his head. "I came to ask for your help."

"If you're looking for more ways to keep her prisoner, I'm afraid I cannot help you."

"You care for her? For my bride?"

Zuran narrowed his eyes. "Is this a trap? I tell you I do, and you take it to Ama?"

"Don't be ridiculous." Olan grumbled, plucking one of the likenesses from a table. She was smiling in this one, her face turned to the side and her hair falling against her neck. "You were always more talented than I could ever dream of being."

The quiet praise made Zuran uncomfortable. "What is it you came for, Olan?"

"I promised her I would personally check on her friends, and since I refuse to put her in danger, I'll be leaving her in the village until I return. I'm on my way now. Could I ask you to look after her in my absence?"

For a moment, Zuran only stared. "You are a breeder."

"I'm aware of my status, Zuran."

"Then you might also be aware that breeders do not go off into the forest. Alone, might I add."

"Will you help or not? My bride trusts you, enjoys your company." Olan set the bust down, turning to face Zuran.

"Keeping the two of you apart has won me no favors with her. I want her to be happy, to wish to remain here."

He shouldn't do this, shouldn't go anywhere near her, but his heart wouldn't listen to logic. "She'll be safe."

Olan inclined his head, but didn't speak right away. He moved past the shelving, his fingers drifting over the more detailed carvings before he reached the open door. "You didn't keep it, did you?"

"Didn't keep what?" Zuran asked with a frown, but Olan disappeared through the doorway without a response.

He didn't have time to ponder Olan's cryptic questions. If he really was leaving now, that meant that Samantha had already been alone for longer than he was comfortable with. Zuran glanced down at himself. Tiny shavings and wood dust clung to his damp skin. He wished he would have gone directly to the pools after leaving Vane, but he would just bring her with him.

Unmated males and family groups milled about the small market, gathering near their huts as they went about their daily routines. He and his hunters provided food and protection for every Seyton who lived within the confines of this village, and yet not one of them even smiled or acknowledged him as he passed. Olan's hut was positioned between the market and the common area where meals were eaten.

He stepped up to the door, fist raised to knock on the wood, when he heard a moan from within. A gasp had his heart racing and his brow furrowing. Zuran knew Samantha's presence, and the fact that she hadn't mated with Olan, had caused a good deal of chaos among the younger breeders. Was it possible one of them had slipped in when Olan sought him out? Could someone have hurt her? The blade at the end of his tail extended as he eased the lever down and stepped into the hut.

Olan's workspace was undisturbed, and he saw no immediate signs of a struggle. A rough, breathy groan made the hairs along his nape stand on end, and tiny sparks formed along his arms. With a snarl, Zuran rounded the wall that divided the room.

What he found wasn't something he had even taken into consideration, and it locked every muscle in his body. Samantha was on top of Olan's furs, the skirt of her dress hiked up over her hips, and one delicate hand buried between her legs. The other was at her chest, her nipple caught between her fingers as it rolled and pinched the flushed nub. His heart hammered in his chest as he watched her back arch, her moan sending a thrill of desire through him. While not a breeder, Zuran wasn't a complete stranger to the pleasure of females.

Solars ago, before the heat had begun to seep into his mind, he had been invited to attend to one of the unmated females. The experience had been painfully embarrassing at the time, but the female had been patient, showing him how and where to touch. If Samantha invited him, if she asked him to tend to her needs, how would Olan react?

He knew he should say something, make a noise to let her know she was no longer alone, but her scent had permeated every fiber of his being and he was helpless to do anything but watch as she took herself higher. Zuran felt his cock harden, begging to be inside her, pleading to take her as if he were a breeder.

Mine.

Her fingers moved faster against her sex, and as her back arched up from the furs, her eyes flew open, locking onto his face. Samantha cried out, her body trembling as she gasped for breath. When her cheeks flushed an even deeper shade of red, and she scrambled up to her knees, tugging her skirt down, Zuran finally found the strength to turn his head away.

"Zuran, I—I didn't think anyone was coming so soon—" She was breathing heavy, her voice shaky as she climbed from the furs. "I'm so sorry."

Sorry? What was she apologizing for? He opened his mouth

to speak, but nothing came out. He wanted to tell her he was anything but sorry, that he would gladly watch her pleasure herself any time she saw fit, but his mouth refused to comply.

"Zuran? Are you okay?"

Say something, you fool! "Bath," he said, turning to face her.

Samantha blinked in confusion. "Bath?"

By the All Mother, add words. Make a sentence. "Need a bath."

"Oh," She caught her lower lip between her teeth, and a pathetic groan fell from his lips. "Yeah, okay. Uh, let me get some clothes."

He waited as she opened one of the trunks and pulled out a dress. It was lovely, no doubt something Olan had created for her. She held it up to her body, checking the length, and when she turned toward him, Zuran felt his breath catch.

Her bridal dress.

It wasn't surprising that she had one. The All Mother had matched her after all, and every female was given one for her ceremony. This one, however, the one Olan had made for *his* bride, was not what he had expected. Instead of the bright colors her mate sported, Samantha's dress was a deep, inky black, just as dark as Zuran himself.

Why would the breeder create this for her? No Seyton female would ever be caught wearing something so dark, but Samantha ran her hands over the material, smiling up at him.

"I watched Olan make this," she said as she moved past him into the male's workspace. "He said the color suited me."

Zuran managed a strangled grunt in response. If he thought anymore about how the darkness of the dress highlighted the paleness of her skin or her blue eyes, the heat would surely take him over. There would be nothing left of him. They walked in silence, and at some point along the way, Samantha's tiny hand slipped into his. Her fingers were interlaced with his and he rubbed the rough pad of his thumb over her knuckles, marveling at how delicate she was.

Seyton females might be slender and willowy creatures, but they were anything but delicate. They had waged wars, defended their families and their villages against rival tribes since the beginning of time. His own mother had been fierce. She had high expectations for her offspring, and when he had come out of his bloom...

Zuran pushed away the hurtful memories, glancing down at Samantha. She would be loving and kind with her young, would never treat them like his mother had treated him.

They took the longer route to the pools so they could avoid the curious eyes of the other villagers. He doubted Ama and Asa would be pleased to learn that he was caring for her. Samantha practically vibrated with excitement when the steps of the pools came into view, a smile overtaking her face as she glanced up at him. His lungs seized for a moment as if she had stolen the air from them.

He could spend the rest of his life wrapped up in her gaze, but he wasn't the one Ama or the All Mother had chosen for her. He had never stood a chance. Zuran helped her up onto the flat surface of the rock, the tip of his tail trailing along her calf as she stepped up beside him. He watched her shiver as she caught her lip between her teeth. Zuran had worried that her confinement with Olan might have turned her against him or broken some of the spirit he found so wonderful, but nothing seemed to have changed.

Tiny sparks licked at his skin and he took a deep breath as he attempted to bring his electricity under control. Just being close to her had the flames of his heat roaring. Watching her in the hut as she pleasured herself had nearly done him in. The temptation to take her, to make her his right there on Olan's furs, had been painful. Could he really bring her back to his hut and not touch her?

The image of her on his furs, within his home, sprang to life within his mind. Her pale legs spread wide, hips gyrating against the hand buried at the apex of her sex. The scent of her arousal would perfume the small space.

"Z? Are you all right?"

He blinked, clearing his vision. "Yes."

"You were growling. I thought maybe something was wrong."

The compassion she showed him never failed to surprise him. After everything he had lived through, after all of the people he had lost, her concern was refreshing. The only other time since his transformation that he had felt wanted and cared for was in the beginnings of their first heat when he and Zyar had clumsily tried to ease it. Compassion from a female, though? He couldn't remember the last time one thought to ask about him or cared about what was happening in his life.

"It's nothing," he said, guiding her away from the edge of the rock. What would she think of him if he told her what had been on his mind? She wasn't Seyton, and had told him herself that she found the treatment of the hunters to be horrible. "I'll bathe first, and then if you wish, you may have a turn."

Samantha lowered herself to the ground, crossing her legs in front of her as she watched him. "Olan mentioned this was the single males' village, but I've seen a lot of families here. Does your family live here?"

He paused, the warm pink water lapping at his calves. Zuran felt his heart clench. "I no longer have a family."

"Oh, I'm sorry to hear that."

"Don't be." He let the water envelop his body.

"Is Olan's family here?"

"No."

"So neither one of you have family here?" He watched as her brows drew down. "That's sad."

"It's not my place to speak of Olan's family, but as far as mine is concerned, I no longer exist for them."

"Did they disown you?"

"Disown?"

Samantha nodded, fidgeting with the hem of her dress. "It's when someone decides to no longer acknowledge you."

"I suppose that is an appropriate term for it." He scrubbed his hands over his face, letting his current loosen the debris. "I haven't seen or spoken to any of them since my transformation. I lost many people that day."

"I really am sorry, Z."

He glanced over, meaning to ask her why she had chosen to call him that, only to feel his tongue stick to the roof of his mouth. Samantha's fingers had worked the knots at her shoulders loose, and as she stood, the pretty black dress fell from her body, pooling around her bare feet. His pulse raced as she stepped forward, crouching down at the edge of the pool before her legs slid into the water. Zuran's eyes traveled up her body as she sank down, finally landing on her face.

Her eyes closed on a moan as she let her head fall back, causing the purple strands of her hair to float around her shoulders. "These pools are magical." She murmured a second before ducking beneath the surface.

She pushed off from the edge, propelling herself forward until he felt her hands on his arms. Zuran stumbled backward just as she resurfaced in front of him, a smile forming on her lips until she saw the shock on his face.

"What?"

"You shouldn't be in here." He tried to turn away, but Samantha's hand clutched at his face, pulling his gaze back to hers.

"Zuran, look at me."

By the All Mother, it was nearly impossible for him *not* to look at her. The water licked at the top of her heavy breasts, revealing the dusky pink of her nipples as she stood up on the tips of her toes. Before he knew what he was doing, his hands were sliding over the curve of her hips as he lowered himself into the warmth of the water. Her arms came up to wrap around his neck and he sucked in a breath of surprise when she pressed her lips to his.

He barely recognized the low growl that rolled up from his chest as he crushed her to him, reveling in the way her breasts pillowed between them. Her gasp of surprise as he spun her around allowed him to sweep his tongue inside her mouth, gliding over hers in a sensual dance he had never taken part in before. Her body arched when he pressed her against the smooth surface of the rock, his hips moving between her open legs as Zuran's cock sought out her entrance through the covering that separated them.

The way she rolled her hips against his had him bucking uncontrollably. This was wrong—he knew that—but when she fisted his braids in her hands and moaned, Zuran couldn't find the strength to pull away.

If this was the only contact the All Mother allowed him, Zuran would die a thankful male.

He *craved* this female unlike anything he ever had in his entire life. The prickle of pain from her nails digging into his skin made his body tingle with the static of his electricity. He throbbed against the heat of her sex as she gyrated, wriggling as if she could somehow bring herself even closer to him.

Something far greater than lust thrummed through his veins. Her sweet whimpers stoked the fires of his heat higher and higher, pushing him closer to an edge he wasn't sure he would be able to come back from.

CHAPTER 13

OLAN

*H*e'd only just started the journey, and already Olan was regretting his decision. The path he had been following had ended abruptly, leaving him to fight his way into the forest. Trees in this part grew close together, giving him almost no room to maneuver around them. Zuran was wider than him, bulkier and more muscular. How in the world did he and the other hunters get through here on a regular basis?

The thought of his old friend caused jealousy to stir within him, but if he was honest with himself, the sadness he felt overpowered that. He had looked around the small hut at all of the beautiful carvings and hadn't found the one Zuran made of him.

Did you expect him to keep it? His mind jeered. Even after everything that had happened between them, Olan couldn't imagine ever getting rid of the carvings on his shelves.

"What is it about Zuran that makes you hate him so much?"

Samantha's question had shocked him, and her words had caused him to look within himself, to judge his own actions and beliefs. Weeks ago, he would have scoffed at the idea that hunters were mistreated, would have laughed if someone had suggested that perhaps their social structure was incredibly flawed, but now? Now, Olan's stomach churned at the way they had all been taught to look at people they had once loved and cared for.

He could remember the look of fear that had flashed across Zuran's face when he had stepped out of the bloom and looked down at himself. Could remember the way the male's family had reacted as if he were dead instead of merely a hunter. It shamed him that over the years he had begun to feel the same way.

"I ought to kick your ass!"

Olan stopped dead in his tracks, his head tilting to the side as he listened. Someone was coming toward him. He crouched down as another voice, this one familiar to him, came from a spot up ahead.

"I would give a great deal to see you attempt that, Star Born. A *great* deal."

A frustrated growl echoed through the trees. "My name isn't Star Born, it's Lucy. Cut the crap and tell me what you've done with Samantha, and I might decide to spare your life."

"Maybe we shouldn't threaten our alien captor," someone else interjected.

Olan stepped around the tree and directly into the path of one of the hunters. He knew Zyar was a friend of Zuran's, but he hadn't ever had the occasion to speak with him.

"Olan," Zyar frowned. "What are you doing out here?"

A small Star Born female with golden hair appeared behind the hunter, frowning as she looked him up and down, clearly not impressed. Another Star Born, this one a male with bright orange hair and odd frames around his eyes, stumbled up behind her, clutching at her arm.

"There are others!" he whispered.

The one who had called herself Lucy rolled her arms, shaking his hand away. "Of course there are others. Did you think this one was the only one on this entire planet, James?"

"These are Samantha's people?"

Lucy's eyes flew back to his face, and she attempted to shove Zyar out of her way as she leaped forward. "You know Samantha?"

"I do."

She glanced sideways at Zyar. "Okay, you weren't lying, but that doesn't mean anything. If she's been hurt in any way, I'll still kick your ass."

Zyar only grinned down at the little female, but he didn't miss the way the hunter's tail came up to curl around the Star Born's ankle.

"No harm has come to her," Olan replied.

"I'd like to see that for myself, if you don't mind." Lucy shook Zyar's tail off, snarling up at him, and she pushed her way between them.

"You're going the wrong way, Star Born," Zyar called. Lucy stuck out her hand, one finger raised, as she spun in the direction of the village. He wasn't sure what the gesture meant, but he assumed it was anything but a compliment. "Lovely, isn't she?"

"You should be careful," Olan warned.

Zyar scoffed. "I don't need your warnings, breeder. I understand *my place*."

"I didn't mean—"

"I have heard the things you spoke to Zuran. Instead of reminding me of what I should and should not do, perhaps you should start by explaining why you are outside of the village."

"I promised my bride I would look for her friends." Olan said, falling into step beside the hunter. The Star Born male struggled to keep pace behind them.

"You left your female behind?"

"She is with Zuran."

Zyar stopped so abruptly that the alien male ran straight into his back, grunting as he fell backward onto his bottom. "You left her with Zuran?"

"She enjoys his company," Olan said, reaching down to help the smaller male to his feet.

"Take a right!" Zyar called to Lucy as she marched ahead of them.

They walked for some time in silence with Zyar calling out directions to the female. He could see Samantha being friends with the fiery Star Born. When the pillars that framed the entrance to the village came into view, Lucy came to a stop, staring up at the carved wood.

"You go ahead," Olan told the hunter. "I need to find Zuran."

Zyar inclined his head, guiding Lucy and the male, James, into the village.

Olan took the smaller, less traveled path back toward Zuran's hut. The door was closed, and when he checked within, it was clear neither Samantha nor Zuran was home. He made his way back into the village, avoiding the market where he could hear the commotion Zyar and both the aliens were causing, slipping into his hut without being stopped.

"Fanahala?" He rounded the wall, and the scent that wrapped around him made his muscles clench. Her arousal was unmistakable. Zuran's scent was here as well, but it was faint, as if he hadn't been inside the hut very long.

Olan turned and stomped from the hut with a sigh. He would check the pools. There was something about that place that seemed to draw Samantha to it. A gentle breeze rustled the leaves on the branches above him as he stepped through the trees that surrounded the pools.

The animals were quiet today, not one of them singing from their perches. The silence made him anxious.

As he approached the stone steps, Olan could hear the stream that ran beneath the outhouse in the distance, but a soft moan from the level above him caught his attention. He moved toward the incline, his head tilted as he caught the sound of a rumbling growl.

Beneath the shade of the trees, Olan could see the dark figure within the pool. He knew without having to see the hunter's face that it was Zuran, and wrapped around his neck were the pale arms of his female.

Olan stepped closer, moving around the pools nearest to him, his eyes never leaving their bodies. He watched as Samantha's hands curled into Zuran's braids, and to his utter amazement, Olan felt his cock harden. Her hips were moving against the hunter's, their tongues tangling in a dance so erotic that he felt the breath slip from his lungs.

He nearly groaned when her head fell back against the stone and Zuran's teeth scraped along the pale skin of her neck. She was beautiful. *They* were beautiful. His hand brushed over his stomach, his hips moving of their own accord as he watched Zuran grind himself between her open legs.

It was wrong to watch this, wrong to *want* to watch this. Samantha was his bride. He should want to stop this, should want to cast Zuran out of the village and never allow him to come close to her ever again, but he couldn't bring himself to actually feel that.

Olan's cock jerked in excitement beneath the leather covering, and his hand trailed down to press against it as his eyes closed. He could feel his lightning pushing toward the surface, sparking along his arms and chest as Samantha's soft sighs of pleasure drifted over him.

"Hey! You're the guy from the forest!"

The voice coming from below startled Olan, and he stumbled backward, turning to see the Star Born female, Lucy, scrambling toward him. Zyar was hot on her heels, a grimace pulling at his face.

"Olan…" He turned back toward the pools, meeting Samantha's wide-eyed gaze. Her cheeks were flushed, lips swollen from their kiss. She was the most beautiful creature he had ever seen. When the golden-haired female appeared over the edge of the stone, Samantha's mouth dropped open. "Lucy?"

"Sam!" The female sprang forward, launching herself into the pool and throwing her arms around his mate. "I can't believe you're alive!" She clutched at Samantha's face before crushing her back to her chest. "That big dark guy said you were here and mated, and I just couldn't believe he was talking about *our* Samantha."

"How many Samanthas do you think I know?" Zyar asked as he approached.

Lucy cut her eyes to the hunter and stuck out her tongue toward him. "You can go now."

"Afraid not." Zyar propped himself against the back edge of the stones that led up to the next level, his eyes following Zuran as the other male climbed from the pool. "Brother."

Zuran merely inclined his head in acknowledgment. His eyes met Olan's briefly before darting away.

"Where is everyone else?" Samantha was asking. "It couldn't have just been you on the drop ship."

Lucy sobered, the smile slipping from her face. "James and I are the only ones who made it."

As if summoned, the Star Born male's head popped up over the edge. The frames he wore on his face slid down, and he shoved them back up, squinting at the females. "Hello, Samantha."

Samantha squealed, crouching down until only her head breached the surface of the water. "James! Turn around!"

The male's eyes widened and he spun around, his hands flying up to cover his framed eyes. "I'm so sorry!" He stammered. "I didn't realize—I wouldn't have ever tried to—"

"I just wasn't expecting you. Either of you." Samantha grinned at Lucy. "Just give me a second to get dressed."

"Turn around." Lucy snapped her fingers at Zuran and Zyar before turning her gaze to Olan. "You too," she twirled her finger. "Turn, buddy."

Olan wanted to protest—she was his bride, after all—but he did as the female asked and gave them his back. He heard the splashing of the water as Samantha climbed out of the pool.

"Oh, wow, Sam." Lucy breathed. "That's lovely on you."

When Olan turned back, he felt his breath catch in his lungs. She was wearing the bridal dress he had made for her. The inky black material clung to her hips before falling away. He had dyed the fabric himself solars ago with no clear purpose for its use. The females here would never accept anything in the color, and Ama would not have approved a bridal dress made from the fabric. It had sat on his shelves until the day Samantha had come home. Olan couldn't have explained what compelled him to make the dress, but looking at her now, he had no doubt he had been right.

He had told her the color suited her, and it was no lie; her pale skin practically glowed beneath the dark material. Zuran's low growl drew his attention away, and he turned to see the other male's eyes sweeping over the garment.

"Thank you," Samantha was saying. "Olan made it for me."

He felt the weight of Zyar's curious gaze on him, but ignored the hunter. Olan didn't owe him an explanation, and he wouldn't have been able to tell him why he had done it anyway.

"Well, wasn't that so nice of him?" Lucy turned her narrowed gaze on him. "We need to talk, Sam."

"We can go back to Olan's hut—" Samantha began.

"Preferably somewhere not surrounded by aliens?"

"If Zuran will allow you the use of his hut, he is welcome to stay with me," Olan said, turning to the hunter.

Zuran's brows furrowed in confusion, but he inclined his head. "You may stay in my hut if you wish."

Samantha looked between them, trepidation clear in her eyes as they volleyed back and forth. Lucy was busy chattering, but Olan didn't hear a word she spoke. His mind was racing as fast as his pulse as he tried to come to terms with what he felt when he found his mate in the arms of the hunter; of a male who had once been his closest friend.

I assume you had not planned to leave them in the forest, outside the safety of the village, unguarded," Zuran said, his arms folding over his chest as he watched Samantha move around his hut.

"No," Olan said.

"I will stand guard tonight," Zyar offered, but Zuran shook his.

"You have been gone for days. Go home and rest. I will see to their safety tonight."

Zyar opened his mouth to argue but snapped it shut when Zuran narrowed his eyes. "I'll be here in the morning to relieve you then."

Olan waited until the younger hunter was out of sight before stepping into the hut. Samantha watched as he came closer, her eyes roaming his face as if she were trying her best to figure out what he was thinking.

Good luck, he thought. He wasn't even sure of that himself.

"Thank you," she whispered as she placed her hand on his chest.

The contact sent a jolt of longing through him. "I didn't actually find them," he admitted. "I was hardly out of the shadow of the village before I came upon Zyar leading them here."

Samantha smiled as she stepped into him, her forehead resting against the bottom of his chest. "It still meant a lot that you did that and that you..." Her head lifted and her eyes found Zuran as he entered. "That you trusted me to stay."

"I will bring the evening meal soon. Enjoy the time with your friends." Olan tipped her face up, lowering himself so that his lips hovered over hers for a moment. He watched as her eyes fluttered shut, and he swore he could hear her heart racing within her chest as he moved up, brushing his lips against her forehead. A soft sigh escaped her, and he resisted the urge to smile as he turned and exited the hut.

"Olan."

Zuran was on his heels before he even reached the end of the small path. They stood in silence, watching one another, not entirely sure what should be said after what happened in the pools, but the words never seemed to come. He should be upset, he should rage, he should be at Ama's hut demanding action be taken against the hunter, but...

He looked into Zuran's face as his mind raced. It was both familiar and alien, with the same sharp angles as it had in their youth, the same slightly upturned wide eyes. He hadn't allowed himself to admit how much he missed this male, but being forced into his presence was making it painfully clear.

"I will bring the meal as soon as I can," he told Zuran absently, leaving the other male to stare after him.

CHAPTER 14

SAMANTHA

"*I* knew they would be more primitive than us, but this is —" Lucy paused as she spun around, gesturing at the interior of Zuran's hut. "A whole different level of primitive."

"Shh," Samantha admonished. "It's not that bad." She froze when she saw the carvings lining Zuran's shelves.

"Holy hell," Lucy murmured. "Are these—are these all of you?" Her friend took one down, studying its intricately carved features.

They were gorgeous. Samantha had never seen herself through someone else's eyes before, and the beauty of the pieces caused the heat to rise in her cheeks. She couldn't help but smile as she brushed her fingers over the carvings, each one of them unique and wonderful.

"Creepy."

Samantha rolled her eyes, laughing as she turned away. Maybe she should feel the same way as Lucy, but she thought it was sweet that he hadn't been able to forget about her. "Yeah, yeah. I saw the way Zyar was looking at you."

Lucy's face immediately flamed. "Whatever. Like I care what that damn caveman thinks. I want nothing to do with him or any of these other aliens."

"To be fair, we're the aliens this time," James interjected. He too was studying the carvings, his brows raised as he plucked a vicious-looking animal from a lower shelf.

"Seems like you have the beginnings of a fan club here." Lucy grinned. "The caveman mentioned you were mated, but he only mentioned one mate."

"I was given to Olan, so technically, he's my only mate."

"Oh? So what you've got going on with Mr. Tall, Dark, and Zappy is just... what? A little something on the side?"

Samantha grimaced. "I don't have anything going on with either of them."

Lucy raised her brow, grinning like a loon in the face of her denial. "Lies. You think I missed the way they looked at you, or that sweet little kiss your *mate* gave you before he left?" Her friend plopped herself down on a large wooden chest, crossing her arms as if she were daring Samantha to disagree with her observations.

What *did* she feel? The fact that she had been given to Olan the moment she stepped into the village made her want to fight against everything that was expected of her, but did she really dislike Olan? Sure, he was bossy, he had literally tied her to him, and didn't let her go anywhere alone, but he had been far kinder than most human men she knew.

That's a disturbing realization... Especially since most of the men she knew would sooner shove you out an airlock than actually pretend they cared about you.

From what little she knew about their customs, she knew Olan hadn't asked to be mated to her. She was sure he hadn't grown up imagining himself shackled to an alien—a female with no wings, horns, or electricity of her own to defend herself. To Olan, she was probably more of a hassle than anything else.

And then there was Zuran. He had been the one to bring her to the village, had captured her the very first time she decided to venture out of the pod. She should probably dislike him as well, but she felt some sort of strange pull toward the gloomy hunter. Being near him made her mind foggy, made her think staying on this planet wouldn't be such a hardship.

And when she was around both of them? It did something to her that she didn't care to think about right at that moment.

"What took you guys so long to get down to the surface?" Samantha asked, redirecting the conversation. "I've been here for weeks waiting to be rescued."

"We had to wait for the investigation after your disappearance, Sam."

Samantha's head whipped around. "My disappearance? What do you mean?"

"You didn't show up to work the day after the meeting. We sent Ramos and Amaran to check on you, but they reported that your cabin was empty," James said.

"There was a ship-wide search for you. No one had seen you since we left the dining hall the night of the meeting." Lucy frowned. "A couple hours later, someone noticed one of the escape pods was missing. Marsel said he checked over the footage and saw you walk in before the pod was ejected."

"Did *you* see the footage?" Samantha asked.

Lucy shook her head. "Marsel claimed something corrupted the footage afterward. We had nothing but his word to go off of."

"What happened that night?" James asked, taking a seat next to Lucy on the chest.

"I don't remember." Samantha shrugged as she paced the small hut. "I remember going back to my cabin after dinner. I was so exhausted that night that I didn't even undress. Just threw myself on my bed and passed out. When I woke up, I was in the escape pod, still in my lab coat. I think I was thrown from the chair during the crash, but I checked myself over and there were no signs of a head injury." She shook her head. There was no way she'd gotten into the pod herself.

"Something smells like a cover-up," Lucy grumbled.

James frowned, his eyes darting between them. "Who would want to get rid of Samantha, though?"

Perhaps she had gotten in far deeper than she had even thought. Would Marsel have actually tried to get rid of her for what she had overheard? "You said at the pools that you two were the only survivors. What happened?"

"Everything was fine until we entered the atmosphere." Lucy stood, her hand trailing over her upper arm. "It was like something just sucked all of the power from the engine. Control panels went dark, lights went out." She shook her head, swallowing hard. "When I woke up, we were on the surface, and there was smoke and bodies all over the place. I found James still strapped into his chair. Nearly all of the tech was useless. Thank the gods the Venium medkits and wands still worked. Those took care of the small lacerations the two of us walked away with."

"Only the Venium tech worked?"

James nodded. "None of the human-made electronics seemed to be able to function here. The communication systems were filled with nothing but interference when we tried to reach the Constellation."

Samantha had noticed this as well. While the communication technology and AI on the ships were things they had learned from the Venium, they were not actual tech made by them. There were things such as the med wands and kits that their alien allies hadn't taught them to produce, and that they hadn't been able to reverse engineer just yet. The large holoprojection machine on board the *S.S. Constellation* was another such device.

"So they investigated, and then what?"

"Marsel selected a field team." James shrugged, pushing his glasses back up his nose. "Many of us were from the team you originally requested, but he replaced more than a few of the science team with his personal security."

Samantha grimaced. "What purpose did that serve? We already had more than enough security."

"The natives," Lucy interrupted. "Marsel kept saying that they couldn't be trusted, that we didn't know what we would be getting into when we landed."

Samantha's stomach soured and she felt ill. This was what she had been afraid of. Marsel could poison the people's minds against the Seyton before she even had time to learn about them.

"Was he wrong?" James asked.

"Yes," Samantha hissed.

Lucy's brow raised as James's head snapped up. "But—but they took you, Samantha." He looked to Lucy for support, but she only shrugged. "And the big guy, Zyar, said that you were mated. I assume it was against your will?"

"None of us have been harmed in their care," Samantha said, avoiding his probing. "And how many times do we need to repeat human history before we learn?"

"The *Constellation* has no doubt already noticed that something is wrong. It's been days since we crashed, and they've had no sign from us," Lucy sighed. "If they send another drop ship, maybe we can get to them and see if their systems are working."

"I don't think so," James huffed. "One escape pod and a drop ship crash land on this planet and experience the same tech issues? It seems likely that it's something within the atmosphere of the planet or within the core itself that's causing it."

113

"Shit," Lucy grumbled, scrubbing her hands over her face. "So what do we do?"

Wasn't that the same thing Samantha had been asking herself for weeks now? "What can we actually do besides get to know the Seyton? If help does come, we'll have a better understanding of the people and maybe we can even convince Ama that humans aren't so horrible."

"Ama is the chieftess, right?" Lucy pursed her lips when Samantha nodded. "We met her when the caveman brought us into the village."

It wasn't long before Olan returned with Asa, both of them carrying trays of steaming meats and fresh fruits. Samantha smiled when she realized Olan had brought all of her favorite dishes. When Asa took her leave, James deflated a little.

"She's lovely, isn't she?"

"She is mated," Olan grumbled.

James's face turned as fiery as his hair. "Right... Of course she is. I wasn't—I didn't mean—" he stammered.

"He was just paying Asa a compliment."

"Right," James breathed. "Just a compliment. I meant no offense."

A grunt was Olan's only response. He ate beside her in silence, placing more food in front of her until she was so full that she had to stop him. When they had finished, Samantha watched him gather the trays and stand to leave. He hadn't spoken to her, hadn't touched her. They had only just gotten over the silent treatment stage, and she felt like they were slipping right back into it.

Olan stepped out of the hut and turned to latch the door behind him, but Samantha wedged herself in the doorway, slipping out as Lucy and James stood from the floor. "Are you going home?"

"I am."

One of the younger mated females from the village, whose

name she couldn't recall, appeared at the end of the path. She took the trays from his hands, nodding at Asa where she rested against one of the trees.

"Olan will take the human male with him tonight until Ama makes her decision," Asa said.

James sputtered behind Samantha. "Decision about what?"

"About where you will be housed." Asa looked at him as if she was explaining something to a child. "You are an unmated male and will require a hut of your own." Her eyes narrowed on him. "*If* Ama allows you to stay."

"Hey, it'll be all right," Lucy reassured James as his shoulders slumped. "We'll see you first thing in the morning."

Samantha looked up at Olan as he waited, struggling with what she should say to him. This would be her first night away from him since she had arrived in the village. She should be relieved, shouldn't she? Aside from the time she had spent with Asa, Olan was constantly by her side. The disruption of their routine, even if it was a bit unconventional, made her stomach churn with anxiety.

"I will be back to escort you to the morning meal." Olan leaned down, his lips brushing her cheek. "Sleep well, Fanahala," he whispered into her ear before gesturing for James to follow him.

Movement within the trees caught her eye, and she turned to see Zuran watching them, his gaze locked on her face.

"Let's get inside."

Lucy tugged at her arm, pulling her attention away from the hunter. She could feel him watching her all the way to the door, and she wanted to turn back, but for what? Samantha sighed, and closed the door behind them. The days on Seytonna seemed to be longer than the twenty-four-hour cycle they kept on the ships and the space station. It was something that had been started when their ancestors had left old Earth, and no one since had felt inclined to change it.

Olan had lit a few candles for them, setting them around the hut so they weren't in complete darkness. Lucy stretched her arms high above her head, twisting to the left and right before letting out a long grown.

"I'm freaking exhausted." She grimaced at Zuran's furs. "No blanket?"

Samantha rolled her eyes. "I'm sure he's got one somewhere." The chest against the wall seemed to be the only storage within the hut. She hadn't missed a blanket since she had been sleeping next to Olan. The male was a furnace and kept her plenty warm, but even if he hadn't, the planet was warmer than any ship she had ever slept on. When she lifted the lid, the contents on top brought a smile to her face.

More carvings, these of animals, were piled on top of one another, many of them unfinished and rough. One among them caught her eye. It was painted white, and just like the one in Olan's hut, it seemed to be a representation of one of the younger males. Zuran must have been the artist behind both carvings, but why would Olan have refused to tell her?

"Man, this guy needs another hobby," Lucy murmured as she stared down into the chest.

"Like you're any better?" A corner of a finely woven blanket stuck out from beneath the pieces of wood and Samantha carefully tugged it out. "How many old paper books do you have stashed in your cabin? If your writing wasn't digital, there would be no room for your bed."

"Well, mark me down as sufficiently called out." Her friend laughed, taking the blanket from her hands and wrapping it around her shoulders. Lucy plopped down on the furs, rolling until she was pressed up against the side of the hut. "Hey, Sam? What do you think happened with the drop ship? James prattled on and on about all of his theories on the way here, but you know I'm not big on the scientific jargon."

Samantha crawled in next to her. "Well, I can't say for sure since I don't have any instruments to run tests, and there was nothing in the data files for X9, but there must have been some sort of electromagnetic interference. Whether that's from the dual sun system or something else entirely… I'd need the lab to figure that out. Nothing about this planet is what I would have expected. I'd kill to get some equipment down here—"

The soft sound of Lucy's snoring interrupted her musings. Her friends had been through so much in the last few days, and she couldn't imagine the horrors they had faced seeing the other members of the field team lying dead on the floor of the drop ship. She turned on her side, her arm pillowed beneath her head, and closed her eyes. They could figure out what to do tomorrow. Tonight, they would rest.

CHAPTER 15

ZURAN

Samantha and the other female had finally fallen asleep within the hut. Outside, wood quanauks sang softly, their wings creating a calming buzz that filled the forest around them. The insects were large, growing to nearly the size of his palm, and put off a brilliant blue light.

In his youth, Zuran had often stalked the insects through the trees, catching them in blown glass jars and taking them to the cliffs to show Olan. They had spent so many nights up there, releasing the quanauk and chasing them through the high grass of the fields until his friend's mama had come calling.

He tried not to think of Olan often, but since finding Samantha, that had become more difficult than he had ever imagined. Zuran shifted on the branch he was perched on, grimacing at himself. His tail thrashed behind him, cutting through the air in the same way he wished he could cut through the damned memories that refused to stay buried.

A sharp tug on the appendage had him snarling and extending

his blade, but instead of an overconfident predatory animal, Zuran glared down at a grinning Zyar.

"You're getting old, brother." The other hunter climbed the trunk of the tree, forcing his way onto the sturdy lower branch. "I don't think I've ever been able to sneak up on you before."

Zuran grunted as he made room. Zyar was only a solar or so younger than he was, but there was no point in reminding him of that. "I was thinking."

"Do you want to tell me about what is bothering you?" When Zuran said nothing, Zyar sighed. "Olan or Samantha?"

"What?"

"Is that broody look on your face about your feelings for Olan or Samantha?"

The male saw too much at times. "Why would you think either of them were on my mind?"

"Because I've hunted with you, gone through miserable heats with you, spent solars of my life with you. I know what you are thinking before you think it most of the time." Zyar tugged at the long forebraid that hung down past Zuran's waist. "Out with it."

"I don't like missing him," Zuran finally said. "And I don't like this... guilt."

"Guilt over what? Over Samantha?"

Zuran nodded. "Ama selected Olan as Samantha's mate, but I cannot stop what I feel for her. The way I've touched her, the way I've allowed her to touch me..." He scrubbed his hands over his face. "Olan could have had me cast out."

"It is none of my business what happened in the pools today, but from the way he reacted, I doubt Olan was thinking of having you sent away." Zyar nudged him with his elbow, his grin turning lopsided.

"He would never agree to share her affection."

"And you know this because you have discussed this with him?"

"I know this because Olan has never deviated from what is expected of him, and allowing a hunter to be with his mate will never be permitted. I would never be more than a pleasurer and I don't know that I could ever settle for that." Zuran growled.

Zyar was silent for a moment, his legs swinging back and forth as he studied the hut in front of them. "You cannot help who you love, Zuran."

"I don't know if love is what I feel for Samantha. It is still so early."

"I wasn't talking about her," the other male whispered.

Zuran's jaw clenched so hard that he was shocked his teeth didn't splinter. He had only spoken of his feelings for Olan once, solars ago during a particularly miserable heat. Leave it to Zyar to remember the little details. "Olan would never—"

"Stop assuming you know what Olan would do." Zyar flung his hands into the air. "The two of you sit here denying everything you feel, wallowing in your misery, and for what?"

"You don't understand him—"

"I understand *you*. I understand loving someone you shouldn't. I understand the fear of rejection, and how terrifying it is to trust your heart to someone." The other hunter shook his head. "Do you think I wasn't afraid to trust Vurso?"

He wanted to protest, to tell Zyar that he was wrong, and that Olan was nothing like Vurso, but how long had it been since he and Olan had spoken more than a few words to one another?

When Olan had shown up at the entrance to his hut earlier, he was surprised that his old friend even knew the location of his home, and having him there had been more than unnerving. He had never told Olan how he felt, not even in their youth when things had seemed so simple. Loving the other male had just come naturally for him. So many nights he had lain awake, wishing he had the courage to tell him, hoping that he might feel the same way, but he had waited too long and lost his chance.

Zyar had always been far too optimistic, but trying to convince him that Olan might harbor the same feelings he did was a new level of delusional. At the end of the day, neither one of them was ever going to be a lifelong mate to the males they cared for.

"Ama spoke with Vurso today," Zyar whispered, his chin dropping to his chest.

Zuran felt his stomach clench at the words. "Do you know what it was about?"

"I haven't spoken to him since he left for her hut, but I have my suspicions."

A mating. Males were rarely called for anything else. "Perhaps she had other business for him—"

"We both knew, brother. It was never going to end any other way." Zyar huffed, his breath disturbing the braids that had fallen around his face. "I was on my way to his hut when I saw you up here. I wanted to give you something to think on before I go." Zyar slipped off the branch, landing nimbly on his feet. "Samantha's bridal dress was not made by accident. Olan selected that fabric himself and presented *your* colors to *his* bride."

He stared after his friend as he slipped into the darkness of the forest, letting his words sink into his already racing mind. Zuran wasn't blind, he had noticed the dress, but he hadn't dared to let himself guess why Olan had chosen it. *I cannot torture myself with what ifs*, he told himself, but... All Mother help him, what if Olan had felt the same way this entire time? What if they had been running in circles for solars?

Do not do this to yourself, his mind roared, but how could he not? He had spent so many solars trying to hate Olan, trying to convince himself he no longer cared, but Samantha had come along and destroyed all of his defenses. He had wanted her so fiercely that day in the forest that it had shocked him.

Watching her be given to Olan had churned up so many of the

emotions and memories that he had thought were buried within him. They had crawled to the surface, burrowing up from the graves he had placed them in, like the mertzhi in the old legends his father had told him. Just like those decaying, undead creatures, the memories and his love refused to die.

What he had done with Samantha today had felt right. Natural. He had not felt like a hunter taking liberties with a female, he had felt like a male touching his mate. It should terrify him, but the memory of her touching him, and the way she had moaned when he'd rocked against her made his cock harden. Instead of pushing the thoughts away like he had been, Zuran propped himself against the side of the tree and let his imagination run wild.

His hand slid down his stomach, the sharp tips of claws scratching the dark skin. He closed his eyes, letting his head fall back as his palm skimmed over the leather cover, growling as his fantasies played out in his mind.

They were in his hut this time, his body vibrating with arousal when his attention was drawn to his furs. Samantha was sprawled over them, her naked body flushed pink as she gasped and moaned, writhing against Olan's hips. The breeder was thrusting between her parted legs, his hands gripping her hips, digging into her flesh. He stumbled forward in his mind, crouching down beside them. Samantha's blue gaze lifted to his, and she smiled sweetly, reaching out to brush her fingers down his chest.

Zuran shifted against the tree as he lifted his covering, fisting his cock in his hand. The smooth tentacles that sprang from the base were normally flush against the appendage, but now they wriggled as if they had minds of their own. They wrapped around his wrist, slipping over his skin as his hand moved up and down the pulsing shaft.

Olan's tail drifted over Zuran's thigh, the tip trailing along his heated skin and sending a shiver down his spine.

The Heat within his blood roared to life, setting fire to his core. The tip of Zuran's tail followed the same path as Olan's, but unlike the breeder's, the blade at the end of his tail sliced across the skin on his chest. He hissed in pleasure, his hands flexing around his cock until he groaned into the humid air of the forest. Though the other male lacked the blade, there were other ways he could inflict the sting that Zuran had come to crave over the solars.

Samantha took his hand, sighing as she placed it on her breast. Zuran plucked at the straining peak, rolling her nipple between his fingers as she gasped and arched her back. He watched them, wishing more than anything that he could take her as Olan was, wishing he could bury himself within her and forget his place in this world.

Sweat beaded his brow as his hips jerked up, and his cock twitched in his grasp.

The scene in his mind began to morph, and a moment later he was kneeling on the floor of Olan's hut. Samantha's arms and legs were wrapped around him, her bare sex hovering over the tip of his cock. Olan was on his knees behind her, his hands sliding up and down her sides before he slowly pressed her down, impaling her on Zuran. She moaned, a deep, guttural sound that nearly had him coming before he had even begun. Olan's palms slid over his chest as he pressed against Samantha's back, the breeder's nails digging into his skin, causing shallow cuts that made his body tense. Like they had earlier in the day, Samantha's hands fisted his braids as she moved her body up and down, taking his entire length into her scalding heat.

Zuran's tail slinked down his belly, cutting small grooves. The tentacles spasmed, gripping his wrist as his hand slid faster along his shaft, clenching it in the way he imagined Samantha's sex would.

With Samantha working herself on his cock, Zuran fisted one hand in her hair and the other in Olan's, bringing the other male close. Olan leaned forward, his hands coming up to cup Zuran's face before his lips pressed against his in a desperate kiss.

Zuran's entire body went rigid, his back arching as his cock jerked in his grasp. A strangled growl rumbled up his throat, and he distantly felt the warmth of his come spray against his stomach and over his hand as he continued to pump.

For a long moment afterward, Zuran lay slumped against the tree, his chest rising and falling rapidly as he attempted to calm his racing heart. In all of his solars, he had never felt pleasure like what he just experienced. He looked down at himself and froze, his brow furrowing in confusion as he brought his hand closer to his face. Instead of the translucent secretions he was accustomed to, the skin on his hand and stomach was painted in bright blue liquid.

Even the consistency seemed to have changed. He should seek out the healer for her counsel, but he feared that if he did, the female would be able to see the heat building within him. If Ama knew how close he was to breaking, she would never allow him near Samantha or the villages. He would be cast out, forbidden from ever returning.

He had kept the madness hidden for this long, and he would continue suppressing it for as long as he could if it meant more time with them.

CHAPTER 16

OLAN

*W*ith his head bowed and eyes downcast, Olan pulled the door to his hut shut and made his way through the village. Ama had returned early yesterday morning, and though she hadn't summoned him yet, he knew she would be expecting an update about the humans. He had hardly spent any time with Samantha's friends, and his time alone with her hadn't yielded all that much. What was he going to tell her?

Would he tell her what he had witnessed in the pools? Could he honestly tell Ama about what Zuran had done and still face Samantha? *Could I face myself if I told her?* If he did, would Ama be able to see that he had actually enjoyed what he had happened upon? That he hadn't interrupted them because he had been so enthralled and aroused by the display? Perhaps it was Ama's connection with the All Mother, but his chieftess often knew things before being told about them.

If she already knew, would she punish him for not telling her himself? What if she took Samantha from him? They had not consummated their mating, and he was sure it was within her right as chieftess to separate them if she saw fit.

Icy dread churned in his stomach as he passed by mated pairs and their families where they gathered in doorways, preparing to leave for the morning meal. A group of younglings ran in front of him, their laughter filling the air as they scurried out of his way.

Olan wished, not for the first time in his life, that he had been born a hunter. He longed for the ability to leave the village, longed for the freedom to come and go as he pleased. Even the unmated females had more lenient restrictions. With their wings and claws, the females were seen as more capable than the breeder males when it came to defending themselves.

When his sister had been born, Olan had listened to his grand-mother's stories about how their females had once lived in the skies, building their homes within the clouds. The first females to come down were the All Mother's daughters, her most guarded treasures. Each of her daughters had fallen in love with those who lived on the surface, refusing to abandon their new families and return to their homes in the sky. Instead of making demands, the All Mother had rejoiced, and blessed their unions.

"The All Mother herself still lives among the clouds, watching over all of her children," she had whispered to him, rocking his sister as she slept in her arms.

Hearing that had made him curious. If the females found love with males already living within the forest, then who had his male ancestors mated with before? Had hunters and breeders intermingled during that period, and if so, what had caused the rift? Had there even been differences between them then? As the current Ama, their chieftess retained many of the memories from those that had come before her, but was she herself privy to the answers?

The chatter of those already gathered for the morning meal interrupted his thoughts, and he looked up to find Ama sitting at the head of the table speaking quietly with Asa. A kind smile lit up her face when he approached, raising his right hand over his chest in greeting. Ama dipped her head to Asa, dismissing the female wordlessly.

"Olan, come." She gestured to the seat Asa had just vacated. "I assume you have come with news for me. Speak freely."

He took the seat, frowning down at his hands where they rested on the table. "I have done as you asked, and I believe that my bride means Seytonna and our people no harm."

"And the others who arrived yesterday? Have you spoken with them?" Ama asked.

"I only spent a short time with the other female, Lucy, during the evening meal, but my bride trusts her, and I trust my mate."

Ama watched him for a moment, her gaze boring into his as if she was reading his mind. "Very well." He felt his muscles loosen some when her eyes left him. The chieftess leaned forward, plucking a gnua berry from a tray. "There was a male found with Lucy."

"James, yes."

"Asa told me he stayed in your hut last night. Did you have any problems with him?"

Olan shook his head. "He gave me no trouble." In fact, James had been far easier to handle than either of the Star Born females they had come across. He hadn't tried to escape the hut, hadn't fought him or argued over everything he was asked to do. Olan fought off the smile that tugged at his mouth when he thought about his stubborn, independent mate.

"Excellent. Perhaps he can make himself useful to us soon."

"Will you allow him to stay within the village?"

The elegant black wings at Ama's back ruffled as she inclined her head. "As he is not Seyton and therefore did not go through the agmari, he was tested against the vilebloom and found to be fertile."

This must have occurred when he left them to look for Samantha and Zuran. That she had even considered testing the male when the hunters were instructed to kill them in the past came as a surprise, but one did not question Ama. If she had done it, then she had a reason.

Although Ama had never been anything but kind and peaceful, easy to speak with and quick to aid, Olan was still attempting to sort his thoughts and emotions and her gaze unnerved him. He couldn't risk drawing attention to the situation he currently found himself in with Samantha and Zuran. It didn't matter that Samantha was female. Even a coveted fertile female would be punished for the things he had seen her do.

"I hope I can count on you to help guide him."

Olan's eyes snapped back to her face. The little grin on her lips told him she knew his mind had drifted, and he silently cursed himself. "Of course." Olan shifted in his seat. "Perhaps, if we are going to bring the Star Born into our village and mate with them, it might be in our best interest to—"

"Hey!"

Olan's head jerked up, his eyes landing on a very determined Lucy as she stomped through the streets. Samantha wasn't far behind, her brows furrowed over narrowed eyes.

"Lucy, seriously!" she hissed, trying to catch the other female's arm.

"I'm not going to sit around in some prison disguised as a hut while they make decisions for me, Sam."

Zuran was frowning at both of them as he followed, sparks of lightning dancing along his skin as he grumbled beneath his breath. "I apologize, Ama," he ground out.

"Samantha, Lucy," Ama greeted them. "What a pleasant surprise."

"We want answers." Lucy crossed her arms over her chest, her face flushed red with what he assumed was anger and frustration. "You can't just assign us to a guy and expect us to live happily ever after. That's not the way humans work."

"So Samantha has said."

"And yet you still gave her away like you had any right to her," Lucy argued.

"Lucy—"

"No, Sam!" The other female held a hand out to silence his mate. "This is ridiculous!"

The silence that followed the outburst was deafening. Every Seyton sitting at the table fixed their eyes on Ama, shocked that anyone, even a Star Born female, would have dared to raise their voice to her.

"Ridiculous?" Ama repeated, sparks dancing between her curved black horns. "These are our traditions."

"*Your* traditions, not *ours*. Humans—"

"No longer have a home of their own? Destroyed their planet? Yes, we have been told." Ama narrowed her eyes and folded her hands in her lap.

"We really are very thankful for your hospitality, Ama." Samantha glared at Lucy, but it didn't seem to faze the female at all.

"Hospitality? They kept you shut in a hut for a week," Lucy shot back.

"That was for her safety," Olan growled.

"You were sent down by your people to determine whether or not this was a suitable place to live, were you not?" Lucy clenched her jaw and inclined her head. "Do your people do this often? Do you simply come into someone's home and decide to take it for your own?"

"We don't want your homes. We want a small portion of a planet. We want to make our own homes, our own villages."

"This world is our home, Star Born." Ama gestured all around them. "The All Mother blessed us with the resources we needed to make our lives and it is She who will judge you fit to stay or not."

"Fuck that," Lucy sneered.

Behind her, Samantha's eyes widened and her mouth dropped open as if she couldn't believe she had heard her friend correctly. Before his mate could speak, Zyar stepped forward, the muscles of his jaw hardened and his fists clenched at his side. He spoke to Ama, but his eyes never left Lucy's face. "I apologize for her insult, and will accept responsibility for her words."

The raised voices had attracted more onlookers, and with the way some of the younger males were shifting and pacing, Olan was getting increasingly uncomfortable having Samantha in their midst. "I am sure Lucy is still adjusting to the idea." He said as he rose from his seat. "Perhaps we can ease the transition by teaching them about our traditions, showing them the cultural importance of the things they do not understand."

Ama was quiet for a long moment as she studied the faces around them, her expression impossible to read. Olan's pulse pounded in his head as he waited. Ama rarely handed out punishments, but he had never seen anyone speak to her in such a way.

"If you want to teach us something that bad, then show us how to survive here." Lucy's hands clenched around her upper arms. "This is temporary—we won't be here forever. The minute we get our tech working, we can leave this planet and your barbaric traditions behind."

Olan groaned, wishing the female had enough self-preservation to stop arguing.

"You wish to learn how best to survive on your own on Seytonna? To learn about the planet and all of the dangers that await you outside of the village?" Lucy nodded, and Ama pursed her lips. "Fine."

The golden-haired Star Born female looked shocked for a moment before she recovered. "Great. Thank you."

"Olan," Ama turned toward him. "Since you proposed the idea, you may lead the first lesson."

He swallowed hard, dropping his chin to his chest in acknowledgment. "Of course."

"Escort the Star Born to the farms so that they can better understand where the food they have enjoyed came from. Introduce them to Urhin and his flock."

All Mother help him, he nearly choked on his own tongue when she mentioned Urhin. The male was one of a handful of farmers who worked to provide food to the village and its inhabitants, but most of his contribution came from the flock of winged samaras he raised. The look his chieftess gave him dared him to protest so he kept his mouth closed and said nothing, nodding again before collecting some of the fresh fruit from the bowls in front of him. Zuran caught Olan's eye, and they both frowned.

"I swear, I didn't know she was going to do that." Samantha muttered as she took the fruit he offered. "Maybe I should talk to Ama, try to smooth things out a little?"

He took her hand in his, pulling her through those that had gathered as they made their way back to his hut to collect James. The sight of his fingers enclosing her much smaller hand made his heart race faster, and each moment that she allowed him to keep touching her gave him hope for the future. "I think we have gotten ourselves into enough trouble for one day. With any luck, Ama will overlook the scene Lucy made and not hold her ignorance against her."

Olan knew this must be hard for them. They had been thrust into a society with traditions and norms that were not their own, and had been expected to go along with whatever was decided. It may have taken him some time to realize he shouldn't have expected Samantha to accept him as one of their females would have, but he would do his best to help her and her friends. He looked down to where their fingers interlocked and felt his chest tighten. Even if it meant having to reject the traditions he had followed his entire life.

CHAPTER 17

SAMANTHA

"You wanna talk about what happened back there?" Samantha asked as she slowed her steps, giving Lucy a chance to catch up.

"I don't know, honestly." Her friend shrugged.

James walked up ahead of them, his head swinging left and right as he took in the changing scenery. Within the main part of the village, the massive red trees were prominent, surrounding the huts and even blocking the view of the pools, but that wasn't the case out here. Wide open fields stretched on for as far as she could see. A few family-sized huts dotted them, but the landscape was dominated by row after row of crops. Even in the giant greenhouse on board the space station, growth like this was not something any of them had ever seen outside the archives.

She could hear James's excited chatter and smiled at the way Olan eyed him, clearly not understanding what the man was feeling. To the right of the closest hut was a small fenced-in area containing what she assumed to be a small herd of domestic livestock. The animals weren't very large, with their heads maybe reaching the top of her hip, but the massive white horns that sloped up from their crown gave them at least another two or three feet.

Samantha recognized their shaggy grey coats from the pile of furs in Olan's hut. She had been more than a little surprised to realize she missed being home with him. *Home?* Samantha grimaced, her eyes trailing over Olan's back. She couldn't afford to get too comfortable, could she? When the others came, surely she would need to get back to her old life. There would be so much work to do. What if they decided Seytonna wasn't right for humanity?

The thought caused an unwelcome knot to form in her throat, and she cursed herself for allowing an attachment to form in the short time she had been in the village. "What happened before you all got to the village? I'm not exactly sure where the drop ship crashed in relation to the pod, but it took Zyar so much longer to bring you and James back than it took him and Zuran to get me here."

Lucy's steps faltered, her brow furrowing as she came to a stop. When her eyes met Samantha's, they were glassy with unshed tears. "We had to bury them, Sam."

Olan stopped up ahead, looking back at her as Zuran came up behind them. "Go ahead," she whispered. "We just need a moment." The males looked at one another before Zuran nodded, continuing down the path.

"We were alone for maybe two days before Zyar and the other woman showed up. They tried to make us leave them, but we couldn't, not until we had seen to all of them." Lucy's hand swiped at the tears that fell down her cheeks. "Some of them were so bad—" Her breath caught and Samantha rubbed her hand over her friend's arm. "I have no idea how James and I walked away with so few injuries, but Yopher and Frone were thrown from their restraints at some point during entry or maybe the crash itself. Laveau had massive head trauma, and I'm pretty sure Ocampo's neck was broken. I've never seen anything so awful in my time working security. Poor James leaves the lab for the first time and ends up crash landing and digging graves."

"I'm so sorry, Luce."

Her friend shrugged, but the tears continued to fall. "We had almost finished by the time Zyar and that other woman showed up. They tried to make us go with them, but I couldn't leave Laveau out there like that. She was a good person who just wanted to find a home. She used to talk about it when we were on shift, about how she was going to be the first one off of that damn ship when we found a place." Lucy's breath hitched, and she shook her head. "She deserved happiness, deserved the family that she had been dreaming of, and now she'll never have it. The least I could do was make sure her body was safe from whatever predators are on this planet."

Burials were a thing of the past for humanity. Since the construction of the space station and the mass evacuation of Earth, their ancestors had few options when it came to disposing of a body after death. Simply sending a deceased loved one out an airlock and into the vacuum of space was illegal, and had actually been that way since before the Venium and Grutex had showed up on Earth.

No one liked a litterbug. Instead, you could choose to be incinerated by chemicals or have your body zipped up in a bag, exposed to cold depths of space until you were frozen solid, and then smashed up into tiny pieces. The bag would be vacuum sealed and presented to your family. It was about as eco-friendly as they could get.

Their whole lives revolved around making everything as efficient as possible, and that included raising families. With the limited amount of space on the station, couples who chose to have a child were restricted to only one. Children were taught the basics of education for the first few years of their lives until the formal testing started. Your entire life was decided based on the results, and if you were a washout in your prospective career field, that meant you ended up doing the things no one else wanted to do.

The shortage of space, not to mention the hit their population had taken after the war, meant that many fields of study had done away with specialties and now promoted a broader education. Sure, there were people who excelled at certain subjects more than others, but that was nothing new.

As one of the children thrust into the science career, Samantha had spent most of her life studying sciences that would aid them in finding a new home. Being placed in a leadership role on the *S.S. Constellation* had been a surprising honor considering the fact that so many others were just as qualified.

While Samantha had gotten lucky and enjoyed her work most of the time, Lucy had always resented the fact that she had been selected for security. She, like much of humanity, longed for the day when they might be free to decide for themselves. Samantha knew that was another reason this loss was so hard on her. Many of these people had been her friends and co-workers and they had the same dreams of freedom.

Lucy sighed, her feet shifting against the dark earth of the path. "I don't want to lose this opportunity, Sam. I want this to work out, and I'm sorry if I made a shitty impression with their chieftess, but it's been a long few days and then we get into the village and I'm already being bossed around."

Samantha grinned as she wrapped her arms around her friend, squeezing her tight. "They are a bossy bunch, huh?"

"The bossiest. I was barely inside the walls before they were thrusting some glowing rock in my hands and proclaiming me a coveted one." Samantha laughed as Lucy pulled back, a grin tipping the corners of her mouth. "They even did it to James. Poor guy was standing there just staring down at it as it glowed. They seemed pretty excited about it working on him."

Samantha made a mental note to ask Olan or Zuran about that. It had been explained to her that the females were tested, but she hadn't heard of this happening with the males since they used the agmari bloom.

"Do you think they will agree to some sort of alliance?"

"I'm not sure, but I'm hoping so."

Lucy grimaced as they began to walk again. "I know I told Ama that I didn't want to stay, that this was a temporary thing, but I'm so tired of looking, Sam. I want it to be over. This place... it isn't like last time. There are natives here who can teach us, who can warn us and prevent the things that happened on—"

"I know," Samantha interrupted. She didn't want to hear the name of the planet, didn't want to have to think about the tragedy of that mission, but the pain still lanced through her. "I don't know why Marsel was so insistent, especially after the last time. He should have been more cautious, but he didn't learn from my mistakes."

She could still hear the screams over the radio; the strangled sounds of their field team as they struggled to breathe. None of the files had made mention of the possibly harmful emissions, and none of the data retrieved from their probes had given them any clue that it would cause such horrible allergic reactions.

Humans had been given many things by the Venium in the years after the war, not the least of which was radiation shielding to help keep the remaining population safe. The space station had been outfitted with special panels and the windows were covered in a film the Venium had crafted.

From what she could remember reading in some of the older published journals from the first inhabitants of the station, there were rumors their alien allies had genetically modified humanity in an attempt to further prepare them for an extended stay in space. Whether or not they knew how long that was ultimately going to be was another matter altogether.

In the early days of their alliance, before Earth had taken a turn for the worse, many humans, both men and women, had chosen to leave and make a life on Venora. The fact that she had been born on the station told Samantha that her ancestors were either stubborn or they had been wary of the aliens, like so many others that stayed.

"That wasn't your fault, Sam," Lucy murmured. "You did everything you could have done to make sure it was safe for them."

"It obviously wasn't enough." The fact that Marsel had been willing to send a team down to X9 so quickly, with no idea about the atmospheric conditions or the makeup of the planet in general didn't sit well with her. Perhaps that was why he had sent her down on her own. At this point, she was convinced he had been the one to order her placed in the pod, assuming he hadn't done it himself.

"Have you noticed how often the planet experiences partial eclipses here?" James asked as they approached.

"I did. I can't imagine it doesn't have an effect on the weather patterns."

"What I wouldn't give for a lab and some decent equipment," he sighed.

Samantha grinned, recognizing the wistful tone. "You and me both. Sometimes there's a chill in the air that makes you feel like you're on the verge of winter, but most days the suns are so bright that leaving the hut makes it feel like my skin is going to melt off." She ran a hand over her already red skin.

"Jeez, I can't believe I didn't think to offer you this sooner!" Lucy twisted, pulling a white tube of sunscreen from a pouch on her hip. "Ta-da!"

"Thank the gods! I could kiss you!" She snatched the tube from her friend, eyeing the Seyton-made pouch it had come from. Unlike Samantha, Lucy was still wearing her human clothing, so why she wore the pouch when she had perfectly good pockets on the black cargo pants was something she wanted to ask about, but it could wait. She popped open the top and squeezed a good amount into her palm before rubbing the cream onto the parts of her body she could reach. Lucy helped with the areas on her back that were exposed. "I've been avoiding the sun like the plague anytime I get out."

"Not very often, was it?" Lucy murmured.

Olan's growl let her know that he hadn't missed the comment, but it made her grin. He and Zuran walked a few steps ahead of them, both silent, no doubt trying to listen to their conversation.

"You weren't wearing your suits when you were brought into the village, were you? What made you leave the ship without them?" It was the first time she had really noticed their clothing was far more casual than she was used to seeing on the field teams.

"They were compromised in the crash," Lucy grimaced. "And with the massive hole torn into the side of the drop ship, there wasn't much of a choice in whether or not to take the risk."

"That's another thing that has me puzzled. You would think with the dual star system that the planet would be below zero," James said as he pushed a branch away from himself. He hadn't seemed to notice the change of topic. The excitement of the world around them and all the new discoveries that awaited them was fascinating, especially for people who had spent their entire lives confined to such small spaces.

This place was something they had barely dared to dream about.

"I thought that too, and it shocked me how lush everything looked from the window of the pod when I woke up. I hadn't gotten a chance to see X9 from orbit, but this planet doesn't seem to support much of what we were taught."

"What could the cause be?" he wondered aloud.

"There are so many variables to consider and without equipment I wouldn't even know where to begin or how to measure anything to gain accurate data. When you were preparing to come down, did the team collect data on the stars?"

James shook his head. "Honestly, when you disappeared, we thought it was over. We didn't know we were coming until the night before. It was absolute chaos."

Something was going on within the ship, and she desperately wanted to know what it was. "I'm thinking that if both of the suns were dim, then it would be far colder here. My best guess is that we've got at least a Class-G and Class-L up there, and that might be the perfect duo to bring about the shifting weather and temps."

"It would depend on the distance between X9 and the suns, and even the elliptical pattern of all of their orbits."

"Right." Samantha chewed on her lip.

"There are so many things to consider here: the makeup of the planet and the chemicals within the atmosphere. I'd love to be able to get some readings on the relative humidity here and compare it with the data from old Earth. I wonder how many similarities there are between the two."

"You two have completely lost me." Lucy complained with a playful pout.

Samantha laughed as she looked out across the fields. Maybe it was the fact that she was outside in the fresh air and sunshine for the first time in days, but her spirit felt light and the heaviness that had been weighing on her had disappeared.

Could they actually have found a place to sustain them? Would she be able to convince her people to forge an alliance with the Seyton, and would their hosts even agree to allow them to live among them? She knew some humans wanted nothing to do with the Venium, and that they may not want to feel indebted to yet another alien race, but this could be different.

"*Oof!*" Samantha huffed when the toe of her shoe smacked against one of the large stones. She stumbled forward, her hands shooting out to brace her as she collided with Olan's back.

"Fanahala!" Olan said, spinning around to steady her. "Be careful."

"What does that mean anyway? Fanahala?" Lucy asked when Olan had resumed walking.

"Olan said it was similar to wife or mate." Samantha explained.

Lucy responded with a derisive snort. "Well, how romantic."

A laugh burst from Samantha's lips. "You write romance, Luce. I always figured this would be the sort of stuff you'd love."

"I write romance. I don't live it."

Samantha grinned as she reached out, running her hand over the feathered tops of the crops growing along the edge of the path. It reminded her of the wheat fields on old Earth with the way the crops swayed back and forth in the breeze. She wondered idly if the soil here would be suitable for the seeds they had stored on the ship.

This could be our home.

No, don't go getting your hopes up, she chided. *It's still early.*

A shriek up ahead caught her attention, and she shielded her eyes against the bright sunlight. A child zigzagged across the path, his laughter ringing through the fields, and on his heels was a terrifying little creature covered in red feathers and dark scales with a mouth full of pointed teeth. Long talons tipped the toes on its scaly feet, but all Samantha could focus on was the open mouth. Like the gators on old Earth, this thing sported a blunt snout, but the double row of teeth seemed more likely to be found within the jaws of a shark. From its teeth to its toes, the little beast screamed danger.

Before she had time to process what was happening, Olan took off, his long legs eating up the distance. He snatched the child up, holding his flailing body high above the ground, out of reach of the jumping gator-chicken.

"Put me down!" The child giggled as he twisted in Olan's grasp, his white skin covered in the dark dust of the earth. "I was winning! Teeth couldn't keep up!"

"Teeth?" Lucy raised a brow. "Seems like an appropriate name."

"You are playing a game with a samara?" Olan asked, frowning at the boy. "They are dangerous."

"He's been around the flock since he was old enough to walk. Probably even before that," a deep, rumbling voice said from within the crops. A colorful male, a breeder like Olan, stepped out onto the path, shooing the samara away. "Away with you, Teeth."

"Aww, Papa, I was going to win this time." The boy's shoulders sagged as Olan placed him back on the ground.

"You aren't worried he'll get hurt?" Olan asked.

The older male shook his head, a laugh rolling up from his chest. "It's obvious you haven't spent much time on the farms. Not many of those within the village do," he said, shrugging his massive shoulders.

"No one comes out here," the boys said, eyeing Zuran and the rest of their group. "They're all too scared of the samaras."

"They are wild beasts, and they deserve caution from outsiders, but when you know how to handle them, the risk is minimal."

Samantha raised a brow as she glanced at the old scars on his hands, arms, and legs. It seemed like he was speaking from a lifetime of experience.

"Still, it seems too dangerous to leave a kit alone with a samara." Olan looked so fiercely protective of the boy, his eyes following him closely as if he was prepared to jump to his rescue again, and for the first time she wondered what having a child here might be like.

For the first time in her entire life, Samantha could actually see herself *wanting* children. They wouldn't be fully human, but there were enough similarities between humans and the Seyton that she could see a little one with this boy's bright white skin running through the forest. Would her child grow up and have dark, shimmery black skin like Zuran, or would they have Olan's colorful scales?

The realization of what she was thinking about nearly knocked her over. *What the hell's gotten into me?*

"He was not alone with the Samara." The male's voice had turned cold, the unsolicited parenting advice was obviously not well received.

"He was having a great time, Olan," Samantha said as she stepped forward, attempting to ease the tension. "And it's obvious he wasn't playing unsupervised." The older male grunted, staring down at her as if he was just now noticing she wasn't one of their females. "I'm Samantha." She stuck her hand out in greeting, but the male only eyed her hand. "I'm one of the humans who crash landed near the village some time ago. Olan and Zuran brought us here in the hopes that you might have some time to help us understand more about the work you do out here."

The change in his demeanor was immediate. A smile broke out across his face, and he gestured enthusiastically, calling for their group to follow him. They spent the rest of the day exploring the farms, visiting the other family huts so that they could learn about the different livestock. Urhin, the father of the boy Olan had "rescued," was the only one crazy enough to keep samaras, but Samantha enjoyed the goat-like olmank and their soft, shaggy coats that some of the other farmers kept.

James was the happiest she had ever seen him. He asked a million questions, dug his hands into the soil, and even braved a few of the samara chicks. "Hey, Sam! Don't worry about me. Urhin said I could stay with his family so that I could get some hands-on time with the managing of the farm." He was grinning from ear to ear, bouncing on the balls of his feet. "If you can work out an alliance with Ama, we could finally have a place to call home. A chance at a real life, Sam."

She watched him run back toward the farmer's hut and sighed, knowing she had her work cut out for her. Life here could be perfect, but they would never be free if she couldn't convince Ama they weren't gifts from the All Mother to be given away like prizes.

CHAPTER 18

ZURAN

*H*e had known he was going to be required to return to the hunt, but returning after being near Samantha and Olan for so long was killing him. There was no doubt in his mind that Ama must have noticed the heat building within him, saw him struggling with his madness, and wanted to keep him away from Samantha and Lucy.

He had foolishly hoped that others wouldn't be able to see that things had only gotten worse the longer he was near Samantha.

Zuran slapped a branch out of his way as he traveled deeper into the forest. What did it matter anyway? Ama would never allow anything to happen between them, and despite what Zyar had tried to insinuate, he doubted Olan would welcome his suggestion.

Maybe things would change in favor of the hunters once the rest of the humans landed. They wouldn't harbor the same resentment against the hunters as his own people did, but until then, he couldn't allow himself to dream of something better. The only way he could prove himself to her in the meantime was to provide, and luckily, it was something he had become incredibly good at over the solars.

The ipsla tracks he was following suddenly veered off to the right through the thicker underbrush, and he crouched down to peer through the branches. The way the thin rays of light speared through the foliage reminded him of the stories Olan's grandmother had told them in their youth of tiny creatures who lived among the trees and shrubs. They looked like balls of light and enjoyed playing tricks on unsuspecting travelers. The old female had known many stories, claiming that they had been passed down to her from her grandmother and all of the females before her.

Days before their ceremony, she had gathered the two of them close and whispered excitedly about how once upon a time, this coming of age held none of the apprehension it currently did. Young males did not fear becoming hunters nor did they worry about disappointing their families. Things were different then, but when they had asked what happened to change that, she had merely shrugged her thin shoulders. He often wondered if it had been caused by the madness, or if the madness was caused by the fallout.

During heats, hunters had been known to hurt one another. Was it possible that one had injured or killed a female? During a particularly strong heat solars ago, Zyar had cut him with the blade of his tail, nothing so bad he didn't heal, but it could have been mistaken as aggression. Intentionally causing harm to a female was a severely punishable offense, but could it have caused a rift of this magnitude?

He rubbed his hand over the tiny scar Zyar's blade had left and shuddered. That had been the first time he had realized that the sting of the wound could heighten his pleasure. The danger of the act, the taboo nature of it, had only pushed him higher.

Zuran braced himself against the small red sapling to his right, his chest heaving and cock hardening as the scene he had pleasured himself to only days ago flashed through his mind. He could almost feel the tips of Olan's nails raking down his chest, and the warmth of his mouth against the skin of his neck as his sharp teeth sank in. What would Olan think if he knew what was in Zuran's mind? He had asked himself that question so many times, and each time it brought a pang of despair with it.

It won't matter what he thinks. Whether he feels the same or not, you are a hunter and he is a breeder.

The best that could come from his confession would be an invitation to pleasure Samantha, but would that really be enough? Would he ever truly be happy in that role?

As he fought the urge to find release, Zuran's ears picked up on the sound of someone or something coming up behind him. His head tilted, eyes closing as he concentrated on the steps. They were heavy and clumsy, nothing like the prey animals he sought, or even the predatory beasts that lurked within the forest.

The snap of a twig to his left had him ducking into the morning mists, his dark skin blending into the brush as he listened to the being draw closer to his position. Whoever this was clearly hadn't spent much time tracking. Perhaps it was a young hunter, one still in his first couple years of training. It might also be someone from a neighboring village coming to investigate after witnessing the ship fall from the sky, or even more Star Born searching for their missing people.

Whoever it was, Zuran was not going to allow them to come upon him. He quietly scaled the tree he had hidden behind, crawling along the thick flowered branch until he could rest on his belly, his blade unsheathed and his tail poised to strike.

Just as the shadowy form came into view, Zuran slipped from the branch, his arms wrapping around the neck of the one following him, the blade pressing into the sensitive skin of the throat as he snarled.

"Wait!" the familiar voice panted. "It's me! It's me, Zuran!"

Zuran stilled, his breath catching in his lungs. His cock hardened instantly with the realization that the body he was wrapped around was Olan's. The curve of the male's ass was perfectly pressed into the cradle of Zuran's hips, and the thick ridge of Olan's tail was trapped between their bodies, wriggling in his panic. Quick, heated breaths of desire fell from his lips and he desperately swallowed the moan that rose up through his throat.

With a muffled curse, Zuran released the male, stumbling backward so that there was some distance between them. "What are you doing out here? This is too far from the village!"

Olan pushed away from the tree he had fallen against, his lightning zapping between his horns as he tucked his tail between his legs. His eyes stayed on the ground as he fidgeted, shifting from one foot to the other as if he were a kit caught doing something wrong.

"I…" Raw emotion flitted across his face for a moment before he met Zuran's gaze, his expression guarded once again. "It is none of your business, hunter."

Zuran physically recoiled at the insult, his whole body going rigid as the arousal that had pounded through him a moment before all but disappeared. His own lightning rose to his skin as his tail swung behind him in a fiery dance. His upper lip pulled away from his teeth in a snarl as he glared at Olan. He might have to follow certain rules within the village, but Olan was in his domain now.

"That's rich, coming from the breeder who has decided to step outside the safety of the village." He growled, taking a step toward Olan. "Everything in this forest is my business, *breeder*." Rage filled his chest as Olan growled. "What did you think you were going to do out here? Have you decided Samantha is too much to handle? Maybe you've gotten yourself lost on your way to the unmated female village? If that's the case, I'd be more than happy to have her."

"Samantha is *my* female!" Olan lunged forward, catching Zuran around the middle and taking him to the ground, but the hunter was far faster. He bucked up, flipping Olan onto his back before pinning him down. His blade extended and he pressed it once more against the male's throat as he hissed in displeasure.

"Do not underestimate me, Olan," he whispered, his face a breath away from his old friend's. "When we are out here, you are at my mercy. You are not made for this place, but this forest has been my home for solars. Run home to your female, breeder. You are meant for mating and nothing more." Zuran shoved himself away, but Olan followed.

"Is it wrong for me to want more?" Fire burned within Olan's eyes as he slammed his fist into the ground. "Is it wrong for me to want to be useful to my mate?" In a surprising display of frustration, the male flung a handful of the dark dirt at Zuran's feet. "I just want her to look at me the way she looks at you. I want to see the same desire in her eyes for me as I see in them for you!"

"What are you talking about?" Zuran frowned down at him as confusion welled up within him. Why would he ever wish to have Samantha see him as a hunter? This was not a life he should envy.

"I want to be worthy, to prove that I am more than a potential father to her kits. I want her to see that I am capable of more." Olan panted softly. "I want her to know I will do everything I can to protect our family."

Zuran's heart clenched painfully in his chest. How many times had he wished that he could show Samantha that he could be more than a hunter? That he could love her the way a breeder could? How many times had the same thoughts run through his mind? Perhaps they were more alike than either one of them thought.

With a resigned sigh, Zuran extended his hand. "I will help you."

"I want a chance—" Olan's mouth dropped open, the words dying on his tongue. "You will?"

"I said I would," he grumbled, pulling the other male to his feet. "But I have conditions."

"Yes. Okay."

"You will listen to everything I say, and you will do your best to stay out of my way." He shouldn't be doing this, shouldn't be helping the male who was going to take away the only female who had treated him with kindness, but Zuran had done many things recently that he shouldn't have. He had only recently allowed himself to remember and accept his love for Olan, and with that came the realization that he would always put the breeder's happiness above his own.

"You won't tell Ama about this?"

"Did you tell Ama about the pools?" he asked, his voice low as if he were afraid someone would hear.

Olan's eyes locked on his, and what he saw for the briefest moment within their depths sent his pulse racing. "No. I said nothing."

With a nod, Zuran jerked his head to the side. "Come, but watch your step." Zuran said just as Olan snapped another branch in half beneath his foot. "You will scare away anything in the area making that much noise."

"It's not as if I've done this before..."

Right, Zuran grimaced. One of the first things you learned as a hunter was how to move through the forest with as little noise as possible. "Avoid the areas on the ground with twigs and dried foliage. Look for spots where the moss has grown or where you see only dirt."

Zuran looked around them and grinned when he saw the tracks of a large milory. The meat from this animal would feed those in the village far longer than the carcass of the smaller ipsla he had been tracking before.

Behind him, Olan picked his way through the brush, his steps still heavy and rushed. He thumped into Zuran's back, when the hunter stopped suddenly. "Do not worry about moving so fast. Take time to stop and regroup, look around you. There is no need to stare down at your feet, unless you'd like to run into me again?" *Not that you'd mind,* his mind jeered. "Eyes up. Stay alert for any signs of danger or your prey. It does no good to find the thing you are tracking just to scare it away."

"Right." Only Olan didn't look so sure of himself.

"Heel to toe, bend your knees slightly. Shift your weight. If you keep walking the way you are, we will come home empty handed. If we need to run, use the balls of your feet."

"Uh, right." Olan frowned. "No problem."

He knew Olan was trying his best, but with no training and the utter lack of any weapon whatsoever to help kill their prey, Zuran had no doubt this was going to be a long day. He ran a hand over his right horn. "Where is Samantha if you are out here?"

"She is with Asa today."

How could he have forgotten about the lessons? Every morning for the last week he had watched Olan walk Samantha to Ama's hut to learn from the chieftess and Asa.

"Has Ama made a decision about where they will be?"

"For now, Lucy and James are staying with two of the farming families. It's hard enough to keep the peace with Samantha living there, and Lucy is not even half as cooperative as her friend." Olan huffed. "Having the Star Born out there, away from the main village, has done a lot to calm the nerves of the hunters and the unmated males."

Zuran stopped abruptly, his hand pressing against Olan's chest, when he heard the soft clicking of the milory as it chomped at the smattering of grass. If he hadn't heard the noise of the beast's teeth, they might run straight into it. He crouched down, gesturing for Olan to do the same. Taking the milory from here would be simple and quick, and they could make it back to the village before Samantha was even finished with her lesson.

He would give the breeder the credit for the kill. *To help him mate the female I want.*

Shaking off the thought, Zuran pushed forward, his eyes focused on the prey in front of him. He tilted his head, listening for any sign of the predators he knew to be in the area. If the herd got spooked, they would need to move out of their way as fast as possible. It wasn't a large herd by any means, but the milory themselves were hefty creatures and being run over by one of them was not something he wished to experience.

With the cold months fast approaching, many of the young had been weaned, and although their meat was tender, they were the future of the herd and not his intended target. He crossed off the dams, who were needed to birth the young, and the younger bucks, who were often seen as too tough to eat. The large older members of the herd were who he was after today. They were often picked off by predators, but there were still some roaming around the edge of the group.

Zuran's body flexed as he prepared to attack, but before he could make his move, Olan launched himself into the small clearing. He landed on the hairy back of one of the old males, one hand gripping tight to the animal's fur while in the other he brandished a tanner's blade. A strangled snarl caught in his throat as he watched the breeder move with a fluid grace he was sure was born of solars worth of dance. The male attempted to stab at the milory's neck, but the tanner's blade wasn't made for anything as tough as that, and the moment the old beast screamed, the rest of the herd panicked, rushing from the clearing.

Zuran could see Olan's grip slipping and propelled himself forward, twisting in the air so that his tail wrapped around the animal's muscular neck before his blade pierced the tender flesh just behind the ear. It was one of the few places around the beast's head and neck that wasn't protected by bony plating. The massive milory grunted once before jerking to the side. Zuran watched in horror as Olan went down beneath it, crushed under the weight.

"Olan!" The other male was huffing and growling as he shoved at the animal. Zuran raced to the other side, hooking his arms beneath Olan's shoulders and tugging him free. "You damn fool!" He yelled, even as his hands ran over the breeder's body, checking for any signs of an injury. "What were you thinking?"

"I want her to love me!" Olan yelled back. "I want to be worthy!"

"You are worthy!" Zuran shook the male before throwing his arms around him. He felt the way Olan trembled as he crushed him to his chest. "We could have lost you." The words tumbled free before he had the sense to stop them, but if Olan heard them, he didn't let on. He wouldn't have been able to handle the rejection, not from Olan, not ever. His throat tightened, and his jaw clenched so hard that his teeth ached.

Zuran could feel his skin heat with his own embarrassment as he pulled away and cleared his throat. Olan's cheeks were flushed, the light skin turning darker than the rosette bud's sunset colored petals. He ran his shaking hands through his short hair, glancing away as Zuran bent down to lift the hind legs of the milory. Olan quickly took the front and together they carried the kill through the trees, all the way back to the path that led into the village.

"Take it," Zuran said, laying the Milory's head on the ground. Olan opened his mouth, but Zuran interrupted, not wishing to hear whatever protest was on his tongue. "Wasn't this the plan? Bring her a kill, prove your worth?" He stepped away, the blood rushing so loudly in his ears that he barely heard himself as he gestured at the carcass. "For Samantha."

He couldn't stay around him a moment longer, didn't trust the emotions that were surging through him. Already, he had revealed too much to the other male. Zuran needed to face the fact that he was barely holding onto the control he had worked so hard to keep over the solars.

Soon, very soon, he would have to turn himself over to Ama.

His feet pounded the dirt as he ran to his hut, the boiled heat in his blood urging him on. He had thought he could remain near them, that he could restrain himself. *You've lasted far longer than many hunters.* But he didn't want to descend into the madness. Zuran wanted to beat it. He wanted to be loved.

So few of us get what we want in life. The last words his mother had spoken to him before she had walked away rang through his mind, and he squeezed his eyes closed as he roared his pain into his empty home.

CHAPTER 19

SAMANTHA

$\mathcal{T}$he sounds of wildlife all around her was something she was learning to love. Small winged animals, similar to Earth's birds, sang from within the trees, and she could distantly make out the sounds of the grazing herds. This quiet wasn't something she was used to, but she welcomed it all the same. The humming of the machines had been replaced by the chirping of various insects, and instead of the glare of the artificial overhead lights, Samantha got to bask in the rays of the dual suns.

Not for long, mind you. The danger of burning was real for her, but she was enjoying what she could.

She was learning that Seytonna and its people were complex and more beautiful than she had thought. Every day for a little over a week Olan had fed her breakfast, watched her pick a dress from the collection he had made for her, and then brought her to Ama's, where she had started what she saw as cultural and basic living courses.

Most days, she shadowed Asa as she tended to her duties.

Like the majority of human women on the station and ships, Asa wasn't merely a housewife. In space, every able-bodied person was expected to pull their weight. Mothers or fathers were given the first few years with their child before they returned to work, seeing their little one off to school.

Here, it wasn't just mothers and fathers caring for their children. Everyone in the village had a hand in raising the next generation.

As Ama's second-in-command, Asa saw to the safety and welfare of her people. If someone had a problem, Asa was there. If someone was struggling, Asa was there. In her downtime, Samantha had discovered that the female taught the children how to paint. She showed them where to find the berries, flowers, and bits of plants to create their own pigments and fascinated them with her knowledge on fashioning brushes made from the tail hair of the shaggy beasts she now knew were called olmanks. They had taken the children to the farms to gather the hair, and she had enjoyed taking a few minutes to catch up with Lucy.

She missed having her friend with her, but they had agreed that the risk of disturbing the unmated males and hunters wasn't worth both of them living within the heart of the village. If she were honest, Lucy looked happier and more relaxed than she had ever seen her.

It all gave Samantha hope that they were headed in the right direction.

Just yesterday, Samantha had sat among the children, a tiny male curled in her lap, as Asa and one of the older females recounted stories of their history. The little ones gasped and cheered during the tales of war and epic battles, jumping up and down in celebration when they ended in victory. Those were her favorite days. Samantha hadn't had much opportunity to be with children while on board the station, and there weren't very many on board the Constellation, but she was finding she loved spending her time with them.

Today, however, she was with Ama, which meant she was learning more about the spiritual and cultural aspects of living among the Seyton. Samantha wouldn't say this was her favorite activity, but the peacefulness of it helped to ease the tension that seemed to have moved into her body over the last few days.

"You are doing it again." Ama's voice sent a shiver down her spine.

"Doing what?" she asked, peering at the chieftess. Like the other women in the village, Ama was scantily clad, her chest covered in nothing but her long braids and colorful strands of glass, stone, bone, and wooden beads. Soft, nearly sheer fabric was tied around her hips, barely concealing her lower body. Olan had tried to dress her in the same fashion, but she liked the privacy the dresses allowed her. Maybe one day she would feel brave enough to follow suit, but today was not that day. Samantha watched as Ama smirked, stringing one of the glass beads onto the thread that coiled between them.

"Your mind is not focusing," she admonished lightly. "If you do not open yourself to the ancestors during your work, then how will you transfer their energy, their protection, into your covering?"

Right. Everything with Ama came back to the All Mother and the ancestors. The necklaces weren't merely for privacy, they told a story. Each color, shape, and material had a meaning, and when they were put together one should be able to tell the history of a female's line.

"I'm not sure my ancestors really cared to stick around after death, and no offense, but I doubt the All Mother cares whether I'm channeling her during the process." Ama's soft tsk made Samantha grin.

"The All Mother cares for all of her children, Samantha."

"Need I remind you that I am human, and therefore not one of her children?"

Ama looked up from her work, her gaze serious as she regarded Samantha. "The All Mother has been watching over you since the moment you fell through the clouds. You may not know her yet, but she knows you."

It wasn't that Samantha didn't appreciate Ama's spirituality, but as a polytheist, she had her own set of beliefs and practices. The fact that the chieftess believed the All Mother was protecting Samantha actually comforted her some. With a soft smile, she shifted on the grass, wiping away the sweat that beaded her brow. Gods, she felt like she was being roasted over flames. Her skin was already red from her farm trek a couple days before, and she groaned thinking about how uncomfortable she was going to be later.

Ama had insisted this was outdoor work—something to be done beneath the open expanse of the sky. The only problem with that was, between her, Lucy, and James, they were beginning to run out of sunscreen. She glanced up at Ama, wondering if she and the other females used some local plant or other natural remedy to protect themselves and the children.

"Do the Seyton not get sunburned?"

Ama raised a brow but didn't look up from her work. "Burns from the suns?"

"Yeah, where you turn red and your skin peels?"

The chieftess turned to her then, a look of concern and something akin to horror coming over her face. "Your skin *peels*?"

"Well, yeah. After the burn heals, a layer of your skin peels off." Samantha ran her hands over the reddened skin of her upper arm. "This is all going to come off within the next few days. Have you never gotten burned?"

"From fire, yes, but the suns have never harmed us." Ama glanced up at them with a grimace.

"We have a cream that's sent down with the field teams called sun block. It helps keep us from burning, but we still try to limit our exposure."

"There is a plant our healers use on burns that may be useful. We will consult with her." Ama tied off the end of the necklace she had been working on so that the beads were secured and placed the piece inside the woven basket she had brought out with them. "Let's continue this tomorrow. There is too much on your mind today, and I fear the suns have already done enough damage to your skin."

How unfair was it that she had landed on a planet that hated her skin tone? The majority of the natives were far lighter than she was with their pale skin. None of them seemed to be bothered by the blistering rays. She had read in the medical archives once that the melanin in your skin was believed to help protect the skin against the harmful UV rays on Earth, but she was lacking in that department. There had to be something their bodies naturally produced that protected them, but without medical equipment and her lab, she wasn't likely to ever find out.

Samantha sighed as she tied off the ends before holding the beads up to the light. The tiny glass balls caught the rays, speckling her skin with colorful dots.

"Olan…" She heard Ama breathe a moment before the light was blocked out by a large shadow.

Samantha lowered her necklace and nearly gasped when she caught sight of the colorful male towering above her. His hands were wrapped around the hind legs of a large hairy animal that he pulled behind him. Blood, sweat, and dirt clung to his skin, but the proud smile on his face tugged at something deep inside her. Even as filthy as he was, this male was dangerously handsome.

"Ama." He nodded to the chieftess who sat frozen, staring at him. "I brought you a kill, Fanahala."

Samantha placed her necklace inside the box with Ama's before standing. "You brought me... a dead animal?"

"Yes. A milory." His grin brightened.

What did you say to someone who brought you a carcass? *Thanks for this*, just didn't seem sufficient. "Well... I can honestly say no one has ever brought me my own dead animal, so..." She chuckled as she shrugged. "Thank you?"

Olan dropped the body of the beast as he stepped closer, his chest rising and falling as he stared down into her face. Gods help her, but she wanted him to kiss her. When he began to lean down toward her, excitement coursed through her body. As much as she had tried to ignore it, all of those pecks on the cheek he gave her were starting to drive her mad. Some crazy part of her wanted to feel the passion from Olan that she felt with Zuran.

What did that say about her? Should she even care? This wasn't the station, the ship, or even old Earth.

Her eyes had just fluttered shut when a massive boom swept through the forest and the small field they had been working in. What she saw when she looked up into the sky made her stomach drop, and terror replaced the excitement she had felt moments before.

The *S.S. Constellation*'s metal siding gleamed, flames shooting from various points as explosions rocked it. Samantha had heard the phrase "time stood still" before, but until this moment, she hadn't ever experienced it. As if in slow motion, she watched as escape pods ejected from the sides, trying her best to count them, to calculate how many of her people could possibly be saved.

The sound of rending steel as the ship began to break apart tore a sob from her throat.

This wasn't what was supposed to happen. They had protocols in place for a reason. The ship was never meant to breach the atmosphere of a planet.

The pods plummeted toward the ground in the wake of the ship. Samantha felt someone grab her hand and turned to see Ama's wide eyes staring back at her. They were running together, back toward the village. When had she started moving? Her entire body was so numb that she didn't even notice when Olan lifted her, sprinting for the cover of the trees.

There were more explosions, more pods falling free. When a section of the ship was blown open, Samantha finally heard the screaming all around her, the panicked voices of the villagers as they hurried to investigate. Tears were streaming down her face as she watched the *S.S. Constellation* slam into the planet, the force of the impact shaking the ground and jarring her bones. Smoke billowed into the air, rising high above the tops of the distant treetops.

How many had been lost? How many more of their people would they bury on Seytonna? Gods, she hoped the children on board had made it off or had taken shelter. Someone was saying her name, shouting it. She turned her head to see Olan and Ama. They were shaking her shoulders and tapping her cheeks.

"Look at me, Fanahala."

"This wasn't supposed to happen. You have to let me go. I *have* to go this time." She heard herself sob. "There were women and children—babies. *Please.*"

Ama grimaced, her head turning toward the smoke. "I will not stop you this time, but there will be conditions." Samantha opened her mouth but Ama raised her hand to silence her. "The forest is dangerous. Having braved it once before, you should know this. You lack the natural defenses of a Seyton female, and I will not have you take risks that are unnecessary."

Olan's tail curled around her waist, drawing her closer. "I will go with her. No arguing," He snapped when she shoved at his chest. "If you want to go see to your people, then I will go as well. You are my mate, and my responsibility."

She wanted to shout at him that she hadn't agreed to be his mate just yet, but there wasn't time to argue, and honestly, she wouldn't have even known where to start. Ama was right; she had gotten better acquainted with the animals, big and small, that roamed the forest and she had no wish to travel alone. It didn't matter who went with her as long as they hurried. Samantha settled for an angry glare instead and pinched the skin of the breeder's tail.

"Find Zuran. Let him know he will be going as well," Ama said as Asa made her way through the crowd.

"What?" Olan hissed. She could feel the air become charged, and the hair on her arms stood straight up as sparks darted between his horns. "Zuran is—"

"Our best hunter and he knows the forest better than anyone else here. He will accompany you, and I will hear no more of your defiance." Ama's eyes flashed with annoyance. "We will speak about your *kill* when you return, Olan." The chieftess turned her back on them, and moved to the villagers that had gathered, her voice calm and assertive as she assured them everything would be fine.

Olan shifted her weight in his arms, but she pushed and struggled against him until he finally set her down. "That's enough, Fanahala." He growled as he wrapped his tail around her wrist. "We will find Zuran and prepare to leave."

Maybe it was the shock of seeing the ship and her people fall from the sky, but Samantha just didn't have it in her to fight him anymore. She allowed him to lead her through the village as she prayed to whoever was listening.

Please let them be safe. Please.

CHAPTER 20

SAMANTHA

*S*he didn't think she had ever cursed her short legs so much in her life. These damn males ate up the terrain with their mile-long legs while she struggled to get through the brush and climb over roots. This part of the forest was much denser than the area she had traveled in before Zuran and Zyar found her. Both Olan and Zuran had offered to carry her countless times, but she had refused. There was no way she was going to participate in the pissing contest they seemed to engage in any time she was near the two of them.

Maybe they wouldn't act like that if you hadn't led them on. You threw yourself at Zuran and then sought attention and affection from Olan. What did you expect? Some snide, judgy part of her sneered in a voice that sounded suspiciously like her mother's.

No. They were full grown men, and while she wouldn't deny she felt an annoying attraction to them, she wouldn't be held responsible for their testosterone-fueled outburst.

A little over a week ago, Olan had caught her in the pools with

Zuran. She had no idea how long he stood there, or how much he saw, but he hadn't seemed angry then. If anything, Samantha had been surprised to see arousal and interest in his eyes before Lucy had barged in. There had been so many nights where she lay there in the furs next to him, struggling with how to broach the subject, but he never brought it up and she had wondered if that was for the best.

There was something between these two, something that went much further back than her arrival in the village.

She had guessed that the carvings in Olan's hut must have been done by Zuran after finding all the figures in the hunter's home, including the mate to the one she had been so fond of. *Fond enough that you shoved it into your pouch before leaving,* she thought to herself. The thought made her smirk as she patted the leather bag Zuran had given her when she insisted she could carry supplies as well.

Up ahead of her, Zuran paused to look back as if he could hear her thoughts, his eyes roaming over her in a way that made her pulse race before he spun around and continued his brutal pace. There was something incredibly intense about everything Zuran did. There had been such an urgency to his touch at the pools the last time that if they hadn't been in the water, she might have worried they'd catch fire.

He had devoured her the way a starving man does his first meal, and she hadn't actually wanted to stop him.

She hadn't meant for things to go as far as they had, but the moment his lips had touched hers she had been lost to him. It was the same feeling she got when Olan pulled her close at night while he slept. The soft purr that rumbled up from his chest when he crushed her to him always sent a thrill of desire through her.

Samantha sighed. Her own emotions were going to give her whiplash. One moment she was ready to shove the two of them over the nearest cliff and the next she was seconds away from begging them to touch her.

Neither of them had spoken to her much since the start of the trek, and it left her feeling uneasy. Zuran had hardly even looked at her. It shouldn't bother her that it felt like he had closed himself off not just physically, but emotionally as well. They hadn't known one another long enough for her to be getting her feelings hurt, but here she was.

The more she had learned about their culture and traditions, the more Samantha began to see that it wasn't as bad as she had initially believed it to be. Sure, she still found the way she had been given to Olan to be barbaric, and she hated the way their society treated the hunters as a whole, but like humanity, the Seyton were not perfect.

The breeders in the village, especially the younger unmated males, gave off a haughty, almost spoiled vibe that she found to be unbearable the majority of the time. It seemed to her that they were used to female attention. That they expected it.

Although she knew Olan wasn't as young as many of them, he too had expected her to fall instantly for him. It didn't matter that he set butterflies dancing in her stomach when he did something sweet, or that he sent her arousal soaring with nothing but a look, she would be staying with her feet firmly on the ground for as long as she could.

A root snagged her booted foot, catching one of the ties and sending her face-first toward the ground. She gasped, flinging her hands out in an attempt to catch herself just as she was swept up into a pair of strong arms.

Olan's aqua eyes were the first things she saw when she swung her head to the side, his slitted pupils dilated as he pulled her close to his chest, adjusting her against him so that she was more comfortable. Claw-tipped fingers ran through her hair longingly as he leaned down to brush a sweet, tender kiss to the tip of her nose. "I've got you, Fanahala."

Her breath caught in her chest for a moment as she stared up at him, her heart racing frantically. The fact that she had literally fallen for him right after swearing she wouldn't was not lost on her, and she smiled at the irony.

"Your face softens so much when you smile." Olan murmured, the tip of his finger tracing her jaw. "I thank the All Mother every day for her blessing."

Annoyance bubbled up within her at the words. "You should have stopped at my smile." She growled, swatting his hand away. "I am not a gift! I am not some reward you got for being a good male."

"Fanahala—" His voice was soft, as if he were trying to placate her.

"Stop that, Olan! I haven't even decided if I'm willing to be your bride, your wife, or your girlfriend at this point." She staunchly ignored the pain in his eyes her words had obviously inflicted and wriggled until he finally released her.

With a huff, Samantha stomped away, brushing past Zuran, who had stopped to watch the scene. After spending forty days trapped inside her pod, she had been thrust into a new world with a culture as unique as the planet and the people living on it. To top it all off, she had been given away to a complete stranger. While she liked Olan, his constant remarks about how blessed he was to have her as his bride drove her insane. She was *not* a thing that could be wrapped up and given away. Samantha was a person and all she wanted was for him to understand that. She wouldn't feel guilty about what she had said. She would *not* feel guilty.

Maybe if she told herself enough times, it would actually happen.

"*A*re you sure this is the fastest route?" Olan asked.

Zuran turned toward them, his brow lifted. "If you know a quicker way, then please enlighten me."

Samantha rolled her eyes, lifting her face toward the sky. From the moment they had made camp last night, the two of them had done nothing but argue over every tiny, pointless thing. They had already disagreed over what to have for breakfast, how to pack the cloth tent back into the pouch, and whether the pace Zuran set was too slow or too fast.

"What shall you disagree about next? Maybe the amount of suns in the sky?" Samantha asked sarcastically.

"Two," they answered in unison.

She pressed her hands to her chest and gasped in mock surprise. "Praise the gods! They have finally agreed on something! It's a miracle!"

"It is not a disagreement. It is a discussion," Olan insisted. "I simply think there has to be a faster way to get there."

"You spent a handful of hours stumbling through the forest, alerting every animal within earshot of your presence, and you are suddenly fit to tell me that my path selection is incorrect."

"What path have you selected exactly?" Olan gestured at the ground beneath their feet. "My bride can barely walk through this."

"For the love of everything holy…" she mumbled. *Here they go again.* Samantha folded her arms over her chest as they continued their verbal sparring. "Might as well whip your dicks out and start measuring them." Neither one of them paid her any attention so she spun away, taking in her surroundings.

It was warm, but still early enough in the day that it hadn't yet reached the miserable heat that could steal the breath from your lungs. The large red-barked trees provided enough shade that she didn't have to worry about her skin burning just yet. She could save the cream given to her by the healer just before they left the village for when they needed to cross open fields.

More growling and snarling filled the air, making the tiny hairs on her body stand on end. Despite the distance he had been putting between them, Samantha noticed the changes in Zuran. Even Olan had made mention of the aggression and his restlessness. The change was so abrupt that it had caught her off guard a number of times since leaving the village behind.

The fullness of her bladder was beginning to get uncomfortable. She had been holding it in for a little while, not wanting to be the one to ask for a break, but with the two of them still going at it, Samantha figured this was probably her best opportunity.

"I have to pee!" she called over her shoulder, not bothering to wait for a response.

The sounds of their shouting and the rumble of their growls would be enough to scare away anything nearby. Besides, she wasn't going far.

Picking her way around the large root system that surrounded the trunk of a gnarled old tree, Samantha inspected the ground, checking for any creepy crawling creatures or for the plants Zuran had warned her about. *All clear.* Her hands raised the hem of the dress she wore, but as she squatted against the bark, she heard the brush in front of her rustle. Her muscles froze as she scanned the bushes.

Maybe it was the wind, or one of the birds. There were plenty of small animals within the forest the noise could belong to. *No need for panic.*

What stepped out of the dark tangle of leafless branches to her left had the blood fleeing from her face. It was built like a monstrous old Earth dog with a thick muzzle, long, strong legs, and paws larger than her hands.

Unlike the beasts that had once been known as man's best friend, this creature's flesh looked as if it had been turning inside out. It oozed something foul, a yellowish liquid dripping from spots that looked like infected sores and open wounds along its sides. Eyes of milky white and devoid of anything resembling a pupil were set deep into the head, giving it an even eerier appearance.

Without pupils, she couldn't see it watching her, but she could certainly *feel* its gaze taking in her trembling body, waiting for her to move. A tongue the color of spoiled meat slipped from its mouth to run over torn lips and deadly teeth as it snarled.

Her knife was tucked into the small pocket Olan had sewn inside of her dress, but could she actually get to it before the creature got to her? Would the small blade even do anything to protect her against this nightmare of an animal? Three more creatures, these slightly smaller than the first, stepped out from behind one of the trees, nipping at each other's sides as they eagerly chattered and whined.

She was going to die in the middle of the forest with a full bladder. That was if she didn't soil herself in fear first.

"Olan, Zuran," she whimpered, her voice barely audible.

The largest of the creatures threw his head back and howled, the sound of it turning the blood in her veins to ice as she scrambled to the side, her feet catching in the roots. She made a desperate grab for her knife, screaming for the males she knew were somewhere behind her. She snapped her eyes shut, shielding her head with her arms as the beast lunged at her, all fangs, claws, and drool, but the impact never came. Instead, a fierce roar ripped through the trees a moment before she heard the thud of something heavy hitting the ground.

When she finally pried her eyes open, she saw Zuran on top of the animal, his tail wrapped around its neck. The deadly blade at the end tore through the nasty flesh, sending blood spraying in every direction as the thing shrieked and writhed. Having witnessed the death of their companion, the other three sprang forward, but Zuran was already reaching for one. He snagged a front leg, claws digging in as he slammed the dog-like beast into the dirt.

The other two managed to dart past him, their white eyes fixed on her. A large red body jumped in front of her just as the first creature jumped, and she screamed as she watched Olan roll to the side. He was growling, his long fingers digging into its neck as it snapped its jaws inches from his face.

"Olan!" She heard Zuran shout as he tossed aside the limp body of the second beast, but his warning came too late.

The last animal locked its slimy jaws around Olan's thigh, its fangs sinking deep into the muscle. Samantha lurched forward on legs that felt boneless, swinging her arm with as much strength as she could muster. Her blade struck the body of the animal, piercing its hide over and over until it fell away. She turned her attention toward the one at his thigh, but Zuran was already upon it, his hands prying its mouth open as the creature thrashed wildly. There was a sickening crack as the bones in its face snapped, and then the bloody gurgle of the animals dying breaths as it drowned in its own blood.

She stared up at him, eyes wide with shock as she took in his blood-covered body. He dropped to his knees to examine the wound on Olan's leg, growling when the other male hissed in pain. "Come here," he snapped at her. Samantha tried to obey the command, but her body refused to move.

Zuran took her arm, yanking her over Olan's body until she was standing in front of him, her hands braced on his shoulders as she struggled to breathe. The sound of fabric tearing barely reached her ears. When she looked down at his hands, they were ripping the bottom portion of her dress, exposing her to mid-thigh. He lifted her again, setting her to the side as he leaned forward to tie the strip around Olan's leg. There were multiple punctures, each one steadily oozing blood.

Oh gods, he's going to die. He was going to bleed out all over the forest floor, and it was all her fault for walking off. "I'm sorry," she mumbled as Zuran secured the knot.

"Up," Zuran said, pulling Olan to his feet carefully. "There is a cave system close by. We will take shelter there."

The hunter slung his arm around Olan's waist, making sure he was steady on his uninjured leg before lifting Samantha up. She curled her arms around his neck, searching for Olan's hand. Her fingers slipped between his, squeezing them to reassure him that she was there, that she wasn't going to leave him. They had come for her in her time of need, and she would do whatever was needed to be there for them.

CHAPTER 21

OLAN

a groan rolled up his throat and out of his mouth before he could even stop it as he stumbled along beside Zuran. It was difficult to think through the panic that raced through him. He might not be a hunter, but he knew about the carnera packs that roamed the forest, and he knew what a carnera bite could do to him if he didn't treat it quick enough.

Calm yourself. Take deep breaths. Focus.

Samantha's hand flexed in his, grounding him as if she could hear his thoughts. She was nestled against Zuran's chest, her head resting on the arm he had anchored around the other male's shoulders. He could feel her body trembling as her breath fanned across his skin. Even with the toxin from the carnera's bite coursing through him, Olan felt arousal and longing stir within his belly. She hadn't said anything since they left the scene of the carnage, and he knew she must be in shock.

There had been times she had spoken of her home, trying her best to explain to him that she didn't live on a planet, but on a thing she called a ship, high above them in the sky. He hadn't been able to form a picture of it in his mind until the moment the massive alien home had come crashing through the clouds. Even now, the idea that Samantha's people could live within it was foreign to him. There were things she did sometimes, ways she looked at things that seemed perfectly normal to him and his people, that made him wonder what it was like living up there.

She had looked at the carnage Zuran had left behind as if she had never seen anything like it. Olan might be a breeder, but he had been exposed to such gruesome sights his entire life. Were there animals on her ship? Did she have to worry about attacks the way they did?

His steps faltered, and he clutched at Zuran, trying to regain his balance as something unsettling occurred to him. Had he really made much of an effort to get to know his mate? Had he asked her about her life, her home, her interests? Was this why she hadn't accepted him? How could you want to be with someone who seemed so uninterested in you?

So much of his time had been spent encouraging her to learn about his culture, about his people and their traditions. He hadn't taken any time to learn those things about her. He had heard Vane's advice, made a promise to himself to heed it, and then had done the exact opposite. Olan had allowed his jealousy and his own mixed emotions to blind him and now here he was with his life resting in the hands of the male he had looked at as a rival instead of an ally. The fear that he had already lost the chance to make up for his mistakes, to show her how much he truly cared, choked him.

If I survive this, he promised her within his mind, *I will ask every question. I will know everything there is to know about you.*

And if there is no time? What then? Will you ask her now when she is stunned, when she can hardly breathe from the fear emanating from her? You are a poor mate. You could not even protect her.

No. He refused to listen to the self-loathing part of him.

All Mother have mercy on him, but he hadn't even bothered to ask her if she had a mate waiting for her. He had assumed not due to the lack of any other scent on her, but he could have been mistaken. What if she had kits? The thought left a sour taste in his mouth. He couldn't see her willingly leaving her young behind. She would be a good mother. He wanted to see her with his young, wanted to watch her care for them the way he had watched her care for the kits within the village.

Had Zuran thought to ask those things? Was that why she had responded to him so eagerly? It wasn't that Olan didn't care; he had just been so consumed by the need to be accepted, to be worthy of her, that he had neglected everything a worthy mate would do.

"Almost there, Olan," Zuran said as the entrance of the cave came into view.

His vision was beginning to cloud, but he pushed forward, hoping the tourniquet Zuran had fashioned would delay the toxin. The small rocks scattered on the ground in front of the cave tripped him up, jarring his wound and making him hiss in pain.

"Easy," Zuran admonished. "There's no point in rescuing you just to watch you bash your hard head on the rocks."

Using Zuran's arm for balance, Olan slowly lowered himself to the floor of the cave, his head falling back against one of the larger rocks as he caught his breath. Samantha was at his side the next moment, her small, delicate hands brushing and touching him everywhere.

"I will be right back," Olan heard Zuran telling his mate, but he was so focused on her that he could hardly concentrate. "I need to gather something to keep the wounds from becoming infected. Do not leave his side, Samantha. Repeat it."

Her wide eyes swung up to the male's face, and she nodded. "Do not leave his side."

Zuran grunted before eyeing Olan. *Don't worry her. Don't scare her. She doesn't need to know what could happen.* He wanted to shout the words, to make sure the hunter knew that the last thing he wanted was to frighten her. A simple nod before leaving the cave told him Zuran understood the plea in his eyes.

Samantha watched Zuran go as she worried her lip, her fingers fidgeting against his stomach where they rested. "Were you injured?" he asked, covering her hand with his.

"Was I..." She shook her head, a dazed laugh shaking her shoulders. "You jumped in front of that thing before it got to me. You and Zuran both put yourselves in harm's way to save my life." Her hand curled around his. "So no, I wasn't hurt, but I'm sorry that you were."

"It will heal." He shrugged, managing a small smile to ease her worry.

By the look on her face, his mate didn't completely believe him. She turned her attention to his thigh, her fingers gently prodding the tender flesh. He watched as her brows furrowed before she leaned down to examine him closer. "Olan, I'm not a doctor, but it looks like these punctures are already starting to close."

Tiny stars were floating around her face, dancing across her skin as she turned to look at him. By the All Mother, she was the most beautiful creature he had ever beheld. His hand moved up to her hair, attempting to brush the stars away, but she turned back toward him. She was saying something. Olan blinked hard, shaking his head to clear the fog.

"Do you always heal so quickly?" Samantha was asking.

"Quickly?" Was this quick? He had never met another race of aliens and therefore had no other experience to go off of. "Yes, I suppose."

"All you damn aliens and your expedited healing." She graced him with a grin. "If you were a human man, we would need the med wand, or at least something to stitch you up and antibiotics to keep it from getting infected. It takes us weeks to heal from something like this."

Weeks for her to heal? When they made it back to the village, he was going to have to fight the urge to keep her locked up in his hut and as far away from danger as possible. "How have you survived this long? Are there no animals, no dangers on your floating rock?"

"There are animals on the station, but not many, and no one is in danger of being attacked by any of them. Most of our animals aren't actually alive anymore. We have their DNA, tissues, and cells frozen to preserve them."

His brain struggled to make sense of her words and their implications. She had lived her whole life without the beauty of a place like Seytonna to call home. Despite the dangers his people faced, he could not imagine a life without the All Mother's creations. "That sounds lonely," he whispered as his tail wrapped around her wrist, pulling her closer. "I'm glad you were unharmed, Samantha."

Surprise lit her eyes and she blinked down at him. "You called me by my name." Her smile made his lips tingle. "I'm not sure I've ever heard you say it. Guess I've gotten used to Fanahala."

The soft strands of her hair hung around her face as she leaned forward, and he couldn't resist the urge to reach up and touch it. "I've done nothing right with you, and I apologize. Let me earn the right to call you mine. Let me prove I'm worthy."

The words had barely left his mouth before Samantha's lips were on his. The contact was like pure electricity shooting through his entire body, making his limbs jerk and twitch. The curtain of her hair brushed against his cheeks, and he burrowed his hands into the strands, cupping the back of her head to hold her close to him. The wet, warm tip of her tongue swiped across his lower lip and he opened to her, drawing her in. He moaned as their tongues danced, his fingers flexing against her scalp.

His Star Born tasted like the nectar of the sweetest fruit; ripe and luscious.

She shifted at his side, bracing her hands against the rock behind him as she carefully moved to straddle his body, avoiding the wound that was now only a dull ache on the edge of his mind. Samantha consumed him, his body and his mind were so focused on her that there wasn't room for anything else.

Had it really only taken him using her name for his mate to respond, or was this born of something else? Heat rushed through him, pooling in his loins as his cock jerked, seeking the haven between her spread legs.

His grip in her hair tightened as he pulled her head back, exposing the skin of her neck to his tongue, biting at the flesh until he felt her tremble and moan. He would mark her here when the time came, right where the smattering of her freckles faded. The thought of claiming her, of branding her where every male could see, left him pulsing painfully.

The breathy way she whispered his name into the cool air of the cave sent chills down his spine and had his hips bucking up into her. She rocked against him, grinding her core into his rigid length until the stars returned to his vision.

Was it the toxins in his blood or his little mate that was bringing the fog back and making every rational thought flee from his mind? What did it matter to him now anyway? She was here with him, touching him, her hand trailing over his stomach to grip his aching cock over the cover he wore.

He couldn't hold onto his sanity after that.

A growl, deep and possessive, tore up through his chest as he released her hair to clutch at her hips, moving her faster against his cock.

When Zuran appeared behind her, his eyes skimming over her

prone neck and the soft curve of her shoulder, Olan snarled. He watched as the male's dark hands moved around to cup her full breasts, heard her whimper as he plucked and twisted the peaks that showed through the soft material of the dress he made her. Samantha's head fell back to rest against his chest as she continued to work herself against him.

"There's a good little female," he crooned. "Let Zuran touch you. Let me watch him take you."

"Yes—" She groaned before she cut herself off, the tempo of her hips faltering as she spun her head to the left and right, looking up into the hunter's face. *His* hunter. "Olan, there's no one else here. It's just us."

"Let me watch him, Samantha," he pleaded.

Her frown deepened and she leaned forward, her cool hand cupping his cheeks and brushing his forehead. "Gods, Olan, you're burning up." Anxiety and fear laced her voice, but her words were fading, morphing into something he didn't care to decipher.

All he wanted was them, his female and his hunter. They were all he needed.

Olan watched as Zuran ripped the dress from her body, his claws tearing through the fabric easily. The sight of her perched above him, her breasts exposed and swaying as she rode him, of her arms raised above her head as she clutched at the dark male's horns was almost enough to have him spilling his seed. The sensation of his cover being removed, of it being yanked from beneath him as Samantha settled her heat onto him was over-whelming.

Behind her, Zuran growled, a low, arousing sound that made his cock jump in anticipation, before he pressed Samantha down. Her breasts pillowed against his chest, and she pressed her swollen lips to his cheeks and neck, muttering things that might have been words. With his eyes locked on Olan's, Zuran fisted his cock, stroking the thick shaft a few times before lining himself up with Samantha's sex and burying himself deep within her body. His mate gasped, her whimpers turning into moans of agonized pleasure as Zuran rocked back and forth.

"Yes," he hissed, arching beneath them. "Fuck her. Take her."

Samantha's face was twisted in pleasure as Zuran pressed himself into her, never once taking his eyes off Olan's. When the hunter's tail wrapped around Olan's cock, the stars in his vision burst open, multiplying until he thought he was going to black out.

He wanted this. He needed this.

"Please," he heard himself beg as he trailed his own tail up Samantha's thigh and into the searing heat between her folds. "Take her, Zuran." He panted, feeling as if he were on the edge of sanity. "Fill her, come for her. Fuck her, Zuran."

CHAPTER 22

ZURAN

"Fill her, come for her. Fuck her, Zuran."

The piece of scorched metal he had been holding in his hand dropped to the ground with a clatter that echoed through the cave.

Samantha spun around to stare at him, her eyes wide, face flushed red as she slapped at Olan's roaming hands. "Help!" She had a leather cover in her hands and was attempting to wipe at the other male's sweaty brow. "I don't know what he's doing, but I can't get him to stop."

"Why is he naked?" He asked, looking between Samantha and an obviously very erect Olan. The scent of their arousals swarmed his mind and stirred his heat, threatening to allow the madness to overtake him.

"He's burning up and I needed something to wipe him down. You tore up a good portion of my dress for the tourniquet, so I improvised." His eyes fell back to the sweat stained cover, as Olan grumbled something unintelligible. "I used the rest of my water skin to soak this. I've done the best I could. Is he dying?" she asked when he stepped forward.

"You have done well, Samantha. It's just a side-effect of the toxin in his blood."

Her body stiffened as her eyes darted to his face. "Just the... There's a toxin?" Beautiful blue eyes narrowed dangerously and he cringed.

All Mother save him. He shouldn't have said that.

"You knew this was a possibility and you didn't say anything?"

"No, I knew for a fact it was going to happen, and I said nothing because this thick-skulled fool didn't want you to worry over him," he grumbled, crouching down next to Olan's undulating body. The blade of his tail sliced easily threw the new skin, releasing the blackened blood that had pooled within the punctures.

"Am I wrong in remembering his blood was purple not that long ago?" She was leaning over his shoulder, her face close to his.

Concentrate. Don't let the heat distract you. "Not wrong," he managed to grind out.

"I knew something wasn't right. He was talking nonsense, swearing you were here when you weren't." Olan grabbed her ankle, tugging until she crouched down beside him. His eyes were glassy and far away, as if he were seeing through them. She brushed his hair from his forehead, murmuring to him as he pulled her against his chest. "Zuran, we have to do something."

He watched her hands caress the other male's face and shoulder. The way her face pinched with worry made his heart clench within his chest. "He will live, Samantha. We will make sure of it." The pouch he wore was stuffed full with the yellow and red illandor and aclate, two herbs hunters used frequently to keep wounds free of disease and infection. Zuran took both bundles and twisted them in half; one he returned to the pouch and the other he shoved into his mouth. His teeth made quick work of the delicate leaves, smashing them into a thick orange paste that he quickly spit out onto Olan's thigh. The male hissed, writhing against Samantha as Zuran packed the mixture into each of the punctures.

"I'm so sorry," Samantha was whispering.

Zuran wanted to comfort her, to cradle her against him like he had on the way to the cave, but Olan's moans of pain tore at him. While the tourniquet had slowed the toxin and the paste would keep the wounds from becoming worse, he would need the added help of the elixir to keep the toxin from taking hold.

From the bag Olan had dropped when they heard the carnera's howl, Zuran pulled out a small cup and the cooking bowl, pouring the remaining water from his skin and the rest of the herbs into it. A small bed of dried leaves and sticks were all that was needed to catch the sparks of his lightning.

"Zuran..." Olan was moaning again, voice breathy and needy as he raised his arm into the air. "Take her..." The male's fingers moved as if he were touching someone, and Zuran felt the flames of the desire roar low in his belly when the breeder's hips began to pump and he threw his head back.

He allowed the tea to steep for a moment longer before the two of them coaxed it into Olan's mouth, making encouraging noises as he swallowed it like a starving kit. Zuran sighed in relief as Olan's body began to go lax and his eyes drifted shut.

"He will sleep for a while. His body needs time to rest and recuperate the strength he lost."

"Zuran?" He glanced up at her as she wiggled uncomfortably on her knees. "I still *really* have to pee, but I don't want to be out of sight again."

Squatting near the entrance of the cave as he stared over her head, she made quick work of relieving herself as his eyes scanned the trees. There was still half a day's worth of light left, but they wouldn't be leaving for some time.

If they were lucky, Olan's wounds would heal during the night, but he would need at least another day to regain his strength and clear his mind. Seeing the male's leg clutched in the jaws of the carnera pup had nearly sent him spiraling into the inky black of the madness. Only knowing Samantha still needed him and that Olan would require aid had pulled him back.

At Samantha's request, Zuran helped her maneuver Olan until his head was pillowed in her lap. She combed her fingers through his short hair, wiping the sweat from his brows with the cover until he replaced it with a clean one.

"When he wakes, we will make no mention of the things he said," Zuran told her.

"Why not?"

"I am confident he will not wish to be burdened with the memory of his words when he is of sound mind again. Never repeat them."

"But—"

"Never, Samantha." Zuran stared her down until she finally nodded, her eyes falling back to Olan's face.

The light from the suns shifted across the floor of the cave as night drew closer. Zuran built a small fire, not for warmth, but to illuminate the interior of their temporary dwelling and to keep any courageous predators from wandering in. He hadn't scented any recent inhabitants when they had arrived, but just to be sure, he inspected as far back as he could go without Samantha losing sight of him and found no signs of life.

The flames flickered, and he watched the light dance across her body as she lay curled against Olan's chest, her head resting in the crook of his neck as her eyes began to drift shut. She had jarred herself awake many times in the last couple hours to check his pulse, or feel his cheeks, as if she needed to reassure herself that he was still alive. The way she held him and comforted Olan even though he wasn't aware of it made his chest tighten with a strange mixture of envy and admiration.

"Hey, Z?" came her sleepy whisper.

"Yes, little one?"

"Thank you for what you did for me today. If you hadn't stepped in, I would have been killed."

The thought of her death made his stomach sour. "I will protect you for as long as I am able." He promised. *Until the day the madness takes me, little one.*

He watched them sleep for the rest of the night, unable and unwilling to let the two most important beings in his life go unprotected for even a moment.

⁂

*A*fter relieving herself the next morning and rinsing her mouth out with the water Zuran had collected, Samantha hurried back into the cave to check on Olan, who remained sleeping. He was no longer hot to the touch and his breathing had returned to normal sometime overnight. They may be able to leave this place sooner than he thought.

Samantha stuffed the bag he had given to her full of items before they left, and she busied herself searching through the contents. "I know I put clean dresses in here."

The small painted wooden figure tucked between food rations and her waterskin caught his attention. He leaned forward, plucking it from her, examining the familiar details. It was the one he made in his youth, the one he had given to Olan just before their ceremony. He thought it had been destroyed or lost, but here it was in his hands all these solars later.

"Where did you get this?" he asked her.

Samantha glanced sideways at the breeder. "It was in Olan's

hut on the shelf the first night I was there." She faced him again. "You made it, didn't you? I saw the other carvings in your hut the night Lucy and James arrived and I knew it was you."

"I did. I thought he had..." Olan had kept it in his hut and had displayed it on his shelf for anyone who had come in to see. That knowledge tugged at something deep inside of him, uncoiling the strands of the darkness that had wrapped around his heart.

"Stop assuming you know what Olan would do." He heard Zyar's voice in his head.

He had assumed the words Olan had been mumbling yesterday were due to the toxin from the carnera bite, but perhaps that wasn't entirely true. A spark of hope kindled within him, but he didn't let it grow too bright.

"Why was it in your bag?" he asked Samantha. The way her cheeks heated as she averted her gaze made his fingers tingle to touch her, to take her chin and turn her toward him.

She shrugged her shoulders, "I'm not sure, honestly. It's comforted me since the moment I saw it in Olan's hut. I didn't want to leave it behind."

The thought that something he made brought her happiness warmed him.

"I saw its mate at your hut."

Zuran stared at her in confusion. "Its mate?"

"The one in that chest that looked just like it. I'm sorry if I wasn't supposed to go in there, but Lucy wanted a blanket—"

"You were welcome to anything within the hut, Samantha."

He could feel her eyes on him as they sat in silence. "Were they carvings of your family?"

Zuran shook his head as he held the figure out to Samantha, placing it carefully into her hand. "The one in my hut was made in Olan's image, while this one was made in my own. I told you they were carved before the ceremony, which is why they were left white. We were young then; free of worry and living our lives in a way that is no longer possible."

"Do you miss being a child?"

"I miss certain things," he mumbled, glancing down at Olan. "But my youth was not always kind."

Samantha rubbed absent mindedly at the breeder's fingers. "Was it your family?"

"Mostly, but I escaped often enough to Olan's that his family became mine."

"Do you ever wish you could see your family again?"

Did he? "I'm not sure." He answered honestly.

"Do you have siblings?"

"Just one, a sister. She will remain with my mother and father until her ceremony." *This solar...* he mused silently. She had been so young when he left and it had been just one more thing that had torn his heart out. "Do you have siblings?"

"No. The majority of human families are prohibited from having more than one child."

"Prohibited? Why is that?"

"Because life is strange sometimes. Humans are on the brink of extinction and should want to make as many little babies as possible, but babies require resources like food and shelter and humanity happens to be running low on those things up in space. Unless you happen to be from one of the wealthy families, you're one and done." She grinned at him, but her eyes were unhappy. "What about Olan? Any siblings?"

"Three sisters."

"Wow. Are any of them mated?"

Zuran shook his head. "They are young still. Only one, Harva, has had her ceremony. Isootro and my sister, Vura, will go through their transformation soon. Bemni is the youngest. She was newly born when Olan and I had our ceremony."

"Asa and Ama explained the separation of the villages during the lessons, but how do families see one another? It's not fair to have to choose between your children. The breeders can't leave the unmated male village, and the unmated females can't leave their village."

"My family would not visit even if they were able to, but many do not like the idea of risking the lives of their families. You have seen the creatures the forest sustains. Imagine if Olan were a kit instead of a fully grown male. The bite would have killed him." She chewed her lip thoughtfully as she brushed Olan's colorful forearm. "Before they have their ceremony, both males and females are too vulnerable. They lack any natural defenses of their own." He grinned at her. "Much like fully grown humans."

"Hey now!" She laughed. "Let me go a couple more weeks without clipping these nails and we'll see."

He took the hand she shoved at him, rubbing the rough pad of his thumb over the blunt, thin nails at the tips of her fingers. "This is how our young are born," he teased. "It is not until they have matured that the nails harden and lengthen." Zuran pushed himself forward so that he was leaning over Olan's body. Samantha's face was so close that he could feel the warmth of her breath. "And these?" he whispered, pushing her lip up to reveal teeth so tiny he wasn't even sure how she tore meat from bone. "These are milk teeth."

"I'll admit to a polite curiosity when it comes to the teeth of your species," she said with a wink.

"They are sharp for hunting, eating, and marking." The thought of getting to mark her skin made him shiver, and he hurried on before his mind lingered too long. "Our females develop wings to escape, hunters have bladed tails to defend and kill, and we're all given the gift of our lightning. But you, little one..." His finger brushed over her bottom lip. "You have none of these things. You need to be looked after and protected." He tapped her chin as he sat back with a grin. "Just like a kit."

"Oh, that's a serious load of—"

"Accuracy," Olan grumbled from between them. "An incredibly accurate assessment."

"Olan! You're awake!" Samantha's smile practically lit the interior of the cave as she threw herself at the other male.

"Awake and unclothed?" Olan laughed as he wrapped his arms around his mate. His eyes turned to Zuran as if he wanted to ask if what he had been dreaming had actually happened. Zuran wished he could ask him if his toxin-fueled dream had been anything like his lust filled fantasies. The things he had heard him saying told him they might have been, but he only shook his head before averting his gaze.

"You were burning up," Samantha told him, glancing up at Zuran for a split second. "We had to keep you cool so I took it off of you."

Olan was still watching him when he turned back, and the things he saw in those aqua eyes made his skin tingle. "We were able to treat the wounds and get the elixir in you quickly."

"Thank you," he said as Samantha dug into the large bag Olan had carried with him the day before, pulling out a clean cover for him to change into. "What happened with the light last night?"

"The fire?" Samantha asked.

"No, it was pink and pulsing. It was strange, like it was alive."

Zuran shook his head. "I stood guard all night long. There was no such light within the cave. It must have been the toxin."

When Olan tried to sit up, Samantha shot forward, her hands pressed against his chest as she attempted to push him back to the floor. "You just woke up! Stop trying to move."

"He is fine now, little one. Let him up so he can regain a bit of his balance." Seyton healed quickly and usually didn't require much downtime. It was vital for survival in a world that was often harsh outside of the village.

"I would love to have equipment to study whatever it is that helps you heal so fast," Samantha mumbled.

Olan climbed up onto his unsteady legs, brushing the dust of the cave floor from himself before he fixed the cover over his hips. "It wasn't the toxin. I know what I saw last night, and I'll prove I'm not crazy."

He wanted to growl at the other male, to tell him he had no idea what he had seen because he had also thought he saw Zuran mating with Samantha as she sat astride his hips, but he pinched his lips together and followed Olan and Samantha toward the back of the cave. They kept Samantha between them where she would be safe.

It was much cooler back here and she shivered, rubbing her hands over her upper arms. The cave curved further back, blocking out the view of the entrance, but something up ahead caught Zuran's attention. A softly pulsing pink light emanated from a large swirling whirlpool set into the floor of the cavern they walked into.

"Holy shit," Samantha breathed.

Holy shit indeed.

CHAPTER 23

SAMANTHA

*T*here was a movie in the archives of the station she had watched with her mother when she was a child. The title escaped her, but Samantha could remember her mother rolling her eyes and calling the main character stupid for walking into what she saw as obvious danger. *"This right here is why humans are dying out, Sammy,"* she would grumble.

If her mother could see her now, she was positive she wouldn't be thrilled with the risks Samantha's mind was telling her to take. The depths of the glowing pink pool were calling to her, begging her to come look within, to discover the secrets it wanted to share with her. Yeah, she was sounding crazy, but she couldn't do anything to convince her body and her mind that this was not a great idea.

Come, Samantha. Dip your hands into the water. Come.

Listening to the eerie voice calling from a whirlpool was surely on a "Top 5 Things You Should Never Do" list somewhere, but that didn't matter just then. It wasn't until she found herself crouching down at the edge of the pool that she realized she had even moved away from the safety of the males. Ignoring the large hands that gripped her shoulders, Samantha cupped the water, gasping at the cold. The sensation of icy vines wrapping up her arms, followed closely by the gentle zaps of static on her skin, made her want to jerk away, but she found herself completely immobile.

Wonderful, her mind jeered. *You have now become a movie heroine statistic.*

She cursed herself, yanking her upper body as hard as she could, and yelping when she was flung backward onto the dusty cave floor. When she turned to look for Olan and Zuran, she realized she wasn't actually inside the cavern anymore, and worst of all, her males were nowhere in sight.

What she saw around her stunned Samantha. Instead of the metal walls of the station and ship cabins or the simple timber walls of the huts she had been living in on Seytonna, Samantha found herself in an honest-to-gods home, similar to the ones on old Earth with smooth white walls.

"Well, hello there. You have finally seen fit to answer my call," a feminine voice at her back spoke, sending goosebumps racing up her arms.

Samantha spun to face the disembodied voice and felt her eyes bulge when they landed on the female. She was clearly Seyton, but instead of the black wings and white body she had come to know, this female's skin was nearly the same deep, inky dark as Zuran. Massive white horns curled atop her head, decorated with colorful beads and tiny bone fragments, and beautiful shimmering white wings rested against her back. It was as if someone had taken Ama and mixed up her colors.

"Who are you?" Samantha asked.

"I have been calling out to you for some time, little female," the female said, ignoring her question.

"I've never heard your voice before I walked in here. Am I dreaming?"

"Not exactly." She smiled. "The Pool of Tears brought your consciousness to me. You have been incredibly hard to reach, child."

Samantha looked down in amusement. She was far from being a child. The feathers at the female's back rustled softly as she moved forward, stopping so close to Samantha that she could feel the warmth her body radiated. "You never answered my question. I have no idea who you are, but you're acting like you know me."

The female offered her hand to Samantha, palm up. "Come with me, and I will show you something."

Sure, take her hand, she thought. *We've already touched the magic water, why not touch the magic lady?*

Samantha placed her hand in the female's and found herself being pulled into her embrace. Her vision went dark as her wings closed around them, blocking out the light and her view of the room. When the feathers parted, Samantha was back on X9. Well, that wasn't exactly true. They were hovering above the ground, looking down on a scene that made her feel like she was encroaching on a private moment.

A Seyton female lounged on the grass below them, the dark body of a hunter beneath her head while a colorful breeder stroked the hunter's long braids. The affection they showed one another reminded her of the trios many humans formed on Venora with their alien mates. Something inside her pulsed with longing as she watched them.

You could have that, a voice whispered softly.

Then the scene changed. The trio stood in a field surrounded by other Seyton. They pointed to the sky, and their mouths moved excitedly as they watched a ship soar overhead before striking the treetops and falling to the surface. The hunter turned to the female, caressing her swollen abdomen as he spoke. He embraced her and the breeder, pressing kisses to their faces and lips as he walked away.

Again, the scene morphed into something new. The hunter charged through the trees, snarling and growling at the tall, lean Venium male who stood outside the still smoking wreckage of his ship. The newcomer raised his hands, speaking hurriedly as he pivoted, guarding himself from the hunter. Samantha could see their mouths moving, but nothing being said was audible.

Days of their lives flashed by in minutes as she watched, enthralled by what she was seeing. The hunter and the Venium warrior worked together, repairing the parts of the ship that were damaged in the fall. It wasn't long before the breeder came seeking the hunter, but he would never find him. Upon seeing the Venium warrior, the breeder attacked and was killed in the struggle. When the hunter returned, he lashed out at the warrior, yelling and pushing him until the male conceded and climbed into his ship.

The hunter, with tears trailing down his face, carried the body of the fallen breeder back to the village, placing him at the feet of the female. She dropped to her knees, her hands clawing at the beads on her chest. Her face was a mask of pure agony as she looked up at the hunter, shaking her head as she spoke. In the next moment, Samantha watched as the hunters were gathered together and cast from the village. Breeders and females, even small children, screamed silently as they stood crying at the entrance.

Had the female banished them for what happened to her breeder? It hadn't been the hunter's fault. Samantha wanted to shout at her, to tell her she had made a mistake, but the scene morphed for the last time, and she watched as the female knelt on the floor of the cavern she had been in with Zuran and Olan, the body of the breeder in her arms as she rocked back and forth. Her tears fell to the floor as her hand clutched her belly.

Darkness closed in around her, and she once again found

herself in the arms of the curiously cryptic female. "Break the cycle, Samantha. You cannot erase the history her grief created, but you can begin to heal the present, and make a better future." Without warning, the winged female shoved Samantha backward.

She stumbled, gasping as she hit the water of the pool. Her arms flailed wildly as she struggled to claw her way back to the swirling surface.

You can break it, Samantha. You can heal them.

The sickening feel of falling tore a scream from her throat, and she felt when she landed with a thud on the dusty floor of the cavern.

"You let her touch it?" Zuran was growling. "There's no telling what is wrong with that water!"

"You were right behind her!" Olan roared.

"Are you two almost finished fighting or should I lie back down?" She asked as she pushed herself up on her elbows.

Two large sets of hands grabbed at her, pulling her up as they turned her this way and that. "What were you thinking, little one?" Zuran hissed.

"Don't yell at her." Olan snarled, pulling her into his arms and cradling her against his chest. "What happened, Samantha?"

"I don't know. I heard a voice coming from the pool and then I was... transported? It's hard to explain, but I was with a Seyton female and she showed things that seemed like memories." She told them what she had seen, and hearing it from her own mouth made her shake her head in disbelief. Olan looked perplexed by the time she finished her tale, but Zuran looked almost angry.

"Perhaps I missed where you were bitten by the carnera? Surely this was nothing more than a hallucination." Zuran told her.

"Look, I know it sounds outlandish, but it was so real, Zuran. I felt her when she touched me. If this is what caused hunters to be banished then we need to speak to Ama."

"Why won't you listen to her, Zuran? If what Samantha saw was true, then the hunters should have never been cast out."

Zuran shook his head, his jaw clenched as she growled. "An Ama would never punish so many of her people for the offense of one. None of the Amas after her would have continued it. This was a dream and nothing more."

Olan frowned, "We will speak with Ama when we return. We will confront her—"

"She would never keep this from our people. I have to believe that, Olan."

The pain in Zuran's voice and eyes broke Samantha's heart. The thought that he and countless others before him for generations had been punished for something that had nothing to do with them was unimaginable. When she reached out a hand toward him, he jerked back as if she were going to strike him.

"Focus on things that are real." He pulled a scorched piece of metal from the bag he had slung over his shoulders. "This is from your rock, yes?"

Samantha nodded as she took the jagged piece of paneling, running her fingers over the lettering. "Yes."

"We are close. If we leave now, we may make it to the ship before nightfall."

She wanted to continue her argument, and wanted to convince Zuran that Ama knew more than she told them, but seeing the paneling reminded her that she also had a duty to her people.

Zuran was right; she needed to focus on the present, on the things she knew were real. When they returned to the unmated males' village, she would question Ama.

195

CHAPTER 24

SAMANTHA

a sigh of utter relief escaped Samantha when the scarred outer walls of the *S.S. Constellation* came into view. She was finally home. Well, it wasn't really home anymore, was it? Entire sections of paneling had come off during its descent and now littered the forest and fields leading up to the actual crash site.

Olan and Zuran eyed the smoking ship with suspicion, refusing to leave the tree line until they were sure it was safe. From what she had heard from them about the other pods they had encountered before she crashed, they had never seen anything this massive.

"Okay, you guys stay here. I'll get in and see what the state of things is like, and then I'll report back."

"No." Zuran growled.

"Z, I'm not so sure it's smart to walk in with two aliens. It's going to be chaotic enough without the addition of strangers."

"It is not safe for you to go alone."

"Listen, I'll have you guys at my back. I know you won't let anything happen to me, but humans have a tendency to be xeno-phobic." She thought back to the night they had made the plans to send the field team down, and Marsel's words still made her uneasy. She had known he wasn't fond of the Venium. What would he think of the Seyton? Samantha had a sneaking suspicion she knew, and it made her stomach sour.

"What does that word mean?" Olan asked, tilting his head as he watched her crouch to tighten the laces of her shoes.

"It means they're untrusting of anyone new or anything they don't understand. We've come a long way, but there are still those who wouldn't react kindly to you simply because they don't know anything about you." She frowned down at the ground, knowing there had been a time in their history when it had been members of their own species that humans had discriminated against because of xenophobia. "I'll be right back."

"Like *vack* you will," Zuran snarled, pushing himself away from the tree he had been propped against. "You will remain with us."

Since leaving the cave, his behavior had become more and more erratic. It seemed like the longer she was in his presence, the worse his possessive and protective behavior became.

A little time apart may do him a world of good.

Samantha admitted that she had formed an attachment to them and that the thought of leaving either one of them brought her painfully close to tears, but after what she had witnessed within the cave, she needed answers before she could make a decision about her future. The caves had been quite the learning experi-ence. Her eyes shifted toward Olan, taking in his weary stance.

Whatever he had envisioned during his fevered dreams had excited him. *Really* excited him. The memory of his cock pressed into her, of it pulsing between her legs, caused the heat to creep up her neck. Her body had reacted the same with Zuran at the pools the day Lucy and James had come. When he had wedged his hips between her legs and ground himself in her sex, Samantha had lost all semblance of control.

Are you seriously thinking about dicks at a time like this? Her mind chastised. Right. She had bigger things to worry about for now.

"The last time I checked, *I* was in charge of my decisions, not you." She narrowed her eyes on Zuran as he growled and spun away from her. *So dramatic.* "It shouldn't take me long. Try not to kill each other while I'm gone, please."

A grin tugged at Olan's lips as she turned and stepped through the patchy line of brush at the tree line. The two of them had been at odds all morning, and she hoped not having her there to act as referee wouldn't end in bloodshed. They had only just healed Olan from his bite.

The clearing where the ship had come to a stop was large, but the nose of the vessel had taken out a good portion of the trees on the opposite end and created massive furrows in the earth. Samantha ducked behind those as she drew closer, peeking up over the ridge to see if she could catch sight of anyone who might be outside.

She sent up a silent prayer to the gods, even including the All Mother in there, that Olan and Zuran would stay put. The last thing she needed was for someone on the ship to mistake them for the demons of the old world's religions.

The damage to the outside of the ship looked horrible to her eyes, but she didn't see any obvious holes in this section. When she reached one of the emergency hatches, she was surprised to see only one armed guard stationed at the entrance

She recognized the tall, broad-shouldered man as Curtis. He

was a good guy, even if he was sometimes a little over-eager to prove himself when it came to his job. His keen eye and imposing stature made him useful on missions and helped to quell any nasty behavior from others on board. She prayed he was someone she could trust.

"Curtis!" she hissed, putting her hands up above her head as she stepped over the upturned earth.

He pivoted toward her, his gun raised. Dark brown eyes went wide when recognition finally dawned on him. "Samantha?"

She released a sigh of relief when he lowered the weapon and rushed down the ramp to meet her. "Yes."

"What the hell happened to you? We all thought you were dead! Marsel was beside himself with worry. Even sent James's team down in the hopes they would find you, but we haven't heard anything from them since they hit the atmosphere."

Marsel was beside himself with worry? Not likely. "He was worried about me?"

"Oh yeah! He had the entire crew searching for any sign of you. When he found the video of the pod detaching, he nearly lost his mind. Had all his men scanning the planet with the viewer to find the pod. What were you doing in there anyway?"

If she didn't believe Marsel had a hand in her disappearance before, she certainly did now. "Do you know where he is? I should fill him on what's been happening."

"Right, of course." Curtis nodded enthusiastically, pulling her up the ramp to the entrance. "I can't leave my post, but the last time I saw him he was in the mess hall trying to keep the peace. Hey, Samantha?" he called as she stepped inside. "I'm glad you're safe."

She smiled at him. "I'm glad you are too. Don't aim that at your feet. You know Lucy would have your ass."

Curtis groaned and threw his back as he chuckled. "A man

clips his toe one damn time during training and no one lets him live it down."

She wasn't sure how he had ever convinced Lucy to let him carry a gun again, but her friend gave him crap about it anytime she saw him. None of the overhead lights seemed to be working, but the crew had attached chemlights to the walls, illuminating the space.

Worry over her males nagged at Samantha as she rushed forward. What if they were spotted? What if Curtis or one of the other security members fired on them out of fear?

My males, huh? She snorted at herself, shaking her head. *They aren't my anything.*

"Lies!" The little devil on her shoulder accused her. He looked suspiciously like Zuran, and she imagined herself flicking him from her shoulder as she stepped up the stairs to the next floor.

You're losing it, Sam. Face it.

She could hear raised voices up ahead, and when she reached the top, she was shocked to find the deck in complete chaos. Crew and families were all over the place, rushing around as if they hadn't been trained for something like this. Someone had stacked crates on top of one another, creating a makeshift stage at the front of the hall where Marsel stood.

"I understand your concerns and I am working to restore the power as quickly as possible. In the meantime, you have all received the chemlights. Keep them close and use them sparingly. We all need to work together to—" His eyes landed on her at the back of the hall, and she swore she saw something like fear flash through them before he recovered himself. "Samantha?"

The massive crowd in front of her turned as one to stare in her direction, and she wished a hole would open up beneath her. "Marsel."

A megawatt smile lit up his face, and he jumped down from

the crates, his long legs eating up the distance between them before he grabbed her around the waist, hugging her close as he spun her in a circle. "I thought I'd never see you again!"

I'm sure you did. "Yeah, well, I thought the same when I crashed on X9."

"Why didn't you try to contact us? What happened that night?" he was asking.

Samantha could feel the curious gazes of the crew on her as he questioned her. "Can we go somewhere else to talk? Somewhere private?"

"Of course." Without releasing her, Marsel steered Samantha through the crowd, promising them he would return shortly. "We can go to my office," he told her when they stepped out into the hall. "The power is out, as I'm sure you've noticed, so we will take the stairs."

All over the ship, people milled about, chatting, passing out emergency rations, tending to children. She couldn't imagine what the crash had been like for the little ones. The door to Marsel's office had to be pried open, and she found herself giggling at the effort he put into it. She imagined Zuran and Olan could have easily ripped it from the wall with ease.

He motioned for her to take a seat as he cracked more of the chemlights. "So? What happened to you? What made you leave the ship without the safety of the team?" He leaned over his desk, his hands spread across the wood as he watched her. "You know what happened on F2 wasn't your fault, don't you? You didn't need to go down alone. What were you trying to prove?"

So that was his angle? He was going to bring up her failure, tear her down so that she felt vulnerable and hope she wouldn't suspect him? Okay, she would play his game and wait for him to slip up. "Honestly, I have no memory of that night. I woke up on the surface inside the pod with no idea how it had happened."

Marsel pursed his lips as he took a seat behind his desk. "We searched for you, but there was no sign of the pod on the surface. After we lost the drop ship, we tried to maneuver the *Constellation* closer to the planet, but something went wrong, a miscalculation by the crew perhaps. The power was zapped, and we were suddenly falling."

"None of the tech in the pod worked either. I actually have a theory on that."

Marsel's brow raised as he leaned forward. "Care to share it?"

Samantha studied his face, amazed that she had once found him to be everything perfect in a man. He was tall, and handsome with a strong jawline and picture-perfect smile. His golden hair was cropped close on the sides, and not one single strand would have dared to step out of line. Baby blue eyes the color of old Earth's sky sparkled, shimmering with an easy welcome that lulled others into a sense of security. He may have looked a bit frazzled at the moment, but nothing much had changed.

"I'm thinking X9 gives off major electromagnetic pulses or it's possible it has something to do with the dual star system. I can't tell for sure without equipment, but I'm guessing none of that is working now." She shifted on the plush cushion beneath her, nearly groaning at how comfortable it felt.

Marsel nodded sagely as if he had any clue what she was talking about. "That makes sense." His brows furrowed as he sat back, his eyes running over her. "Even the old school compasses were going haywire. The only thing still going is the damn Venium tech. How did you survive so long down there if nothing was working?"

"I stayed in the pod I woke up in for the most part, rationed my supplies, tried to conserve what little bit I had with me." She shrugged. "It wasn't too bad until I ran out and had to decide between starving to death on the pod or risking my life outside in the forest to find something to eat."

"You were very brave, Sammy."

Sammy? He had never called her that before. The longer she sat there, the more uncomfortable he was making her. "Thanks, Marsel." She twisted the fabric of the dress she wore. "That brings me to where the whole situation gets really interesting. When I finally left the pod, I was discovered by the natives we knew were present."

"Animals, no doubt," he grumbled.

"Well, those too, but no. They're sentient beings, Marsel."

Marsel leaned forward, his jaw setting. "Aliens?"

"Well, if you want to get technical, we're the aliens in this situation," she said, thinking back to what James had said in Zuran's hut. "We knew it was inhabited, but they aren't anything like what I expected."

The chair creaked loudly beneath him as Marsel stood, raking his fingers through his short hair. "Are they anything like our *friends* back on Venora?"

"I'm not sure what you mean by that, but tech-wise, no. They call themselves Seyton. From what I got to experience while I was among them, they aren't bad people. They seem peaceful."

A laugh burst from Marsel's mouth, but it wasn't the cheerful one she had grown used to over the years. This one dripped with hatred. "They told you this? That they're *peaceful*?" The look in his eyes caused the hair on the back of her neck to stand on end. "You could communicate with these aliens?" At her nod, he frowned. "I thought you said all electronics would malfunction? If the translators are working then maybe it's these people screwing with our systems. Or maybe the Venium know them and are doing this on purpose. Maybe it's the reason they banned this place to begin with."

"What? These people don't have any tech, Marsel. How could they possibly do that? Besides, the translators are made organically now. Didn't you pay attention in the medbay when it was given to you?"

The man huffed, his eyes rolling toward the ceiling, "Sammy, darling, these are things I figured I would never need to know."

So much for that. "I'm telling you, the Seyton aren't bad. A little different, but I think we could benefit from a good relationship with them. They are willing to talk."

"Hah! Relationships with aliens? The only things humans get from that are hybrid children. We've lost enough women to aliens who wished to *help* us." The disgust in his voice had her chin lifting in defense.

"It wasn't only women the Venium valued. Many human men left too." He didn't acknowledge her. "Marsel, we need this."

His eyes snapped up to her face and he smiled, his lips thin as he pressed them tight together. "I'm sorry, kitten. This is a subject close to my heart." He reached out a hand to caress her chin, and she had to stop herself from recoiling. "Forgive me?"

There was something in those whispered words that soured her stomach and made it hard to speak, so she just nodded. Warm lips pressed against her forehead, and this time she couldn't help the jolt of surprise.

"I, umm… I brought some of them with me."

The smile slipped from his face slowly. "Back here? Are they on the ship now?"

"Not on the ship. I've asked them to stay put somewhere within the forest. I didn't want to cause a panic." *And I didn't need you or your men shooting them dead before we even had time to speak.*

He nodded slowly, lips pursing as he thought. "How many of them are waiting for you to return?"

"Two. Would you be willing to speak with them? Olan and Zuran travelled all this way to bring me back. At least give them an audience."

"Of course, kitten." Both the smile and the ridiculous pet

name were back, and she wasn't thrilled with either one. "I'd be happy to do almost anything you ask."

Samantha couldn't put her finger on it, but something in the air had changed, and she wasn't sure it was for the best for the humans or the Seyton. Gods help them.

lan

Olan shoved his fingers through his hair as he paced back and forth across the dark terrain. He had put on a brave face and let her go back to her people on her own, trusting that she would return.

The more he clung to her, he'd noticed, the more distance she desired to put between them. Samantha was teaching him each day that she was not going to bend to the way of his people simply because he desired her to do so. Honestly, he was finding he rather liked her rebellious nature. Almost losing her to the pack of carneras had nearly destroyed him and had almost certainly shaved solars off of his life.

"You should have let me go! It is my job as a hunter to protect!" Zuran snarled angrily, pacing back and forth.

"When did your heat start to become so uncontrollable?" he asked softly.

Zuran stilled as he cut his gaze to Olan. "What do you mean?"

"I've been trying to figure out what is wrong with you, what has changed since you brought Samantha into the village. You're starting to go mad." Zuran huffed as he shook his head. "I can see it, even more so while we were traveling." He kept his words gentle, not wanting to upset the other male. Succumbing to breeding heat was something every hunter eventually dealt with, but watching Zuran was physically painful for him.

"You have no idea what you're speaking about. I'm fine."

"Liar." *So much for keeping it gentle*, he chastised himself. "You are almost fully in the grips of it." The end of his tail crept up to touch the hunter's shoulder. "This is why you want Samantha the way you do, and why you cannot accept what she saw."

A growl tore through the air, and Zuran moved faster than Olan had anticipated, snatching him by the tail and yanking him forward so that they stood chest to chest. Zuran had always been the slightest bit taller, but the way the madness had taken over his body, he seemed to grow in height.

Teeth bared, the hunter snarled, "It is *not* the reason I want her! I want her because I *love* her! Because I can feel she is mine in my soul."

Olan's heart clenched painfully in his chest, and he looked at the male in sympathy. By the All Mother, he didn't wish to see the pain that swam in Zuran's eyes. Even before his fever-dream about the male he had been craving him, but he had always been afraid and a little bit ashamed to admit it.

If what Samantha saw in the cave was true, then this opened up new opportunities for hunters to join breeding pairs. They could be more than pleasurers. The idea that Zuran might join them, that he could have the male he had always wanted and the female who completed both of them gave him hope.

Just as he opened his mouth to tell him as much, there was a rustling of branches and a loud thud as something heavy hit the ground behind him. He spun around, preparing for a confrontation with yet another animal, but instead, his eyes landed on the Seyton female sprawled in the dirt.

"Asa?" Her wings were in disarray, hair tangled around her horns, and her tail caught up and twisted within a few of her once carefully done braids. The sight was far more comical than he should have found it, and he tried his best to choke down the laughter that bubbled up within him.

"Sweet All Mother! The two of you are supposed to be on alert! Can you not keep your voices down?" she hissed, her ears falling flat against her head in what he was positive was acute embarrassment.

Olan bit the sides of his cheeks to keep from grinning, but the laughter died on his tongue the moment he looked at Zuran. The male was in a defensive posture, his tail coming around his side, with the deadly blade fully extended. The darker male's body was taut and humming with his lightning.

Before Asa had a chance to notice the offense, Olan placed himself in front of Zuran, blocking her view. Threatening Ama's second-in-command was a sure way to end the hunter, and Olan wasn't through with him.

"We weren't expecting you."

"I'd imagine you weren't."

A rather undignified snort from the female had a smile tugging at the corners of his lips. Standing up as gracefully as she could, she brushed the dirt from her body before tucking her wings behind her, which seemed a little difficult with all the twigs and leaves poking out from between feathers. Olan always appreciated Asa's presence, but with Zuran as far gone as he appeared to be, now was not the time.

"Why are you here?" Zuran growled, his tail thrashing behind Olan.

"It isn't your place to question what I do, *hunter*," she snarled, her ears twitching and lightning cracking along her body. The current caused her wings to fluff up, the debris from her fall igniting and producing small wisps of smoke before they turned to ash.

"I'm sure he meant no offense, Asa," Olan murmured, his chin touching his chest respectfully. "What can we do to help you?"

Zuran growled, but instead of continuing the confrontation, he turned to pace away from them.

The female's ruffled feathers started to lay flat, her eyes softening toward him. He noticed the way her body naturally turned in his direction, and she began to calm down, her whole demeanor becoming much more approachable. The sparks of her electricity settled as she wrapped her own tail around her right ankle, ears flickering in an almost playful manner.

"Ama asked that I follow you and make sure the humans are not a threat. I will report back to her with whatever I find when I fly over." She looked down at her feet, shuffling them slightly before mumbling, "I just got a little caught up in the tree when I saw the two of you down here without Samantha."

His eyes crinkled as a chuckle burst from his lips. "I can see that," leaning forward, he plucked a twig from her wings that had managed not to go up in flames. How long had she been watching them? "As of right now, there is no update. Samantha has asked that we stay here and wait for her. So far, these aliens seem to be either very peaceful or very naive. There is only one guard posted outside of the rock, the thing Samantha calls a ship. No one has come or gone since we arrived. They don't seem like much of a threat so far."

"Even the most innocent looking beast can be deadly if you turn your back on it," Asa warned.

"Ah, like you?" The words brought a smile to her face. "Zuran and I are more than capable of dealing with the aliens and reporting back. I can't imagine it will take us long to handle this situation, and I'm sure Vane is waiting for you to return home."

"Well," Asa glanced around, her lips pursing as she thought. "All right, but I expect your report the moment you return to the village. If neither of you are back before Ama leaves, I will personally come hunt you down."

"You have nothing to worry about." Olan dipped his head and watched as Asa's wings extended before she gave a few mighty downward strokes, lifting herself into the air high above them.

"Well, at least she treated one of us like we were more than an animal." Zuran's words were laced with disgust.

"Excuse me?" He watched as the hunter brushed at the blade on his tail. "What is that supposed to mean?"

"*Nothing*."

Samantha had mentioned that they treated the hunters like beasts before. He tried seeing the situation through Zuran's eyes. With a heavy sigh, Olan crouched down and watched the other male. "You know something? I don't understand you." It was obvious that Zuran was no longer himself, on the edge of losing it all.

"Of course you don't! No breeder ever could. You all can do no wrong. You are *perfect*."

"Perfect? We are far from it." Olan laughed humorously, turning just in time to see Zuran's fist as it slammed into his face. The pain radiated across his cheek and jaw, ripping an anguished snarl from his throat as he fell backward on his tail.

Don't respond with violence, he told himself. *He doesn't know what he is doing. This is the heat talking.* Getting caught up in the other male's emotions wouldn't do either of them any good, so he merely sat where he was as a bladed tail wrapped tightly around one of his arms.

"You are accepted, celebrated. You are able to intermingle with the females, with the other members of our tribe without being looked down upon, without being treated as if you were nothing!"

Frustration tore through Olan. He didn't doubt that breeders were treated better than the hunters of their tribe, but his life wasn't all Zuran thought it was. "You have no idea what I deal with."

"Oh, forgive me, you have so much to deal with. Being embraced by the people around you, being *wanted*. You have the opportunity to have a family."

"Yes, and I'm not able to leave the village, not able to explore the forest whenever I wish. I lack the freedom that you have." Olan shook his head. "You still have not learned, have you?"

Olan thought back to the day things had changed between them, the day that everything he had truly cared about had been taken from him.

nxiety coursed through Olan as he walked toward the central forest. It was almost time for him to enter his agmari. The thought that he would be deemed a hunter or a breeder soon made his hands shake, and he tried to hide it by rubbing his palms along his sides. A tail curled around his, and he was pulled into the side of the other young male.

"We'll be all right. We always are," Zuran assured him, throwing a lanky arm over his shoulders.

"You only say that because you know that you will be the best breeder any female has ever had," he smiled at his best friend, knowing that this male would one day make an amazing father.

"Me? I doubt that."

"How could you? Just last summer, you saved my life."

They both winced at the memory of Olan's brush with death. He'd been incredibly lucky to have Zuran there that day to pull him back from the edge of the cliff when he'd fallen and been too weak to climb back up himself. They had been nearly inseparable since that moment, and he was thankful he had his best friend next to him now to share one of the most important moments of their lives. Together they walked into the clearing, choosing agmari blooms that grew side by side.

Olan stepped up into his bud and turned back to see that Zuran was still outside of his, staring into the open center. "Aren't you getting in?"

"I don't want to be a hunter, Olan. I don't want to be infertile." The fear in his eyes was something Olan had never seen before.

"You are the worthiest male I've ever met. There is no reason the All Mother would choose to make you a hunter." He smiled, urging his friend on. "Get in! You have nothing to worry about."

The bud had closed up around them, encasing the males within, transforming them. When the buds opened, revealing his friend's changed body, he regretted his words. Zuran looked down at himself and gasped. Where he had once been bright white, he was now a deep black. A hunter. His best friend's dreams of becoming a breeder, of having a family of his own, were over. Confusion was written all over his face as he turned wide white eyes on him.

"You're a breeder," Zuran had muttered, before his face went completely blank.

$\mathcal{O}$lan shook himself from the memory. He had known at that moment, all those solars ago, that their lives would never be the same. They had once been as close as brothers, but their relationship had dwindled over the solars. Zuran had left the village to engage in the hunts, and he had found a job within its borders helping to prepare bridal dresses.

Once upon a time, he had imagined that he and Zuran would

prepare their brides' dresses together, but that hadn't come to pass. Maybe that was why he had chosen the silky black material for her. It reminded him of Zuran's hair and skin, the way it looked against the twin suns.

As much as he hated to admit it, he missed his friend more than anything. The loss of that friendship still caused his heart to ache.

CHAPTER 26

ZURAN

"*You still have not learned, have you?*"

Rage clouded his vision, filling his mind as he stared at the male who had once been his closest friend. It was getting harder and harder to ignore the pull of the breeding heat. The flames of his desire licked at his loins, causing him to suffer through intense dreams that had him waking up covered in sweat and other bodily fluids.

He was growing more aggressive, to the point that even he had noticed. The more he looked at the unfairness of his life, the worse the feelings became.

It's not fair! his mind screamed. *Olan got what you wanted.* Rationally, Zuran knew that his longtime friend had no part in his transformation, but he had been so jealous that he had found it hard to even look at the other male at times. Samantha had been the only being, besides his fellow hunters, to treat him as an equal, to see his worth beyond his looks, but she had left and still hadn't returned.

"What haven't I learned, Olan? Please, enlighten me." He knew he was pushing the male, that he should let this go, but the anger coursing through him wouldn't allow it.

"There is nothing more I wish to say to you right now."

"Ah, there he is. The spoiled kit who gets anything he wishes for."

Olan rolled his eyes, reclining back on his elbows. "Zuran..." the other male warned, but Zuran didn't care to heed it.

"Too good to converse with the hunter, huh? I don't deserve the same respect as you and your ilk. Not worthy to be in your presence, not worthy to live among you. Not worthy of your friendship."

"You have done it to yourself!" Olan yelled, jumping to his feet. "You make it so damned hard to approach you that no one even tries anymore! That *I* don't try anymore!"

The words stilled Zuran, the anger and resentment cooling within him for the moment. Was he really so unapproachable? Had the self-hatred he carried around inside of him been the thing getting in the way of their friendship this entire time? Almost every interaction over the last few days ended the same, with him becoming defensive and aggressive. He had anticipated mistreatment, prejudice, and had reacted negatively without even being provoked in most cases.

"You're right," he admitted. "For the most part."

"What?" Olan's eyes widened in disbelief, looking like they might actually pop out of his face.

All thoughts fled from his mind when he caught sight of their beautiful female as she approached. He didn't know when his subconscious had decided that she belonged to both Olan and himself, but over the last few days, strange as it was to admit, Samantha had gone from "mine" to "ours." He was surprised to find that this didn't bother him as much as he would have thought.

Her violet hair hung loose, barely brushing her shoulders,

while the black bridal dress she wore clung to each of her soft curves. The skirt almost wasn't long enough to cover everything he thought it should, but she looked stunning in it.

Need coursed through him and he took a step forward, wanting nothing more than to pull her into his arms, to hold her. Samantha's blue eyes locked on his, a smile curving her lips as she closed the distance.

Zuran wrapped his arms around her waist, pushing his face into her neck and taking a deep breath, drawing in her scent, committing it to memory. "Well, hey there, handsome. Did you miss me?" Her soft laughter was music to his ears. He felt the press of her lips against his ear and shivered.

"Yes." He whispered into her hair. A frown marred his face when he caught a whiff of something—someone else—clinging to her. Whatever it was, it intermingled with her familiar sweet smell and left a bitter taste in his mouth.

Samantha squealed as she was plucked from his arms and pulled tightly against Olan's chest. "Samantha." He sighed. "You came back to us."

"I told you I would," she murmured, pressing her lips to his forehead.

Something just on the other side of the bushes caught his attention. Someone was watching them. With a snarl, Zuran pounced on the vegetation, striking out quickly at the startled creature. A shrill cry rang out as he gripped the alien around its throat, hauling it off of the ground until they were face to face. Another human. He sniffed, and his eyes narrowed.

This was who he had detected on Samantha. Was this one here to try to lure her back? To spy on them?

If the alien was here for Samantha, then he would have a fight on his hands. She belonged to them. He couldn't change the fact that Ama had blessed the union with Olan, but he could still keep her safe. "Who are you? Why have you followed our female?"

"Samantha! Help me!" the male gasped out, his fingers clawing frantically at Zuran's hand.

"Samantha!" Zuran bellowed, his eyes remaining on the alien he had caught. "Is this alien familiar to you?" A fog was settling over his mind, and he shook his head in an attempt to clear it.

Olan was right. He was going mad. He wasn't going to be able to control himself much longer. The fact that there were unmated males around the female he considered to be his mate was making this harder and harder to dispel. The strong, over-powering scent of pheromones filled the air around them, triggering his lust and making him feel as if his skin was going to catch fire.

"Zuran!" Samantha's voice slipped into his foggy mind, slowly clearing the haze. "Let him go! He can't breathe, Zuran!" His vision cleared suddenly, and he blinked at the purple face of the alien in front of him. He wasn't supposed to be this color.

The human dropped to the ground the moment Zuran released him, gasping like a faloui water dweller that had been thrown onto the shore. He watched as the alien scrambled away from him, hands clutching at the dirt as he shook. "Are you all right, Marsel?" The alien didn't answer as he gasped some more.

"Zuran." The deep voice at his side belonged to Olan. He looked over at the other male, taking a deep breath to steady himself. The madness had never come upon him that quickly. A tail wrapped familiarly around his own, sending a calming jolt of electricity through his body, clearing away the rest of the fog. "Are you back with us?"

"I am."

"Is everything all right, Z? You looked like you were in a trance." Samantha brushed her hand down his arm then slipped it into his own.

"It's nothing." His eyes narrowed on Olan when the other

male opened his mouth to protest, but it quickly shut on a frown. Zuran wasn't ready to come clean about what was happening.

The alien male had made it to his feet and was standing with his body pressed against one of the trees. *"These* are the *peaceful* aliens you asked me to speak with?"

"You weren't supposed to follow me, Marsel. If I'd have known you were there, we could have avoided this whole scuffle," Samantha told the human male. "Zuran didn't mean to hurt you. He was just looking out for us."

Marsel, as Samantha called him, glared across the open space at him. He knew he hadn't won any favors with this one. "I apologize." The words tasted like dirt on his tongue, but he should at least attempt to smooth things over with the human male. A carnera cry pierced the air, coming from deep within the forest at their backs. The twin suns were getting lower in the sky, and they would need to find shelter soon if the male denied them entrance to the ship.

"Well, I suppose I should have made my presence known." Marsel brushed dirt from his clothing.

"It will not be safe to linger here much longer." Zuran tugged his tail from Olan's, flicking it lightly against Samantha's leg.

Olan rumbled from his other side. "We should find shelter soon, Samantha."

The darkness came swiftly on Seytonna. There were all kinds of dangers lurking in the shadows, biding their time. He had scars on his body that served as reminders that this planet was unforgiving.

"Could we come back to the ship?" Marsel began to protest, but Samantha grabbed his hand, squeezing it.

Growls from both Zuran and Olan had the alien's eyes darting up to watch them closely. There was something about this human male that neither of them seemed to trust. "Oh, kitten, you know I can't say no." The human smiled at them, patting their female's hand. He didn't trust this male at all.

*he human ship was not at all what Zuran had expected. It was small, the path that led throughout was barely wide enough for him and Olan to walk abreast. There were doors hidden within walls, and the living spaces of the human families were practically piled one on top of the other. There wasn't much actual space in the thing they referred to as a "space vessel."

The entire thing looked like it was constructed from a glimmering silver metal, like the kind they used in the village. There were small windows and blocks with colorful circular protrusions that he made a mental note to ask the names of once they were finished speaking with Marsel. Some spots were missing entire sections of the wall from where other parts of the ship had fallen off.

Zuran watched as the human pushed at one of the doors, struggling to slide the slab into the wall. He stepped around Samantha and gave the door a nudge with his hand, raising his brows when the thing shot back into its crevice. Marsel stumbled forward from the force, falling less than gracefully into the room. He turned to glare up at Zuran, "My apologies, human."

"I knew that door would be a piece of cake for you." Samantha laughed as she squeezed past him.

"Yes." Marsel smiled as he straightened. "Piece of cake, indeed. Please, gentlemen, have a seat." Zuran and Olan, who had just entered the room, glanced down at the small chairs. "Hah, perhaps you would prefer to stand? I don't think our seats are large enough."

"Standing will be fine." Olan nodded and took up a spot just behind Samantha, leaving a space for Zuran to join them.

Marsel took the seat behind the large wooden table in the center of the room. He was sure it made the human feel important, like a chieftess, ruling over his tribe of homeless people. On Seytonna, this would be laughable because villages were governed by females, not weak-smelling males who had no spines.

Their females would eat this male alive.

The way the human's eyes were running over Samantha made him want to reach across the table and pluck them from his skull. He knew exactly where the male was looking because his gaze was being pulled there as well. Every shift of Samantha's legs made the black material ride up a little higher. Just thinking about the heat nestled between her thighs made his pulse quicken and his mouth salivate. The memory of it pressed against his cock was still fresh in his mind.

"I don't know what you all here have found out, but I worked day in and day out on the console on my ship, and I got nowhere. I don't think there's an immediate way off of X9. Sorry," she glanced up at them, "I mean, Seytonna."

"What do you suggest we do for the time being?" The human leaned back in the chair, his feet coming up to rest on the table in front of him. "We have limited resources. Without power on the ship, we can't operate food dispensers, med bay is practically useless, the bathing chambers just barely work. We will soon be out of the emergency rations. People are going to riot in the halls."

"I could teach you how to survive here," Zuran spoke up. "You would learn to grow your own food, hunt. I could teach you which creatures to avoid and how to avoid them." If he could befriend them, then he might be able to escape his people and their oppression.

"And you would do this, why? Just out of the kindness of your heart? Assuming you have them, that is," Marsel sneered.

"I would do this for acceptance. If you bring me into your tribe, I would be willing to provide you with any information you need to survive this place. I am a hunter among my people. This carries a certain... stigma."

"The Seyton are not perfect. We have done our hunters a great disservice, but Zuran is right. No one knows the land better than our hunters. If you accept his offer, the tribe will surely support him," Olan said, eyes cutting in his direction.

The human male nodded as he tapped the tips of his fingers against his legs. "Well, that is certainly something to consider. We should have a sit-down, talk this out." His eyes slid over Samantha. "Hey, kitten? Why don't you go ahead and get cleaned up? I'm sure your new friends and I can hash this out. No need to bore you with the finer details."

"I really don't mind staying—"

"Samantha." There was a smile on Marsel's lips, but Zuran could see the annoyance hovering in his eyes. "Go on. We'll be fine here. Take the time to relax. We'll call for you when we finish up."

"All right. If you're sure?" She glanced back at Zuran and Olan, who nodded softly.

His mate stood up from the chair, pushing a hand into her hair nervously as she moved past the table. Marsel's hand snaked out to grasp hers, and he pressed a kiss on the back of it, smiling up at her with blunt white teeth. "I think we may have used your old room as emergency quarters, but you may use mine. You remember it? I still have some of your clothing in the closet." Heat lit up his eyes. "Maybe I'll come and get you myself when this is over with."

Samantha frowned and snatched her hand back quickly. "Uh, sure."

"We will see you soon, Fanahala." Olan looked as if he was barely holding onto his control.

Zuran gave her a reassuring smile, his hand brushing her arm as she stepped out of the room. They stood with bated breath, listening to her footsteps as they faded. The human looked at them, a smirk pulling up the corner of his mouth. He obviously didn't understand his offense or else he wouldn't be finding this so amusing. A current of electricity flowed just under his skin as Marsel began to speak.

"She's gorgeous, isn't she? *Great* fuck, would highly recommend it. Hard to believe I ever let her out of my sight." He shook his head, dropping his feet to the floor. "Seems like we're going to be stuck here for a little while. There's an old Earth saying, a quote by a doctor, I believe his name was Hertzler. He said, 'The only way to keep a woman happy is to keep her barefoot and pregnant.'" A laugh burst from his mouth as his head fell back. "This time, she won't be able to argue that her job is more important than us having a family."

"You should rethink your words, human," Olan warned.

For once, Zuran agreed with his old friend. He growled low in his throat, his currents zapping and snapping freely around him now. "Stop while you still have a chance for redemption."

"What's wrong? Did you really think she could love beasts like you?" He laughed again, his hand slamming down on the wood in front of him. "Did she let you kiss her?" Marsel's hot, putrid breath wafted between them. "She likes that. Likes to play with men before she tosses them away. You're nothing but a toy to her, something new and shiny. She is a human. She will never want creatures like you."

"You don't know what you are talking about."

"Oh, don't I? While you waited for her in the forest, she let me spread her thighs right here on this desk, let me slip inside her body and fuck her until I found my release." He tried to appear unafraid, but Zuran could hear the frantic rhythm of his heart in his chest. "She told me she couldn't wait to get away from the hideous monsters this planet had spawned right before she came all over my cock."

Anger shot through Zuran, leaving him so raw that he nearly leapt over the table at the human. From the way his heart was pounding, the human had to be lying. Samantha would never say or do that. Would she though? How many times had she said she didn't want them? That she only wanted to go home? No, something had changed between the three of them. She couldn't kiss him like that, touch him so gently, be so kind to him and still be the woman Marsel was saying she was.

"Aww, what's wrong? Can't stand knowing you meant nothing to her?" Marsel narrowed his gaze on Zuran. "It was you, wasn't it? You're the one she *whored* herself out to." He leaned back in his chair, hands resting on the back of his head. "Well, I for one am thankful as hell that these translators aren't affected by the atmosphere on this god forsaken planet of yours, because it pleases me to no end to be able to tell you to your face just how little you mean to Samantha. I'll make sure to put in a good word for you both when I'm fucking that pretty pussy tonight."

A dam seemed to burst in both Olan and Zuran at the same moment. They dove across the table, both reaching for the human male. Blackness clouded his vision as his tail whipped forward to wrap around the column of Marsel's throat. Olan reached a sparking hand forward just as the human pressed something hard and cold against the middle of Zuran's chest.

"Uh, uh, uh, I wouldn't do that if I were you," he tsked, wheezing slightly from the pressure on his throat. "One wrong move, and I'll blow a hole through your heart."

CHAPTER 27

OLAN

Zuran's pacing in the cage was quickly driving him mad. It made him anxious and on edge, the last thing they needed was for both of them to act irrationally. Olan had always been the calmer of the two, but even he was feeling the effects of his pent-up rage. The bars on the cage were too strong for them to break; they had spent the first hour after being locked inside trying.

Sighing loudly, Olan pushed to his feet and grabbed Zuran's shoulders, yanking him back hard enough to throw him off balance.

"You pacing this way is not going to get us free from this cage."

"You should have let me kill him for what he said about our mate!" Zuran spat, slapping Olan's hands away angrily. "You don't even deserve to call her Fanahala."

"Had I not stopped you, he would have killed you." He tried to remain calm, hoping it would help Zuran's rising anger. The fact that he had called Samantha theirs was slowly making knots twist in his stomach. Could he actually have them both?

"Would that have been such a bad thing for you? Samantha would be yours and only yours. Just the way you want it. A lowly hunter is no great loss."

"Do you think that losing you would make her happy? She cares about you, Zuran." He cupped the angry male's cheek so that he couldn't look away. "*I* care about you. I wish you would let me help."

He ignored Olan's plea. "You will abate her sadness, I'm sure." Zuran's tail flicked in agitation.

"It doesn't matter what I do! She wants you as well, Zuran! Why are you so stubborn?"

"I can never give her kits! I can never marry her! I can never be with her! You can."

"Samantha doesn't care about any of that! You might know this if you paid any damn attention. This is ridiculous. Get over it!"

"Get over it? *Get over it?* Like you got over me being less than you?" Zuran's words stung like venom in a wound. "Like you just seemed to forget my existence?" He ripped his chin from Olan's grasp, stepping away.

"Are we really on this subject again?"

"This subject is all I can think of! *My* whole life was ruined because I saved *your* life!"

"What?" The word came out as barely a whisper, the pain of hearing the confession searing his heart. Did Zuran really regret saving his life? Did he really mean so little to the male? The current that he had been holding back disappeared as his ears flattened against his head.

"If I hadn't saved you, I might have never become a hunter. There are whispers among the elders that it's possible to tell which of the younger males will emerge as hunters by how strong their protective instincts are. Had I not saved you that day, I could have…" Zuran winced as if he had only just considered how his words affected Olan.

"Well, go on, say it!" Olan choked back his emotions as he grasped Zuran's hand and sent a pulse of electricity down his arm, forcing it into him. "Say it, you *vacking* faloui!"

The air was knocked out of his lungs as Zuran tackled him, taking him to the ground with the force of his weight. The other male pushed up and sent a fist into Olan's face, raining blows down on him like a kit throwing a tantrum.

This time, Olan didn't hold himself back. He wrapped his tail around the other male's neck and yanked him backward, a snarl ripping from his throat as they rolled across the floor, jumping up to pound his fists into Zuran's body.

Blood smeared down his face as lightning crackled danger-ously between them, singeing patches of skin. Claws tore into his flesh, and he let out a grunt of pain. Olan tried to ignore it as he cocked back his arm and sent his fist flying at Zuran—only the other male caught it before he made contact. Zuran's free hand moved to curl into Olan's hair as he yanked him down and crushed his lips in a firm, rough kiss.

The shock of the kiss rooted him to the spot for a few heart-beats, but he didn't want to stop it. Instead, he eagerly fell into the bliss of the moment, letting his honest emotions flow freely through him for the first time in so long.

A soft groan ripped from him as his tail wrapped around Zuran's, the male's legs coming up to lock around Olan's hips. Zuran ripped his mouth away, tugging Olan's head back to bare the column of his throat so that he could nip at the sensitive skin. Heat flared between them as the current went from threatening to sensual, licking across their bodies.

Zuran twisted his hips, flipping them so that he was hovering over Olan's body, his white gaze burning brightly before he leaned down for a softer, sweeter kiss. Their tongues danced, brushing and retreating, not in a competition for dominance, but in the same way a Seyton moves around their mate during the Festival of Light.

The two of them had always been close, since the day they were born, one never too far from the other. Losing Zuran after the Choosing Ceremony had left a gaping wound inside of him that he never thought would be filled again. Right now, at this moment, he felt nearly whole. All that was missing was Samantha.

Nothing had ever felt quite like this. Definitely not the time he and Asa had tried—and failed miserably—to become lovers. He was glad she was now happily mated to Vane. This felt right, like it was always meant to be. Their horns clicked softly against one another and the urge to perform the dance for Zuran nearly consumed every one of his thoughts.

This wasn't how they were taught it was supposed to be, but it felt right. The knowledge that Zuran was a hunter didn't matter. He knew that it never should have mattered to him and the guilt ate at him. Olan knew in a place far deeper than his heart that he belonged to Zuran just as surely as he belonged to Samantha. Looking back on their friendship, it was obvious that it had always been this way.

"I'm sorry," Zuran whispered, his forehead pressed to Olan's. The other male's breath fanned across his mouth as he panted heavily. "I don't regret saving you. I never did. Even when I tried to blame you for everything that happened, I knew I was just fooling myself. I would beg your forgiveness."

Olan brought his hand up to brush back one of the long braids that had fallen over Zuran's shoulder. "You know you have it, as long as you forgive me for my part."

"Oh, gods, you're fucking *gay*?"

The males turned quickly to glare at the unfamiliar human

male who stood in the doorway. Olan's ears flattened against his head. He wasn't sure what "gay" meant, but it sounded like this human was using it as an insult. He tried to pull away from Zuran, curling in on himself in an attempt to hide his stiff cock.

Zuran's tail squeezed his comfortingly as if he were trying to tell him he didn't care what their company had to say about the position they had been found in. Male companionship wasn't frowned upon among their people, but it also wasn't something he had seen much of in his lifetime. The tip of Zuran's blade emerged from his tail as his eyes flashed in irritation. "When are we going to be set free?"

"Set free?" The human threw his head back and laughed. "Why the hell would we set you free? Marsel just asked me to check up on you two since he's a little caught up with Samantha at the moment. Been a while since they've had a night together. Lots to catch up on. Know what I mean?" The male closed one of his eyes in a gesture Olan wasn't familiar with, but he knew what the human's words were alluding to.

Marsel wanted to mate their female. He couldn't let that happen.

There had to be a way to get out of this cage. An idea dawned on him, and he pushed himself to his feet, shaking off Zuran's tail as he stepped closer to the tall bars. A current of electricity flowed over his skin, sparking and dancing along his arms and up his chest. He locked eyes with the male, watching as he shifted nervously from one foot to the other, and began to sway. Sparks shot up between his horns, snapping softly. These humans were so tiny, so soft and weak with no natural defenses. How had they ever survived? Heat whispered through his body as he allowed the dance to overtake him.

The human blinked, frowning as he watched Olan twist and gyrate. "Are you... coming onto me?"

Olan faltered, tilting his head in confusion. It didn't seem to have any effect on this one, not like it had on his sweet Samantha. He had been practicing and perfecting his mating dance since he was only a small kit. More than a few times, he had snuck into the forest to dance among the trees and had even run off to the soaring cliffs a time or two to feel the strong winds rush over his body as he swayed.

That's what he had been doing on the day that Zuran had rescued him from certain death. He'd been distracted, wishing to have the freedom the hunters enjoyed, to experience the thing he heard the males whisper about when they brought in their bounties late at night. Thank the All Mother his friend had been there. Solars of practice and this human merely stared at him like he had sprouted wings. He would be lying if he said it didn't irritate him.

"Well, all right. Good luck with your... seduction," the human sneered, sliding a tray piled with what he assumed was some sort of human food into the cage through a small gap at the bottom. "Eat up. Wouldn't want you to starve to death before Marsel is finished with you. Oh," the male spun back toward them, "you're gonna get some company. Found one of those feathered women snooping around in the woods."

A female? All Mother, help them. It couldn't be Asa. He had told her to leave, to go back to the tribe. Had she stayed behind to make sure they were doing what they had been asked?

"Not sure why you'd screw around with each other when you can get with a literal angel." 'Angel' was another term he wasn't familiar with, but Olan's attention was pulled away by the loud bang and dragging sounds that echoed from somewhere through the door. "Huh, sounds like your company has arrived."

Two slightly larger human males pushed through the door, a Seyton female held between them. One of her vivid black wings was bent at an odd angle, the tip bloody and dangling in a way that made his stomach turn. Her body was nude and covered in dirt-smeared cuts and scrapes, the white hair that most females wore long had been shorn short near her shoulders. Dull yellow eyes met his, and his hands gripped the bars so tightly that he didn't know how they didn't crack.

A pained whimper escaped her when they dropped her to the floor of the cage next to theirs. Olan and Zuran rushed to the side closest to her, rumbling softly. With how small her straight horns were, this female looked to be fresh from her Choosing Ceremony. She was so young, barely even an adult.

The door to her cage slammed shut and she scrambled closer to them, eyes wide and fearful. It tore at his heart to see the evidence of how horribly she had been treated by these people. The female sniffled, clutching at their arms as they reached through to soothe her.

"Ah, my least favorite aliens. Enjoying your stay? How are you finding the accommodations?" Marsel sauntered into the room, his fingers running through the short strands on the top of his head. He stopped in front of the female's cage, smiling eerily down at her. "Well, look at you, sweetheart."

"Please..." Her claws dug at their flesh as she tried to pull herself up.

"*Please*," he mocked, laughing when she sniffled. "Oh, little angel."

Olan growled, wishing more than anything that he could reach the human and tear his throat out. The two males who had brought the female into the room and the one who had delivered the food walked in, standing just behind Marsel, who pulled out a thin piece of metal. He slid it into the door of the cage and it swung open easily, allowing the four of them to step inside. Olan's stomach dropped.

"Bring her here," Marsel ordered, the males around him surged forward, grabbing the young female by her legs and dragging her away from the bars.

"Don't touch her!" Zuran bellowed, slamming himself into the metal.

Though he held her tightly, the female's hand slipped from Olan's, he snarled as the humans pinned her arms and legs to the ground. She cried softly as her mangled wing was pressed into the ground, and she tried frantically to bring her electricity to the surface of her skin. It was more than obvious that she was newly bloomed. Most females took months to learn how to control their currents, and she was barely able to create a spark.

"I wouldn't do that, angel." One of the humans holding her arm poked at the broken wing, and she cried out in pain. "Remember what we said. Be a good girl, and we won't rip the whole thing off."

Marsel stood over her, his hands reaching down to work himself free of his clothing as he stepped between her spread legs. "This," he whispered, stroking his cock as he got down on his knees, positioning himself over the body of the female, "is what happens when you touch what belongs to me."

Beside him, Zuran was beating relentlessly on the bars, growling, pacing back and forth, but Olan was frozen. He had never imagined there would be a day when he would bear witness to the defiling of a female—had never even heard of a male committing such an offense before.

There was crime among his kind, but this? Never.

His tail snuck through the bars, wrapping around her fingers, the only part of her that he could reach. He felt them curl around him tightly and stared into Marsel's face. He was going to kill this human. And he was going to enjoy every moment of it.

Zuran squeezed next to him, the tip of his tail barely reaching her, but she grasped at it, holding onto them like lifelines. Her whimpers tore his heart open and he felt the wet heat of his own tears as they fell down his face. He looked into the face of each of the humans as they took their turns with her, memorizing every feature. Each time they switched, Zuran would pound his fists into the bars, his blood painting them both as he opened fresh wounds on his hands. He wished he could propel his currents the same way mature females could, but his just sparked across his skin angrily.

When they finally released her, the female flipped herself over and crawled weakly toward them. Two sets of arms wrapped around her as she shook with the force of her sobs. "Until next time, angel," Marsel taunted before he led the other males from the room.

The female's sobs grew louder as they sat quietly with her, allowing her time to process. "I should have never left the village," she whispered when her tears were spent. "I should have listened to my father, and stayed out of the mist."

"This isn't your fault," Olan told her.

"It is!" Her small fist slammed down on her leg. "I wanted to investigate the rock. I'd never seen one so large fall from the sky... and I was curious. Curious and stupid."

"What is your name, female?" Zuran asked softly.

"Vasa."

"Vasa, what they did to you was not your fault."

Olan watched her chin tremble. He couldn't possibly begin to imagine what she was feeling. Zuran's bloodied hands held hers, and he rested his head against the bars. Olan leaned into Zuran, his head falling onto the other male's shoulder as they all took comfort in one another.

"I am going to kill them all," Vasa whispered, her yellow eyes staring across the room to the door. "I am a daughter of the All Mother."

"Let us know how we may help," Zuran growled.

Vasa turned her head to look at him. "Thank you, hunter. I won't forget this." She nodded at Olan before resting her head against the bars.

Not knowing if Samantha was safe ate at him as they sat on the floor of the cage. It seemed like hours had passed, and Marsel never came back. No human did. This waiting, not knowing what was coming next, made him restless.

The sounds of shouting and pounding feet reached his ears, and all three of them bolted upright as it echoed through the path outside. Someone was coming.

CHAPTER 28

SAMANTHA

*F*uck! Samantha's eyes flew open and she shot up, her legs tangling in the sheets as she sleepily tried to roll out of the bed. "Shit!" she screeched, catching herself on the bedside table. She hadn't meant to actually fall asleep, but the lure of an honest-to-gods mattress had been too much of a temptation after her quick shower.

While she was thankful that the water on the ship was still working, the lack of power meant that it was freezing cold. The space station she had grown up on once had a malfunction with its heating system, and even that hadn't been as bad as this. She imagined it was what the old ice-covered lakes in places similar to Alaska would have felt like if she had dived in.

She had never seen things like that with her own eyes and was only familiar with them because she spent so many hours poring over the old photo books. Much of the landmass on the planet was underwater now thanks to the melting of the ice caps. It had begun to recede in a few places, scientists were hopeful that the combined efforts of humanity and the Venium would mean they could return to their planet of origin within the next few generations. She would never see the planet her grandparents had been born on, but she could do her part to ensure her great-great-great-grandchildren had a place to go back to.

Assuming she ever had children, of course. Samantha stretched her arms high above her head, twisting from side to side to work out the kinks. It didn't look like Marsel had made it back yet, which worried her some. He was either still in talks with Zuran and Olan, or he had finally taken the hint and realized she wasn't going to sleep with him again. Once had been more than enough.

Nose scrunching up in distaste, Samantha smoothed out the dress she wore. It was one of the things Marsel had insisted she have when they had *very* briefly dated. So brief, in fact, that she wasn't even sure it could be counted as dating. The fact that he had kept them in his closet to collect dust when he replaced her with another woman the same day she ended the relationship was a mystery.

All the dresses he had bought her were a little too revealing for her taste, and she hadn't been upset about leaving them behind. *Oh well*, she shrugged. *Beggars can't be choosers.* Better to have something that showed off her cleavage and thighs than something covered in the dried blood of the flesh-doggy that had attacked her in the forest.

The door to the room was slowly pushed open and Marsel stepped inside quietly, a soft smile pulling at his lips when he saw her standing near the bed. "Kitten. You're awake already?"

"Already? Marsel, I'm pretty sure I've been out for hours."

"You needed your rest," he said sweetly, brushing his knuckle down her cheek as he pressed a kiss to her forehead.

She pulled away as politely as she knew how, trying to put

some distance between them. "I'm sure Zuran and Olan are wondering where I went. We should get back to them."

"Nah, they're fine." Marsel pulled her into his body, his arms wrapping around her waist as he walked her backward. His face lowered to her shoulder, and he pressed tiny kisses to her skin as one of his hands snaked down over her hip toward the juncture between her thighs. Samantha wiggled, dodging his fingers.

"Where are they? Did you put them in one of the guest cabins?"

Marsel laughed, "I don't want to talk about the aliens, Samantha." He pressed her harder into the wall, his hips grinding the hard length of his cock into her stomach. "No more teasing, Kitten. Let them wait it out in the cells."

The cells? He'd confined them? "Stop it, Marsel!"

"What's the matter with you? Out there spreading your legs for those animals, but you won't let me in?" His hand fisted in her hair, yanking her head back hard so that she was staring up into his twisted face. She had never seen him this way, his once handsome features wholly evil and terrifying. "You're just like all those other alien fuckers who abandoned humanity."

Where was this coming from? She had known he wasn't exactly thrilled about the prospect of working with the Seyton, but this was obviously something he had been harboring for a long time. "I don't know why you're so upset, but the Seyton haven't done anything to us."

"An alien is an alien, Samantha. All they want is this—" He forced his hand between her legs, cupping her sex roughly. "I won't give up another human woman, whether it's to the Venium, the Grutex, or the fucking Seyton." His hot breath seared her skin as he panted excitedly against her ear. "You are mine, and I won't let them have you. I was a fool for sending you down in the pod to die, but I couldn't let you tell everyone about the planet. The ship was dying, this planet was our last hope. I wasn't going to call the Venium. I'd rather see every last one of us dead before asking for their aid."

Samantha struggled against him, kicking out, but he gave a hard tug on her hair. Tears sprang to her eyes from the pain on her scalp. She clamped her mouth shut and closed her eyes, willing this all to stop, hoping it was a nightmare she was going to wake up from any moment now.

"Open up, Samantha. Be a good girl, and maybe I'll let them live a little while longer." He tugged at the material of her underwear; she both heard and felt them tear beneath his assault.

The knife. She had clipped it to the inside of her bra after the shower. If she could reach for it without him noticing she could get free. Biting her lip, Samantha took a deep breath, willing her muscles to relax, allowing his hand to slide further between her thighs. She felt his fingers brush her exposed cunt and had to swallow the bile that threatened to spill into her mouth.

You can do this, Sam. You can do it.

"That's a good girl," he panted.

She felt him pull away to undo his pants. When he looked down to tug at the stubborn button on his trousers, Samantha reached for the knife, releasing the deadly blade as she pulled it free of her dress. With as much force as she could muster, she thrust the blade into Marsel's side, just below his ribs, yanking it out then quickly burying it into his stomach once, then twice. He stumbled backward, clutching at his wounds, as blood seeped from between his fingers.

"Kitten..." he breathed, falling to his knees, his blue eyes wide in shock.

"Fuck you." She felt tears fall from her eyes, the knife shaking in her grip as she pointed it toward him. Her lips trembled as she watched him gasp and fall forward onto one of his hands before he slowly sank to the floor. Blood pooled beneath him, soaking into the carpet tiles as it spread quickly toward her feet.

Breakdown later, her brain told her. *Get to the cells. Get to your guys.*

Samantha turned on her heels, bolting out of the open door, sprinting down the hall toward the emergency stairs. She made it down to the level where she remembered being told the cells were set up, sliding as she took the turn into the hallway, and nearly collided with Curtis.

"Samantha? What's the hurry?"

There wasn't any time to answer him, and there was the small issue of her not knowing whether she could trust him or not. Had he known what Marsel was planning? Had he helped him send her down to her death? Had he helped to detain her males?

If the situation hadn't been so dire, she might have laughed at herself. She had been fighting her attraction, blocking out the little voice in her head that insisted these aliens were exactly what she needed, that this place was where she was always supposed to end up.

Her shoulder slammed painfully into the side of the wall as she dodged him. A hiss ripped from her, but she shoved away and pushed her body to its limit. *BRIG* was printed in large letters on the sign above one of the open doors. *There!* The sound of feet pounding the ground behind her made the hair on the back of her neck stand on end. She swung herself into the room, stumbling to a stop when her eyes landed on the familiar black and red bodies of her aliens.

"Fanahala!" Olan rushed to the front of the cell, his arms reaching out for her as she fell into the bars.

Yes. That's who she was. She was Olan's bride, and she didn't care what the hell the rest of the Seyton thought, she was Zuran's mate as well.

She gulped in lungfuls of air, running her hands over his face and then turning to Zuran to do the same. Her hands gripped the bars as she shook them with a frustrated growl. "Gods damn it!" Tears pricked her eyes.

There was a soft jangle of keys from behind her. She spun around to see Curtis standing in the doorway, his eyes trained on the cell beside her. "I didn't know, Sam." He frowned and turned to her. "I'm sorry. I—I just got on shift and…"

"It's okay, Curtis. Help me get them out."

"Right." He nodded and flipped through the ring that held all the old Earth keys.

"Open the other cage first," Zuran urged.

Samantha had been so focused on her aliens that she hadn't even noticed there was someone else in the brig. She gasped, her hand slapping over her mouth when she saw the Seyton female huddled in the corner against the bars. She was covered in dirt and blood with bruises beginning to bloom across her arms and legs. Olan was crouched down beside her, whispering.

"It's all right, Vasa. This is Samantha, our Fanahala." Their eyes met. Butterflies took flight in her stomach at the use of 'our' in reference to her.

Curtis jammed the key into the lock, twisting it sharply until the door opened with a pop. Before Samantha could even move, Curtis was running to the female. Vasa snarled, clutching at Olan, who growled threateningly. Currents of electricity snapped weakly along her arms and upper chest, but Curtis ignored the warning and scooped her up from the floor.

"Get away from her, *human!*" Olan warned.

"I'm trying to help you!"

"We have had enough help from human males," Zuran snapped, gesturing around them at the cell he was still locked inside.

"Curtis wasn't a part of that." Samantha frowned at the

younger man. "I'm trusting you, Curtis. I swear to the gods I'll gut you if you're not telling me the truth."

"I wouldn't lie to you." He winced when the female lit up with another current.

Samantha pulled the keys from the cell door that had held Vasa and quickly opened the one holding her guys. Olan and Zuran practically jumped out, sandwiching her between them as they each fought to touch her and press kisses to her hair and face. "As happy as I am to see you two, we need to get off the ship before someone finds Marsel's body and starts looking for us."

"His body?" Curtis asked, his brows furrowed in confusion.

"I didn't stop to check his pulse, but there was a lot of blood and…" Her throat constricted; she felt nauseous, sweat beading along her brow. "Please, I just want to get the hell off this ship."

Olan's jaw clenched, and he smoothed a hand down her hair before nodding. "Show us the way, human."

Holding Vasa tightly against his chest, Curtis jerked his head toward the door. "Stay close and move fast."

Zuran lifted Samantha into his arms, squeezing her tight for a moment before he followed after Curtis and Olan.

CHAPTER 29

ZURAN

*Z*uran and the rest of their small group shuffled wearily into the single female's village, staunchly ignoring the whispers, gasps, and stares from the Seyton milling about the streets. The trek here had been hard on Vasa, who hadn't let go of the young human male since they had left the ship.

Samantha had clung to Zuran, reaching out a hand every so often to brush it against whatever part of Olan was close enough for her to reach. The two of them had decided that no matter what, if Samantha agreed to it, they would both be mated to her. Neither one of them wanted anything less.

The females of the village jumped out of Zuran's way as if he was in the throes of madness, staring at the little alien in his arms. Samantha only cuddled closer, burrowing her face into his chest, her little nose nuzzling against his skin. She sighed as she twisted one of his longer braids around her finger, twisting and stroking the beads. The human male, Curtis, wasn't far behind him.

"Vasa?" Zuran looked up to see the village healer watching

them. The small sack she had been carrying dropped from her hands as she rushed forward.

"Mama!" Vasa gasped, urging Curtis to set her on her feet. The healer ran her hands over every part of her daughter, crying when she brushed over the wing and drew a hiss from the younger female. "I—I'm fine."

"How did this happen?" She narrowed her eyes on Curtis, bristling dangerously before Vasa took up the space between them.

"He helped save me, Mama." Her one good wing curled around him, and she leaned weakly into his body. She smiled softly when he placed his hand gently on her back.

"Then we are in your debt." A hunter stepped through the gathering crowd, his white gaze falling softly on Vasa as he grasped one of the healer's hands.

"Papa..." The young female stumbled forward and threw herself into the hunter's arms. "I'm so sorry I didn't listen to you."

The dark male rumbled softly, wiping the tears from Vasa's face as he pressed a kiss to the top of her head. "You are safe now. Come and let your mama look you over before she falls to pieces."

"I'll stay with Vasa for now. Meet up with you later?" Curtis asked.

Zuran nodded, watching as the human male ran to catch up with the family. That was a story he wished to hear, but it would have to wait until Vasa was taken care of—and until he had resolved the issue of his breeding heat.

The madness lurked at the edges of his mind even now, and with Samantha in his arms, it was getting harder and harder to push back. An all too familiar rage surged inside of him when he looked down at her. She smelled strongly of Marsel. He wanted to ask her if what the human had said was true, but there had been something in her eyes when she spoke of the male that told him now was not the time.

Olan stood close to his side, his tail wrapped tightly around Zuran's. Zuran wasn't completely sure which one of them Olan was trying to comfort, but he was thankful for the contact. A very familiar scent called to him, and he spun, quickly searching the crowd for the source.

"Zuran." Olan tugged on his tail gently. "We need to find Ama."

He would set out later, once this was all settled, and confront his past. They found the chieftess in the central hut where she sat upon a large pillow; material was gathered around her and she held up a bride dress, inspecting the stitching closely. The dress would be worn by a newly mated female during the Festival of Light, and it was Ama's job to make sure each one of the brides had something that was unique to their union.

As always, Ama seemed to sense their presence. "No."

The trio came to a halt just inside the doorway, Zuran nearly running into Olan's back. "No?" Zuran repeated.

"Correct." She continued her assessment of the dress in her hand. "I will not bless the union, hunter." .

"These humans are dangerous," Zuran growled. "You are going to need every hunter in the tribe to protect you. I for one will not fight for someone who would deny me my mate."

Ama spared him a brief glance before lifting up the dress. "I'm sure we will manage to survive without you."

"Perhaps you can," he ground out between clenched teeth, "but how many other hunters do you think will follow you once they learn that the humans do not view them as lesser beings, that their females may be willing to accept them despite their status among the Seyton?"

"We may lose many to the temptation," she conceded with a

nod. "The humans will also gain many enemies once the hunters discover what has been done to Vasa." Her eyes bore into his.

He was away from the village so often that he sometimes forgot about the eerie link the chieftess seemed to share with the members of her tribe. She knew how dire this situation with these aliens was, and she was still refusing to end the alienation of a large number of their people.

Frustration and rage bubbled up inside of him. He handed Samantha over to Olan when he felt the electricity push against him, testing his control. A growl worked its way up his chest as he took a step closer to Ama, sparks lighting up the interior of the hut. He was losing the battle with the madness, slipping into the darkness again, and this time he wasn't sure he would be able to claw his way back.

CHAPTER 30

OLAN

*O*lan looked on nervously as Zuran stepped toward their chieftess. For the first time in his life, he was genuinely concerned that his friend might do something he couldn't come back from.

"Ama," he addressed her, stepping in front of the other male, hoping to distract them both, "with respect, I cannot obey your wishes this time. If you will not bless this, we will proceed without your permission." His stomach twisted violently at the disobedience. He had never done anything like this before. It was terrifying and exciting all at once. "We need to show the humans that we are unified, that we are linked with one another. This division within our own people is detrimental."

"We will not be divided." Ama handed the dress she held to a female at her side and picked up another one from the pile, running her hands over it.

Samantha patted his chest and wiggled until he set her down on her feet. He watched as she turned toward Ama, her little hands fisting on her hips. "I know this isn't how it always was, Ama. I don't know when that Venium killed the breeder, but I know the hunter was blamed and I know that's the reason your people treat them so poorly."

Ama's eyes rose slowly, trailing up Samantha's body until they reached her face. "Which breeder are you speaking of?"

Samantha narrowed her eyes on the chieftess. "You know which one, Ama. You always know everything before you're told." He listened again as Samantha launched into the story of the memories she had witnessed. Ama sat quietly, her hands folded in her lap as Samantha recounted the sad tale. "I saw what happened," Samantha said when she had come to the end. "I know it wasn't the hunter's fault, and I want to know exactly what is going to be done about it."

"What was it this dark female said to you?" Ama asked.

"She said she had been trying to reach me and that I was hard to get a hold of. She told me that I was going to break a cycle, but none of that made any sense to me." Samantha frowned up at Olan, but he was watching the grin spread across Ama's face.

"You may not know her yet, but she knows you," she said, watching Samantha intently.

Olan turned to his mate in confusion. He had his suspicions when it came to the dark female she saw in the whirlpool, but he had held his tongue. Who but the All Mother would have known the things Samantha had been told?

"Okay, but—" Samantha's eyes widened and her mouth dropped open. "Oh. That was—"

"The All Mother works in mysterious ways." Ama smiled, but when her eyes landed on Zuran, she turned serious again. "You will want to sit for what I have to tell you." They didn't hesitate to do as she asked, sitting together on the floor in front of her, pressed against one another like they needed the comfort of the contact.

"I knew the night I sent Zuran and Zyar out that something about this new rock was different. There was a change in the air. When you brought her back to the village instead of killing her, it only confirmed my belief that this Star Born was unique, that she was the one I had been seeing in my dreams for weeks before. One of these dreams was a memory from a past Ama." She shook her head as she sighed. "It was so unimaginable and heart breaking. I didn't want to believe that an Ama before me—a female who was supposed to see to the fair treatment of all her people— would do something so horrible. But the All Mother had her hand on Samantha from the moment she fell through the clouds. She would not allow another mistake to happen.

"Zuran, you made the first connection with Samantha, bonded yourself to her, but the All Mother saw fit to include you as well, Olan. Your connection with one another was forged long before your transformations. Perhaps she saw this as a way to begin the mending of our people."

"But why would the All Mother choose me?"

Ama held a hand up to silence their female. "Do not interrupt, Samantha. What you saw in the pools did, in fact, come to pass, but before you can understand that, you must know more about the beginning. The daughters of the All Mother once lived with her in the sky, safe from all of the dangers on the surface below. But the promise of safety could not outweigh their curiosity, and they eventually gave up their immortality for the love of the males they found. For them, this was the ultimate sacrifice.

"As a gift to her daughters and the people they now lived among, the all Mother planted the agmari blooms. The males and females could transform to better protect themselves and their families and so the first of the breeders and hunters of the Seyton were born. The females would soul bond with a hunter, who in turn would bond to a breeder by the will of the All Mother. For many, many, generations our people lived happily this way."

Ama eyes locked on Zuran's as she paused. There were tears on her cheeks, and she shook her head before wiping them away. Olan felt the agony in his heart grow as he listened, knowing there had been a time when they could have gone into their ceremonies without fear. There was once a time when the love they had felt for one another would have been celebrated instead of morphing into something that had torn them apart.

So many generations of hunters had suffered, and for what?

"What happened?" he asked, hoping she would continue.

"This Ama that Samantha saw lived long ago. She was pregnant with the kit of her breeder mate, their first, when the rock fell from the sky. She sent off her hunter, her warrior mate, to see what this new threat was. I have no knowledge of what the hunter discovered when he came upon the first Star Born, but hearing that they worked together, that they seemed to have formed some sort of friendship leads me to believe that they were trying to return him to his home." She shrugged her shoulders. "Unless the All Mother blesses us further, we may never know the truth."

"Do you know why the breeder left the village?" Samantha asked.

"The Ama would have never allowed her breeder mate to leave on his own, but she had grown worried and spoke of her anguish over the fact that their mate had not returned." Ama's eyes narrowed on Olan, and he knew she had not forgotten his jaunt into the forest. "That night while she slept, her breeder set out to look for him. The next time she saw him was in the arms of her hunter. Their mate told her the sad tale, of how the breeder had assumed the Star Born killed him when he came searching for him, how he had attacked the Star Born and been killed in self-defense.

"His female would hear none of it. She blamed him for what happened, using the fact that he had been suffering through his heats and the rage they could bring on, and ultimately banished all of the hunters, decreeing that they were far too dangerous to be allowed near the females and their breeder mates."

Ama knelt down in front of Zuran, placing her hand over his as she continued. "It was her agony and her grief that drove her to make such a horrible decision. She brought the body of her breeder to the cave in which they had spent their first night together as a triad and laid him to rest. Within the tears she cried was her connection to the All Mother, and when she shed them, she lost the ability to hear her. I suspect this was how Samantha was able to speak to the All Mother. Perhaps she has taken on the powers of the Ama who lost her way."

Zuran yanked his hand away from Ama's. "You knew this, and you continued treating us this way? How many generations of Amas have passed and allowed this to happen?"

"We didn't know everything, only what the previous Ama was willing to tell us. We share memories, but many generations means that it takes longer to find information that far back. I knew she blamed him and his heat, but that was all. I cannot make up for the actions of the Amas before me, Zuran, but I can help to break the cycle of wrongs done to you and all the others from this day on."

"So will you bless our union now?" Olan asked, wrapping his tail around Zuran's

"Are you going to bring the hunters back into the fold now?" his bride asked at the same time, looking at Ama with narrowed eyes.

"No, I will not bless the union."

"I don't understand what the hell is up with this fucked up, backward-ass way of thinking you guys have! Humanity may have its own downsides, but we can at least say we don't deny people the freedom to choose who they want to spend their lives with. If I want to mate with both of them, then I sure as hell will. They're mine, whether you like it or not. And the other hunters deserve to find someone who will accept them too."

Ama's gaze cut to Samantha, and her voice was cold when she responded. "This is not your world, little one. You told me yourself that your people destroyed the world that created you, that humanity was so careless with what they were given that they were forced to leave and seek out a new home." The chieftess narrowed her eyes. "It is partly due to these *'fucked up, backward-ass ways of thinking'* that our world still thrives."

The walls of the hut felt as if they were pressing in on him and he drew in deep lungfuls of air as the anger over her words raced through him. He opened his mouth to argue, but a snarl reverberated through the hut. It wasn't from him though.

Turning his head to his left, Olan's eyes widened when they landed on Zuran. Electrical currents ran up the length of his curved horns, snapping furiously between them. "Impossible…" he whispered in awe. Only breeder males and females, as far as he knew, were capable of such a thing.

"Samantha. Is. Mine," Zuran hissed angrily.

Ama's eyes lit with excitement, a smile overtook her features as she watched the spectacle unfolding before her. The last bright rays from the twin suns peeked through the windows of the hut, but they seemed dull in comparison to the currents Zuran was pushing through his horns. "That she is."

"She is?" Olan frowned in confusion. This entire meeting had been one strange turn after the other.

"Correct." She nodded. "There are old texts that speak of the hunters. I haven't been able to translate them all. But one in particular speaks of unions among them. Soul unions."

"Soul unions?"

Ama's head tilted curiously. "Did you know you have an interesting habit of repeating me?"

Samantha's brows furrowed, and her mouth twisted to the

side. "You have an interesting habit of saying things that don't exactly make sense."

Head thrown back, Ama laughed loudly. "I like you very much, little one. I have something for you." She looked to the female at her side, who rushed to retrieve a folded bundle. "Come, take it."

Samantha took a hesitant step forward, lifting the material from the female's hands and held it up in front of her. It was a black bride dress, similar to the one Olan had given her, but this was accented with red and aqua swirls running up the sides. It was beautiful.

"Our colors," Olan breathed. "You knew?"

The chieftess smiled softly. "The All Mother spoke to me. It wasn't my place to bless the union because Samantha had to decide for herself whether she wanted both of you or not."

"So, that's it?"

"Your unions have been blessed. You are Olan's bride and Zuran's soul bride." she looked at Samantha "As for your question, it is up to the hunters to find the one who calls to their soul. I'm only the voice of the All Mother when she needs it."

Olan stood in shock. He had a bride *and* a bondmate. Excitement welled up inside of him, and he turned to look at Zuran, who seemed to be completely focused on Samantha. He saw the shiver that worked through her body when she looked back at the other male, the aroma of her arousal permeating the air of the enclosed space.

"I expect a full report on what happened with the humans after your unions have been sealed," Ama was saying. "You should go now before Zuran falls much farther into his madness."

"Thank you, Ama." He bowed his head to the chieftess and scooped his Fanahala up into his arms. "Zuran." His hand brushed against the other male's face, and he saw some clarity return to Zuran's eyes. Zuran blinked, glancing down at Samantha before plucking her from Olan's arms and disappearing through the door of the hut.

Ama snickered softly when he turned to grin at her. "You had best catch up with them. And Olan?" she called as he moved to leave.

"Yes, Ama?"

"Take one of the blankets with you."

He laughed and plucked up one of the brightly colored throws from the table before he stepped out into the fading light of the evening suns. Olan inhaled deeply, closing his eyes as he let his mind process what had happened. A ripple of anticipation thrummed through him and he smiled. He didn't need to look far for his mates. Olan and Zuran had grown up in this village, and he knew exactly where his bondmate had taken Samantha. The cliffs.

Although it was the scene of one of the most terrifying moments of his life, the two of them had so many fond memories of the windswept bluffs that he couldn't find it in his heart to stay away. With a smile playing on his lips, Olan set off after them.

CHAPTER 31

SAMANTHA

*S*amantha curled up against Zuran's side, her body wedged beneath his arm as she gazed out over the swirling pink-hued waters of one of Seytonna's oceans. Her boots lay discarded near the edge of the cliff and she wriggled her bare toes; enjoying the breeze on her feet. She had thought the water had been beautiful from the observation deck of the *S.S. Constellation*, but seeing it in person took her breath away. The twin suns were sinking slowly on the horizon, casting red and orange light across the undulating surface. She was already planning on talking the guys into taking her down to the shore so that she could dip her toes in, and maybe she could sneak in some samples.

A noise and movement to her left caught her attention; she turned her head to see Olan walking up the hill toward them. There was a colorful blanket thrown over one of his shoulders, a small grin tugging at his lips when his eyes fell on her. Beside her,

Zuran shifted, reaching out to catch one of the corners of the material as Olan laid it out next to them.

Samantha crawled into the middle of the blanket, running her hands over the soft, intricately stitched details. The males took up positions on either side of her, their hands caressing her skin softly. Zuran's teeth nipped at her shoulder, and she shuddered, gasping quietly as her stomach clenched.

Samantha had been waiting for them her entire life, and going another night without them honestly wasn't something she was willing to do at this point. Olan's lips ran over her other shoulder and up the side of her neck, his tongue snaking out to lick at the lobe of her ear.

Gods, she was going to combust—and they had barely touched her!

Her hand came up to Olan's cheek, and she turned her head to brush her lips over his, pressing a soft kiss to them before turning to her other side and trailing kisses across Zuran's jaw until she reached his mouth. He didn't settle for the light brush; instead, he pressed into her, taking her bottom lip gently between his sharp teeth. The prickle of pain excited her, drawing a ragged moan from her throat.

"Samantha," Olan breathed against her neck.

She could barely keep her thoughts straight. "Hmm?"

"Did you mean what you said to Ama?"

Why in the world was he asking her questions that required her to remember how to speak? "I meant every damn word I said to her."

"Even when you said you wanted to mate me *and* Zuran?"

"Gods above, Olan. Stop asking me questions and start touching me. Please." The idea that these two were meant to be her mates was still a little, well, alien. She supposed it shouldn't be all that foreign considering the fact that the Venium had fated human mates as well.

Olan laughed, his hands sliding up the inside of her leg. The panic that shot through her made her recoil.

"I'm sorry, Fanahala." Olan rushed. "Did I hurt you?"

Samantha squeezed her eyes shut, taking deep breaths as she tried to shake the memory of Marsel's touch from her mind. *He's gone,* she told herself, but it didn't stop the tears. "Marsel," she choked out. "Before I found you all in the cells..."

Zuran growled, a terrifying sound that made the hairs on her arms stand at attention. "He hurt you?"

She shook her head, swiping at the tears that slid down her cheeks. "Not really. He came to the room after I woke up. The things he said... they were awful... I didn't know what he'd done to you two, and he was trying to..." Her chin trembled as she took a deep breath. "He was touching me, and I couldn't get away from him at first."

"Fanahala..." the word sounded pained.

"I had my pocket knife on me, inside my dress. He stopped to take off his pants, and I stabbed him with it, three times I think."

"Good," Zuran hissed.

"He deserved far worse, Samantha." Olan brushed the hair back from her face. "I'm sorry we weren't there to rip him to pieces, but I'm glad he died by your hand." He kissed the tips of her fingers softly.

"We can stop," Zuran whispered.

She turned her head so that she could look into his eyes. The madness was there, swirling around the outer rim. She didn't want to stop. Zuran needed her, and she needed them. "I won't let him win from the grave, Zuran." Her hands framed his face, drawing him close for a sweet kiss. "I don't want to stop. I just needed to tell you."

Olan shifted at her side, pushing himself to his feet, a current of electricity sliding along his arms. "You trust us, Samantha?"

"Of course."

He nodded and she watched as the tiny sparks of his current jumped along his skin, lighting up like the little fireflies she had once read about. He swayed slowly in front of her, a side-to-side motion that she recognized from the day they met. She felt the heat bloom in her chest first before it slipped down, curling low in her stomach, and finally pooling between her legs. Pressing her thighs together to relieve the pressure, Samantha moaned. Her pussy pulsed, clenching as she dug her fingers into the fabric beneath her.

Beside her Zuran's current crackled and his breathing grew labored. He was enjoying the dance as much as she was; that knowledge had her moaning again, her eyes closing for a moment as her nipples hardened against the fabric of her bra. While both of the males were quite large, bigger than any human man she had ever met, they were both lean with compact muscle hidden beneath the smooth expanse of their skin. Skin that Samantha was feeling the need to rub herself against, to bite, to lick.

Olan stepped closer, reaching out his hand to Zuran expectantly, but the other male frowned at it. "Come dance with me, Zuran."

"I'm a hunter."

"That isn't all you are though." Olan's head cocked to the side. "You are Samantha's mate, my bondmate."

Samantha smiled and nudged Zuran with her shoulder. "Show me what you've got, Z."

Olan pulled Zuran to his feet and tugged him off of the blanket. *Double the dancing? Yes, please.* She reclined back on her elbows, biting her lip as she watched Olan move Zuran's stiff body around. Tails entwined, the two of them found a rhythm, caressing one another as their currents flickered.

The familiar heat was back, twisting inside of her body, making her squirm restlessly. Electric sparks bounced between their horns, and she felt the same pull she had that first time Olan had danced for her in the village, the same overwhelming need to be close to him and now Zuran.

"Please," she whimpered, her breath catching in her chest. "I'm really, really enjoying this show, but I need... *something*." Her mind was getting foggy.

"What do you need, Fanahala?" Zuran asked.

Oh, gods, she just *needed*. "You. I want you," she finally managed to pant. The growls that burst from them raced over her skin, and she felt like she was on fire. Eyes closed, head thrown back, Samantha reached down to trail a hand over her covered stomach and along her breasts. This dress had to go. Her skin was so damn hot, and she wanted to touch it, to run her fingers over every sensitive spot she possessed.

Reaching down, Samantha pulled the hem of the dress up, exposing her body to her males, grinning when she heard them moan softly. She tossed the garment to the side and reached back with a practiced hand to unclasp her bra, tossing it away before bringing her hands up to cup her breasts. She sat naked on the blanket, having tossed her ripped underwear not long after escaping into the forest.

Olan and Zuran stepped closer, sinking to their knees on the blanket in front of her. Their hands brushed up her legs, drawing invisible patterns on her skin with the tips of their fingers. Samantha reached for Zuran, tugging at his cover, but he stiffened, his hand going to hers. "I'm not a breeder, Samantha."

"Do you think that matters to me?" When he didn't respond, she pushed up on her knees, taking his face into her hands. "I want you, Z. What your society has labeled you doesn't mean a damn thing to me." She took his hand, placing it on her bare breast, sighing at the warmth of his palm. "Touch me. Please."

He didn't need to be asked twice. Zuran's hand tightened on

her flesh, his thumb brushing across the sensitive peak of her nipple, sending a shiver throughout her body. She reached for his covering again, and this time, he didn't try to stop her. Excitement thrummed through her as she tugged at the strings that kept it fastened, fumbling with it before another pair of hands took over.

Olan grinned at her, dropping a kiss to her shoulder. "Let me help."

The knot came undone beneath his quick fingers. She gasped when Zuran's cock sprang free. "Oh."

It bobbed gently as she stared down at it. Samantha had known that first day when she had been hanging upside down with her face practically pressed to it, that his cock would be impressive, but she hadn't counted on just how fascinating she would find it.

The entire length was as dark as the rest of his body, with a few of the small electrified dots scattered along the base. The shaft was thick, and three fleshy, almost vine-like tendrils were wrapped around it. They pulsed and the longer she watched, the more she was sure they were wriggling. At the tip, just below the bulbous head, was a cluster of softly rounded bumps that glowed with his current just like the little dots.

She reached out, her finger grazing the swollen head and trailing down over the bumps. One of the fleshy tendrils wrapped around her fingers, causing her mouth to drop open. *That's gonna be interesting.* She felt Olan at her back, his hands brushed her hips, sliding around to her stomach. Her head fell back against his chest and she gripped Zuran firmly, stroking her hand up and down the length.

"I want to watch Zuran take you, Fanahala," Olan whispered against her ear, his breath fanning over her skin. "Will you let him?"

"Yes." She moaned, arching her back, pushing her breast into Zuran's hand as she squeezed him. Behind her, Olan pressed his still-covered cock into her lower back. She felt it twitch and reached back, searching for the ties, but he stilled her hand.

Bringing it to his mouth, he nipped at her fingers. "I'll wait my turn." Olan brushed one of his knuckles across Zuran's jaw and rumbled against her. "Take her, Zuran."

Not needing to be told twice, her dark, broody mate snaked his arms around her, dragging her forward so that she straddled his hips. "You're mine." He growled, his hands fisted in her hair, yanking her head back. She felt the tip of his cock push through her folds and tried to impale herself on him, but he had her by the hips.

The tendrils on his shaft rubbed against her, fluttering over her clit before they spread her open. With a snarl, Zuran thrust his hips upward, burying his length within her warm, wet pussy. A moan was forced from her throat as a gentle current brushed her walls, making her clench tightly around him.

The wriggle of the tendrils within her had her crying out loudly. She held onto Zuran's shoulders as he pounded up into her, the tips of her nails digging into his skin.

"You're so beautiful, Fanahala."

She turned her head as far as she could with Zuran's hand still fisted in her hair and moaned when she saw that Olan had removed his covering and kneeled beside them, glistening cock in hand. He stroked it from head to base and back again, squeezing a drop of milky liquid from the slit at the top. Oh gods, she wanted to bend down and lick the drop from his flesh. Zuran growled beneath her, lifting her off of him and spinning her around so that her back was flush against his chest before he drove himself back into her cunt.

Samantha felt his lips against her neck a moment before his sharp teeth closed over her skin. Chills spread over her, and she sighed softly when Olan crouched down in front of her. Her breath came out in panting whimpers as she watched him. One hand fisting in Zuran's hair, her other one reached for Olan, pulling him to her for a rough, hot kiss. Tongues twisting together, teeth nipping, she met Zuran's thrusts, moaning into Olan's mouth.

He pulled back suddenly, gasping, his head thrown back, mouth hanging open. Wrapped tightly around his red and aqua cock was a dark black tail. She shivered as she watched, noticing that their cocks looked nothing alike. Olan's was not only a different color, but it lacked the tendrils and bumps that Zuran's had. It was long, curving up slightly toward his stomach, and glistened with its own slickness.

She bucked her hips, biting her lip as she watched Zuran's tail pump up and down Olan's shaft. The way they groaned together was one of the most erotic things she had ever witnessed. Olan's hands trailed up her sides until they reached her breasts. He pinched her nipples between his fingers, drawing a gasp from her.

Zuran released her throat, lapping at the marks before he moved to her ear. "Come for me, Fanahala."

His frenzied thrusts jarred her entire body, and she threw her head back, hands braced on Olan's arms as she cried out. Samantha was pressed tightly between her mates when Olan leaned forward to crush his lips to Zuran's. A tail slipped between her legs to rub along the slippery folds. When it flicked lightly against her clit, Samantha jerked.

"*Yes!* Oh, gods, please do that again!"

The males growled in unison, tongues tangled with one another's, and the tail between her legs rubbed harder, nearly vibrating. She rested her head against Zuran's broad shoulders as the tendrils on his cock caressed the sensitive spot deep inside her. They lost themselves in the maddening rhythm. The males broke apart, panting heavily as they worked together to deliver her release.

"Samantha," Zuran growled, slamming her down on his length.

Her breath caught in her chest a moment before a current licked the inside of her pussy, sending her spiraling into a screaming orgasm that locked up every one of her muscles. Zuran's cock pistoned within her, and she felt the frenzied dance of his tendrils against her pulsing walls, felt the way he seemed to swell impossibly larger, stretching her body to its limits.

The sharp pinch of Zuran's teeth sinking into her neck made her eyes widen. His body slammed into her one last time before he stiffened, his cock jerking and swelling at her entrance. His warm cum shot into her, and he moaned against her skin.

Olan leaned into her front, pressing her between the males again. His curved cock replaced the tail on her clit, and she felt the head slide along her swollen flesh, rubbing against the base of Zuran's cock where they were still joined. Both males moaned, stroking her arms, torso, hips, anything they could reach.

"I cannot wait to be inside of you, Fanahala," Olan whispered, thrusting gently against her.

The pressure was building again, each pass of his cock across her clit reigniting her need. Her pussy fluttered around Zuran. She felt the swelling begin to abate, his cock slipping free as his cum dripped down along the inside of her thighs. He pulled his mouth from her skin, licking her wounds gently.

As if they were of one mind, the males lifted and spun her around so that she was once more facing Zuran. Olan slid his cock along the slick folds between her legs, his hips pressing against her ass.

"Please, Olan." She was so close to coming again. She just needed him to move a little more—just a tiny bit.

He laughed softly near her ear and she shivered. "You want to come again?"

"Yes!"

Zuran grinned at her, trailing a claw-tipped finger over her nipple. *Gods above.* Olan's claws dug into her hips, the tips pricking her flesh as she ground her cunt against him. She had never felt so much pleasure, so much need, in her entire life.

"She wants to come again, Zuran," he whispered, his tail snaking up her thigh to spread her legs wider.

Zuran watched her, his white eyes hooded as he reached down to take Olan's girth into his palm, stroking it slowly. His mouth lowered to one of her nipples and he sucked gently, making her gasp and buck. Behind her Olan hissed, thrusting into Zuran's hand. Holy fuck, this was hot. She felt the tip of a cock push into her and looked down to see Zuran guiding her other male into her needy body. A whimper rolled up her throat as she was pulled down onto his length agonizingly slow, her pussy clenching greedily around him.

Olan sank fully into her with a groan, but he didn't move. Instead, he reached out for their mate, his thumb brushing over Zuran's lips before his hands moved back to her body, trailing from the inside of her thighs, along her sides, and swirling around her breasts. With her feet planted on the ground, Samantha rose up just enough that Olan almost slipped free before she dropped back down.

"Again," Olan grunted.

She obliged, pushing herself up and down a few more times before he stopped her. Zuran leaned forward, pressing sweet kisses across her chest then nipping at her breasts. The familiar tingle of pleasure built in her lower belly. *So close.* Olan leaned back, pulling her with him so that she was reclined on his chest, her legs spread wide and bent at the knees. Slowly, Zuran's lips trailed down her body, his tongue dipping into her belly button before drawing a wet path to her hip. Samantha twisted, grinding herself onto Olan.

"Watch him, Fanahala," the male at her back growled, swiveling his hips against her.

"Fuck!" She gasped when Zuran's mouth sealed over her throbbing, swollen clit, his tongue flicking quickly back and forth over the nub. His tail, the blade just barely visible at the tip, ran up her leg, the pressure of the sharp point just enough to raise goosebumps along her skin.

Samantha's eyes fell closed as she arched up against the assault, her pussy gripping the cock inside of her as it pulsed with a tingling current. A sharp smack on the side of her ass had her eyes snapping open as she turned to stare up into the face of her brightly colored mate. He'd spanked her.

She wanted more.

"I told you to watch, Samantha." Olan's voice was demanding, hard. It sent a thrill coursing through her, heightening her pleasure.

Her gaze slid down so that she could watch Zuran, finding that his eyes were locked onto her face. Olan began to pound into her with desperate, jerky thrusts. The electrical current that ran up his length intensified, her pussy clenching as the sparks licked at her walls. Just days ago, the thought of their currents touching any part of her body had given her reservations, but she had spoken the truth when Olan had asked if she trusted them. She did, completely, knowing they wanted nothing more than to bring her as much pleasure as they could.

The currents flowed through her again, a little higher than the last time. She cradled Zuran's face in her hands, grinding her pussy against his mouth as her entire body locked up, eyes rolling back in her head as a ragged scream tore up and out of her throat.

The sting of another bite, this one on the fleshy part of her shoulder, barely even registered through the blinding pleasure of her release. Olan was panting roughly in her ear. She looked down to see that Zuran's mouth had moved to the exposed base of the other male's cock, his tongue tracing over the swirling aqua streaks. The sight set off another orgasm, and this one finally seemed to trigger Olan's release. He thrust up into her one last time before tearing his mouth away, grunting with each jerking spurt of his cum within her.

Samantha tried to speak, but her throat felt raw. She wasn't even sure she had words for what had just happened, so she just closed her eyes, her head falling back to rest against Olan's chest as his tongue soothed over her newest wound. He wrapped his arms around her, pulling her down onto the blanket with him.

Zuran crawled up next to them, taking up a position on her other side and dropping feather-soft kisses along her jaw. "You are ours, Samantha."

Nuh-uh, she thought, *you two are* mine.

---

*T*he twin suns were just beginning to peek up over the tops of the trees in the distance, the first rays dancing across the naked skin of her males. They were gorgeous. Olan was curled against her back, his arms wrapped around her torso, fingers brushing her stomach gently.

In front of her lay Zuran, his hands slowly trailing through her hair and along the side of her face. She turned to press a kiss to his palm, and for the first time, she noticed that the sides of his hands and fingers were scabbed over with dried blood. The wounds looked painful and angry.

"What the hell happened here, Z?"

He tugged his hands from her grip and turned his face away sheepishly, "Nothing."

"He tried to get to Vasa, to help her," Olan whispered.

She wasn't sure exactly what horrors the Seyton female had been put through, but she had some idea. "Oh, Z." Her lips brushed over each of his knuckles, every tiny abrasion she could make out against the darkness of his skin. "I'm so sorry for whatever they did to Vasa. For everything they put you all through."

"I don't want to think about those monsters right now, Samantha." He pulled her close, his arm sliding beneath Olan's so that they caged her in. "Let us love you."

She sighed, closing her eyes as she gave in to the request.

CHAPTER 32

OLAN

*O*lan grinned down at his mate as she danced away from the waves as they lapped the sandy shore. In one hand was the glass jar she had requested, and in the other she held the hem of her bridal dress, trying her best to keep it from getting wet in the surf.

His bondmate sat on the rocks not far from her, laughing as he watched one of her feet sink down into the sand all the way to her ankle. Samantha yelped as the water in her jar sloshed down her front, but Zuran scooped her up, pressing a kiss to her lips before carrying her up to dry land. Olan should be talking with Ama about what would be done with the humans, and he needed to see his family to introduce them to his triad.

Samantha had expressed a wish to return to her ship so that she could try and convince her people to leave. The ship, she said, was dying, and soon it would not be able to support them. Collecting her things from the place she called her lab and her personal quarters was merely a bonus of the trip. Olan had asked her if she wanted to return to the male's village, but she seemed just as drawn to the cliffs and the shore as he and Zuran had been in their youth.

With a nod to his bondmate, Olan turned from the edge and made his way back toward the village. The festival was in full swing here, with males and females dancing and moving in between the huts. Low whispers and giggles drifted out from behind the closed doors, making her smile.

This might have been what his festival would have been like had Zuran not found Samantha and brought her home. He may have been happy with one of these females, but he would have never been complete without the love of his triad. Ama stood silent in the field just outside the pillars of the village, her eyes fixed on the billowing smoke in the distance.

"Ama? What is it?"

She shook her head in dismay. "Something is wrong, Olan. Terribly so."

As he stepped toward her, Olan noticed movement at the tree line. When the first of the males stumbled forward with kits in their arms and females walking wearily beside them, he felt his stomach drop. Lucy broke off from the group racing toward them, and just behind her, struggling beneath the weight of her mate, was Asa. He rushed forward, his pulse roaring in his ears as he took in the sight of Vane's bloodied chest and torso.

"Get the healer!" Lucy was screaming. "We need a doctor! Get someone!"

A call went up behind him from those gathered in the street who had caught sight of the others. Lucy was gasping for breath as she stumbled to a stop, falling to her knees as she stared up at him. Her face, like those of the Seyton that now ran toward them, was covered in ash and dirt. Ama stood frozen in place behind him, wide eyes locked on Asa.

"Help…" Asa begged.

Olan lunged forward, lifting the other breeder into his arms. Small holes dotted the male's chest and blood flowed freely from them. Why wasn't he healing? The punctures he had received from the carnera were larger and had healed within an hour of the attack.

Something wasn't right here.

He knew that there had been accidents on hunts that resulted in hunters dying. Wounds could be too bad to heal out in the wild, but something like this? Vane should have been almost completely healed by now. The healer would know how to fix this. The All Mother would not take his friend, not like this.

The spell Ama had been under must have lifted because he could hear her calling out directions. Niva had also appeared, and her sharp commands rang through the air as she cleared the streets.

"Stay here, Vane," Olan told him as he hurried to the healer's hut. "Stay awake, do you hear me?"

The male groaned in response. Lucy darted past him, wrenching the door of the hut open. In the center of the room as a fur covered examination bed and Olan placed Vane gingerly on top of it, pillowing his head as Asa appeared on the other side. Her hands cradled his face, caressing the stripes along his cheeks as she whispered to him.

"What happened, Asa?"

"We were attacked. I went with Vane this morning to the tanning hut. He wanted to show me something, a gift he had made..." Tears rolled down her cheeks. "I'd discovered we are expecting a kit and his gift was perfect." She pressed her hand to her belly, cupping the tiny swell. "A cradle he'd carved. There was someone outside, and when he went to investigate, he was overtaken."

"By who?" Ama's voice had turned icy with rage.

"Humans," Lucy whispered from the door, her face pale as she watched Vane's chest rise and fall.

"They had strange weapons with them. Vane tried to protect us, but they pointed them at him. There was a loud noise, like thunder, and he fell."

"Guns. They had old Earth guns on them, and they fucking shot him," Lucy's voice trembled.

"Lucy was close," Asa continued. "She heard the noise and came running. The males fled when they saw her, but they were not the only ones there. More of their group attacked the village, setting the huts on fire, destroying everything..." She choked back the sob. "All of our homes, our lives were there and now it is all gone."

The healer burst into the room, her face serious as she began examining Vane's injuries.

"All Mother, please..." Asa was openly crying now. "Please don't take him from me. I cannot do this alone."

Ama pulled her into her arms as the healer began her work. "Shh, Asa. Come pray with me. Olan, retrieve Samantha. Lucy, come here. We may need your knowledge of the weapon."

With little time to hesitate, Olan ran from the room, heading toward the cliffs where he had left his mates. Samantha and Zuran were climbing back up the natural stair structure when he reached the shore.

Zuran took one look at the dried blood on his skin and dropped the pouch he'd brought with him. "Olan? What's this? What happened?"

"Ama needs Samantha."

"Is this your blood?" Samantha asked as she reached him, her hands prodding his chest and stomach.

"It's Vane's." Olan grabbed her by the wrist and pulled her toward the village.

"Vane's? How the hell..."

"The male village was attacked. Human males wounded Vane and burned it down."

"Holy shit." Samantha picked up the pace, sprinting beside him until they reached the healer's hut.

"I was too late, Sam," Lucy told her when they entered. "I was able to scare them away from the farms, but I couldn't get to the tanner's fast enough. They shot him with old Earth guns."

"Where the hell would they have gotten those?" she asked, but she shook her head as she moved past them. "Marsel. He had a stash, but I didn't think they were still in working condition and I definitely didn't think he was dumb enough to have ammunition for them."

The healer's hands were covered in blood and she dug her instrument back into Vane's chest, pulling out a small metal ball. This tiny thing had taken his friend down? Ama and Asa sat nearby, their hands joined in prayer as their lightning sparked frantically.

"I don't know what you need. I'm not a doctor or a nurse. Lucy and I have basic medical training, but this is far beyond that," Samantha said.

Lucy came forward. "I tried to use the medwand on him, but it did nothing. The wounds would start to close, but then they'd open right back up."

"Do these things contain a toxin, Fanahala?" Olan asked.

"I don't think so."

"Maybe it's a reaction to the metals? My dad used to watch these shows in the archives about the history of weaponry, and many of the bullets made near the end of the war contained lead."

"You think it might poison him?" Zuran asked from behind him.

Lucy shrugged. "Anything is possible."

"Hunter!" the healer called out. "The illandor and aclate. Quickly now."

Zuran grabbed the herbs from the shelves, the same ones that had been used to save him, and without being asked, began chewing the leaves for the paste. Olan stood back, watching the scene in disbelief. How could this have happened? How had Ama not known?

When Vane's wounds were cleaned and the paste tucked inside the holes, the healer stitched them together as best she could. "There is nothing more I can do for him. We will wait for the All Mother to make her decision."

Asa crawled onto the furs, curling up beside her mate as he rested. They left her like that, following Ama out into the center of the village where everyone had gathered to tend to the kits and the others that had been wounded. Most of these were small burns or abrasions from the journey, and they would heal on their own.

"Our way of life must change today," Ama announced. "Our tribe will no longer live separately. All will stay within the village. We cannot afford to lose anyone."

"What about the heat?" someone called out.

"Our females need to be protected!" came another voice.

"I will ask our males to be mindful of themselves. It is time they take responsibility for themselves. We cannot risk the separation as we have before. The unmated females will return to their family huts to make room for those who have been displaced." Ama raised her hands as voices rose. "We will make it through this if we put aside some of this selfishness and care for our friends and family."

Olan looked to their chieftess before asking the question he knew everyone was wondering. "And the humans?"

But before she could answer him, a cry of pure agony came from within the healer's hut. He watched her expression harden. "If Vane dies, we will kill them all."

"There are families there! Children!" Samantha protested.

"They attacked our people. If they cared for their families, then this would not have happened." Ama turned away from the crowd. "See to it that everyone has a place to stay for the night," she snapped at Niva as she walked by.

*W*hen the suns rose the next morning, Olan scrubbed his hands over his face. Samantha had stayed up all night pacing as he and Zuran watched her. They were all worried about Vane. His mates followed behind him as they weaved through the crowded streets of the village to the healer's hut. Olan knocked softly on the wood, announcing their presence. Ama answered, ushering them inside.

Olan was shocked to see Vane's eyes open, but the male's chest shuddered with his labored breathing. A shaky hand rose up to brush against Asa's tear-stained face while the other gently cupped the swell of his mate's stomach. "She is calling me home, Fanahala," he whispered. "I can hear her voice."

"No. No, Vane," Asa sobbed. "Do not leave me. Please. I cannot do this without you."

"Take me to the agmari, Fanahala. Let me go home."

"I cannot do this without you!" she whimpered.

"You are so much stronger than you believe. I have been so blessed to call you mine and to see you have the opportunity to bring another life into this world." Asa's body trembled with her sobs. "You will find happiness again."

"No, Vane."

He smiled at her, wiping away her tears. "My heart. I love you."

"Vane…" Asa shook his shoulders as his hand fell away and his breath shuddered from between his lips. "No. No!" She fell across his chest, her face buried against his neck as she screamed.

The sound went straight through his soul. It was pure heartbreak, an agony he had never known, and one he hoped to never feel for as long as he lived. The healer stepped back, shaking her head as Ama crouched next to Asa.

"You can't take him!" she screamed. "I need him! We need him! Give him back to me!"

"Asa," Ama cooed as she rubbed the female's back. "The All Mother has welcomed him home."

"She cannot have him!"

"Vane requested to be returned. Come, do as he has asked." Ama pulled her away gently.

Asa keened, the sound of her grief filling the room. When she saw Samantha move forward to take Olan's hand, the female snarled, hissing at her as she shook Ama off. "This is *your* fault! We should never have trusted you! We should have killed you like we did all the others who have invaded our home!"

Olan stepped in front of Samantha, blocking Asa's attempt to come closer. "I know you don't mean that. I know this is your grief speaking." He pulled her into his arms, rocking her from side to side as she wailed. "Don't let it take you, Asa."

He rocked her for some time, letting her cry until she was hoarse, and when her legs wobbled with exhaustion, Olan helped her to the ground. "I'm sorry," she whispered into his chest before lifting her head slowly. Her red-rimmed eyes sought out Samantha. "I'm so sorry for what I said."

"I don't need your apology, Asa." Samantha told her, crouching down next to them. "You have every right to be upset, to be furious over what they did. I promise I'll do anything I can to help you."

"Come, Asa," Ama reached out her hand for the other female to take. "It is time to return him."

Zuran stepped forward, lifting Vane's limp body into his arms. The tears in his bondmate's eyes fell down his cheeks as he turned and walked through the door of the hut. Olan took Samantha's hand, following behind Ama and Asa. The entire village waited in silence outside. They lined the path to the blooms, kneeling to show the fallen respect. Some reached out to touch Asa, just a brush of their fingers meant to remind her she was surrounded by support, wrapped in love.

Olan felt an emptiness in his chest, a deep, gaping wound where his friend's light had once been. As if she felt his pain, Samantha gave his hand a little squeeze and rested her head against his arm.

"Olan? Why did the Ama I saw leave her mate in the cave? Why didn't she return him?" she asked softly.

"Maybe she blamed the All Mother as well as the hunter. If she was angry with her, she may not have wished to give him back. It could have been her way of keeping him even after he was gone." He shrugged before pulling her into his side. "We lay our people to rest within the blooms to nurture and give back what the All Mother has given us. In the end, we are all returned to her arms."

Samantha was quiet for the rest of the walk, no doubt mulling over his words. Olan stopped on the outskirts of the clearing where the blooms grew, giving Asa distance for her final good-byes. She pressed a kiss to his lips, brushing back his hair.

"My love, my mate," she whispered to him. "I will not let you be forgotten. Our kit will be safe and will always know how much they were loved by you."

Zuran stepped up to the open bloom and lowered Vane's body into the flat center. The green leaves trembled before they slowly rose, coming together to seal the male within.

CHAPTER 33

ZURAN

"*I* already told you Marsel is dead. Why do you want to go back there so badly?" Samantha's blue eyes narrowed on him as she crossed her arms stubbornly over her chest.

"We have unfinished business with your humans, Fanahala," Zuran told her gently, tucking a few unruly strands of hair behind her ear. As much as he wanted to bask in the glory of having a mate, he knew they would need to deal with the issue of Marsel and the other human men who had harmed Vasa and the ones who destroyed the village. Ama demanded their deaths.

His breeding heat, though tempered for the moment, was still very much a problem. Like Olan, he had thought their night with Samantha would mean an end to the constant hunger and irritation, but they were wrong. The bloodlust still raged through him, even now.

"Not every human on that ship thinks like Marsel, Z."

"That may be true, but even one in agreement puts the Seyton at risk. Humans are dangerous."

"Am I dangerous?" One of her dark brows arched in a challenge.

"Samantha…"

"What about Curtis? Is he dangerous? Or Lucy and James?" When he only looked at her she sighed, rubbing at the sides of her head. "We're examples of humans who are *not* dangerous, who've helped the Seyton. There are more like us on that ship."

"Be that as it may, we are still going back to confront them."

His little mate let out a frustrated moan, plopping down on the blanket Olan had brought with him last night. "Who is 'them,' and where the hell is Olan and his damn diplomacy when I need him?"

"The 'bad' humans, if you wish." He shrugged the way he'd seen Samantha do many times. "And Olan is helping to gather the war party."

"The war party?" Her mouth moved like a water dweller's for a moment. He knew he shouldn't find it amusing, but he wasn't perfect. "Z, I just told you there are children there, babies!"

"Ama has offered sanctuary for any who are willing to coexist peacefully. The only humans we want are the ones who harmed Vasa and those that took Vane away from his mate and kit. They will need to pay for their crimes."

She sighed in resignation. "So why do I need to go? I could stay here. I'm sure I can be useful." A shudder worked through her body. "I know I said I wanted to go back the other day, but I'm not so sure now. If I never have to see that place again, it'll be too soon."

He understood her reasons for wanting to stay behind, and he didn't want to risk her safety either, but they would need her on the front lines. "We would never ask you to return if it was not important, Fanahala." He crouched down in front of her, his hand engulfing her little ones as he plucked them from her lap. "If your people decide to come peacefully, having you there, a familiar face among the Seyton, will comfort them." He tipped her chin. "Besides, how will I know what equipment you want from your lab or where to find the room you lived in?"

"You're going to use my equipment against me? So low."

Her shoulders drooped as he leaned forward to press his forehead against hers. She was hurting. He wished he could take that from her. "I know this is hard, but if we do this now we may be able to stop many unnecessary deaths." A purr rumbled in his chest, a sound he hadn't ever made before, but with the way Samantha shivered at it, he was going to make it as often as possible. "The sooner this mess is taken care of, the sooner Olan and I can bring you back here and taste that pretty cunt again."

The musky smell of her arousal was so strong, he swore he could taste her already.

"Right." She swallowed thickly, her cheeks flushing a deep crimson. "L-let's get this over and done with."

The network of hunters that had moved into the outer edges of the village came together as quickly as possible when they heard what had happened. Zuran recognized many faces and was glad to have them with him in the event the aliens decided not to go peacefully.

The trek back wasn't nearly as hard as it had been to try and convince Vasa she needed more time to recover. She was insistent that she should be present for their punishment and Curtis, who had become her shadow, championed her fight. Despite the protests of the hunters and her family, Vasa had eventually won and now walked alongside them, her broken wing bandaged and bound tightly against her body. Her hunter father stayed a few steps behind the couple, his sharp white gaze never straying too far.

When they were close enough to the ship to smell the acrid

smoke, Ama called for them to stop and sent out scouts. They returned, reporting that a small group of human males stood guard at the front. When they described the weapons in their hands, Samantha sighed in frustration. "They've got guns, but it sounds like only a handful."

"We cannot risk it after the way Vane's body reacted to their weapons," Ama said.

"We can lure them to us," Vasa's father said. "Draw them in and then disarm them."

"Zuran, ready a group of hunters. The rest of us will fall back and wait. If they cannot be disarmed, kill them." Ama took Samantha's arm, tugging her away from him.

"Be careful, Z." She told him before she turned to follow the chieftess.

Zuran watched them go for a moment before turning back to the hunters. They all wanted to help, to see to the punishment of the males who had wronged them, but he selected five and sent the others back to wait. "Into the trees," he told them. "We will create a disturbance to draw them in. Once we have them close enough, we will subdue them. Do not let them point their weapons at you. No more losses."

Zyar nodded, his jaw set as he leaped into the nearest tree, scurrying up the trunk to hide within the branches. The others followed suit, shielding themselves within the thick cover of the leaves. It brought back the memory of the day he had pounced on Olan thinking he was a danger, but Olan had been neither armed nor dangerous that day.

Once each hunter was in place, they took turns rustling branches and making the animal calls they used during hunts. He recognized the call Zyar was famous for. His calfling milory was one of the best and it seemed to do the trick. The humans crept toward the tree line, their eyes wide as they scanned the forest in front of them.

The smaller of the two turned to the larger male before shoving him forward. "Well, don't just stand there looking like a fool. Let's check it out."

Zuran's tail twitched as the blade slid free in preparation of a fight.

When the largest male was directly below their group, Zuran signaled for them to launch their attack. The six of them dropped from their branches, knocking the humans to the ground. There was a shout and then the loud, deafening sound of thunder Asa had spoken of. Zuran lunged forward, wrapping his tail around the human's throat as Vasa's father subdued the other. With the weapons safely out of their possession, the human males were no more a threat to them than an angry kit would be.

Zyar hissed, clutching at his upper arm. When he pulled his hand back, it was painted in his blood. "What is this? Were you hit?"

"It's only a scratch, brother. I wasn't fast enough to avoid it."

Zuran jerked him around, checking for himself. He sighed in relief when the bleeding stopped, a clear sign to him that the wound would heal itself. "I would not want to explain to Vurso how we lost you."

One of the younger hunters called for Ama, letting her and the others know it was safe to come forward. Samantha raced toward him, her face pale as she ran her hands over his chest.

"I heard the shot. Were you hurt? Is everyone all right?"

"Settle, little one. Zyar received nothing more than a scratch, but it looks as if it will heal fine." He took her hand in his.

The men narrowed their eyes when they saw her. "Bitch." One of them spat as she walked by. Zuran snarled, gnashing his teeth together as he stepped between the males and his mate. The pungent smell of urine satisfied the beast within him.

"They worked for Marsel," she told him. "I mean, I guess we all did, but they were loyal to him."

When they moved into the clearing, a call went up. Zuran blinked in surprise as he looked out over a field filled with Samantha's people. Human males, females, and kits, all filthy and nearing a state of exhaustion, were pouring from the ship. Families huddled together carrying all of their belongings in bags or stuffed in their arms. They must have been waiting for the armed males to be dealt with. Had they been held captive all this time?

A gray-haired male stepped forward, his hands raised high in the air. "Samantha," he said with a sigh before turning to Ama. "We don't want any trouble with you and your people. We heard what happened from some of the ones that made it back here and want no part of it."

"How do we know this isn't a trick?" Zuran asked Ama as she came to a stop next to him.

"I don't think it is," Samantha insisted. "I know him. That's Egmond Troy. He's a proponent of the Alien-Human alliance. That means he's pro-alien and nothing like Marsel. They never got along very well."

Ama met the human halfway, Samantha on her heels with Zuran not far behind. "Any who are willing to surrender on our terms are welcome within our village."

Egmond nodded. "I'm not willing to fight a war because humans made the wrong choices again. I won't leave my children fatherless. We'll hear your terms, but I can tell you we would agree to almost anything to stop this."

"The first is that you leave behind any human weapons you might have." A murmur ran through those gathered close by, but no one openly protested. "The second, and most important, is the promise to hand over the beasts that dared to hurt one of my daughters and those responsible for the death of one of my sons." The voice that came from Ama's mouth wasn't her own, and Zuran watched as the human male's eyes widened as he stumbled backward.

"W-we don't know where they went."

"You don't know?" Zuran's eyes narrowed.

"Some said they headed to the place your pod was said to have crashed at," he told Samantha. "We didn't know what had happened at that point. There was no reason to stop them."

Ama tilted her head as if she was trying to decide if she was going to believe the male. Finally, she turned, her hand brushing Samantha's shoulder. "We will bring all who wish to come back to the village. Have them gather their things and prepare to depart." She glanced at Zuran. "Ready your hunters. We will track down these monsters."

Zuran nodded and set about his task. When the humans were ready to leave, Zuran found Samantha watching them, mumbling as groups of her people passed by. He had thought the peaceful turn of events would have made her happy, but she frowned as she fisted her hands on her hips. "Something isn't right, Z."

"It isn't?"

"Nuh-uh. Hey, Curtis?" She called to the young human male who was assisting an elderly female. He excused himself and ran up to join them. "How many men did you all lose during and following the crash?"

"Twenty-four, I think. Not counting the ones who got to the pods before we broke up."

She shook her head. "There's far more than that missing here."

Curtis shrugged as he looked out over the crowd. "We won't know for sure until we can get a full head count."

Zuran said goodbye to Samantha once they reached the forest where Olan waited to take her back to the village. He had one more thing to take care of before he could begin his new life. It took only a couple hours to track the males. They were slow and did not know the forest well enough to get too far in such a short amount of time. Judging by the scent they left on the shrubs and trees they had passed, at least one of them was severely wounded. When his group of hunters and Curtis finally caught up to them, they all stopped short at the strange sounds of screaming and the eerie call of a carnera.

"Please, have mercy!"

"Call it off! It wasn't anything personal!"

"Marsel forced us to do it!"

"Shut the fuck up, you idiot!"

The sound of Marsel's pained voice shocked Zuran. Samantha had been so sure he was dead when she left him. Before he could decide on a course of action, Curtis was bolting past him into the small clearing.

"Curtis! Wait!"

When Zuran burst through the trees after him he found a strange sight. The four human males he had seen in the cells were all attempting to scatter up trees and away from a massive, gnarled carnera. At the beast's side stood Vasa, her yellow eyes blazing as she sneered, seemingly unaware that they had stumbled upon her.

"You are a pack of liars, unfit to even be considered monsters," she snarled, and the carnera growled as if it agreed with her assessment. "I will bear scars for the rest of my days because of you!" The beast leapt forward, snatching one of the men from a low hanging branch. Its jaws crushed bone and muscle, ripping the male's limbs from his body. His dying howls were drowned out by the terrified screams of his companions as they were forced to watch.

A second male's leg slipped over the edge of the branch he had climbed onto. He didn't recover nearly fast enough and became the next victim of the beast. His screams died as quickly as they began when the carnera's teeth cut through his throat.

The third human, the one Zuran remembered bringing them the tray of food, and who had made the snide comments about

Vasa, became so scared that he tried to climb higher. Zuran watched as he slipped like the male before him, his arms flailing wildly as he fell to the ground, landing with a loud crack that echoed through the trees. He didn't move, but the carnera pounced on him all the same, its deadly claws digging into his soft stomach as it shredded his body.

"And you." Vasa's entire body seemed to come alive, currents rippling up and down her body as Marsel scrambled on the ground before her. His torso was wrapped in dirty bandages, and he struggled to breathe as the beast paced toward him. "You thought you broke me, but I am a daughter of the All Mother. I will not be broken."

At the flick of her wrist, the carnera pounced, its teeth ripping into the muscle and bone of the human's legs. Marsel screamed, a blood-curdling howl of agony as the beast began to devour him slowly, drawing out his death. Vasa reached toward the ground, lifting one of the branches that had broken off the tree during the struggle.

She stepped forward, her arms raised high above her head before she swung. All of her rage, all of the hatred for this vile beast powered her blow, and when it landed, it filled the forest with the sickening crack of bone splintering. She didn't stop there. Over and over, she brought the branch down on his face until there was nothing left of him to identify. The forest was silent, the only sound in it being Vasa's labored breathing and the soft growls of the carnera as it stood at her side.

She stumbled back from the corpse, and just as her legs gave out from beneath her, Curtis was there. He caught her up in his arms, cradling her to his chest as his hand smoothed over the back of her head.

"I lied," Zuran heard her whisper as her body shook with her sobs. "I *am* broken. So broken…"

"Tell me what you need, Vasa." Curtis's soft response brought on more tears, and Zuran retreated to give them privacy.

The carnera licked at its bloody muzzle as Zuran stepped around, giving the creature a wide berth. It was an old female, battle-worn and weary. One of her ears had been lost, and her right eye was beginning to cloud, a sure sign that she was going blind. Zuran wasn't sure how Vasa had come to befriend the beast, but he sent up thanks to the All Mother for unlikely bonds.

"Take good care of her," he whispered before leaving the clearing.

CHAPTER 34

OLAN

*O*lan had known from the moment he stepped out of the pod on the day of his Choosing Ceremony that his whole life, like his physical body, had changed. He was expected to mate, to have kits that would carry on his family's blood. These things were a part of regular life for many Seyton breeders.

Love, though wonderful and encouraged, was not seen as being necessary in a union. A soft sigh brought his attention back to the present, back to the female curled up in his bed. She lay on her side, her face turned toward him, faded violet hair spread across the blankets. Zuran was behind her, his arm slung over her hips, tail curled around one of her legs.

If someone had told him all those solars ago when he stepped out of the bloom that he would be here, he would have thought them mad. To have the love of not just Samantha, but the male who had been his closest companion growing up was more than he could ever have hoped for.

They had salvaged what they could from both the ship and the other village, but it wasn't much. Even the fields where the farmers lived had not gone untouched. He learned that many of the animals had been turned loose when the fires were started, and this had most likely saved them. In fact, nearly all of them had found their way to the village, to the utter amazement of the farmers. Even Teeth, the little samara, had strutted into the village in search of his ecstatic kit. It had been a week since their rescue of the humans, but it hardly felt like any time at all had passed.

"What are you thinking about?" The deep voice of his bondmate rumbled along his skin, and he smiled.

"You and Samantha."

Zuran stretched, arching his back. "So sentimental today."

"It's an important day." Olan squared his shoulders in mock offense, but a smile spread across his lips as he leaned over to rub his face along his bondmate's arm. Today, he would get his piercing. It was something that wasn't practiced as often as it had once been, but Olan had been looking forward to this for many solars.

"We should wake her up." Zuran murmured, his lips pressing against the scars on their mate's skin where she had been claimed. They never failed to excite his blood.

In the weeks since the alliance with the humans, life had settled into a new normal. They had set to work building Samantha a hut close to the cliffs so that she could watch the suns set over the water every night or sneak out with a blanket and recreate that first night they shared with her.

Instead of spending his nights alone, staring into the darkness wishing for something more, Olan spent his nights making love to the two beings he cared for more than anything else in this world. Each day they were learning new ways to please each other, and each day, Olan thanked the All Mother for bringing Samantha to them.

His hand slid over her hip and he danced his claws along the flesh of her belly, a tingle running through him at the thought that someday she would carry their kit within her. They had spoken about the possibility and what that meant for all of them. Even though Zuran was infertile, Samantha was adamant that any kit— or child as she said humans called them—was going to have the two most amazing fathers on the planet. Looking at Zuran as he gently brushed his hands over Samantha's hair, he knew she was right.

"Fanahala," his bondmate whispered. "The suns have risen."

"Good for them." She moaned before turning her face into the soft blankets.

Olan laughed, slipping his hands underneath her to lift her into his lap. "It's time to wake up. We cannot be late this morning."

"Late for what, exactly?"

"Olan gets his cock piercing today." Zuran reminded her as he rolled out of bed naked, his own cock bouncing excitedly.

She gasped, twisting to look up into Olan's face. "That's today?"

"It is, and you have tried to sleep the morning away."

Laughter bubbled up her throat. "Hey now, who kept me up all night?"

"I'm pretty sure Olan and I were the only ones up." Zuran gestured toward his hard length, and he felt Samantha shiver just before she whimpered quietly.

"None of that," Olan chastised. "Get your pretty behind out of this bed before we have to listen to another lecture from Vasana about never being on time."

Samantha's laugh rang through their hut. He had gotten an earful from the healer the last time they showed up late thanks to her distractions, and he didn't want to be taken to task again.

Later that day, after he had given himself time to heal like Vasana had instructed, Olan heard Samantha's curious voice call out to him. "Olan? Is it time to take it off yet?"

Olan looked up from his spot on their bed to see Samantha's head peeking through the door. With a laugh, he waved her in, sitting up so that he could look under the bandage. "How about we check on it?"

Samantha came to sit down next to him as he pulled back the red seaweed wrap Vasana had applied following the piercing. While the Seyton were exceptionally quick healers, especially compared to the humans, the seaweed accelerated the process. The piercings he had gotten just that morning should have fully healed. He rubbed his hand over the metal balls that attached to the bars sitting just underneath his skin, five in total stacked horizontally along the underside of his length.

"Oh, Olan! They look amazing!" She exclaimed, leaning forward to examine the decoration more closely. "Do they hurt?" He shook his head, his cock beginning to harden under her gaze. Her brow arched, a smile tipping the corners of her mouth. "Can I touch them?"

A growl rumbled through him, and his cock jerked upward. "Please do."

Soft, warm fingers brushed lightly over his flesh, making him shiver and drawing a moan from him as his eyes closed. This little female could set him off with nothing but a look.

Samantha's hand closed around him, pumping slowly, her thumb rubbing along the metal. He felt the warmth of her mouth close over the head and his eyes shot open, immediately locking on Zuran where he stood watching the scene from the doorway, his cock already in his hand. These two were going to be the death of him.

Samantha moved her mouth along his shaft, her eyes peeking up at him from beneath her lashes as she gripped his thighs for balance. Olan's pulse pounded in his ears, as lust raced along his skin, lighting a fire in its wake. He threaded his fingers into her hair, cradling her head as she moved along his length. A shudder worked through him as she hollowed her cheeks and began to bob her head faster. With a growl of frustration, he yanked her back, pulling her from his cock as he slid from the furs.

"I need to be inside of you." His hands moved to her dress, ripping it down the middle. "I need to bury myself in that wet heat, to feel you come around me."

Zuran moved closer to them, his tail sliding up Olan's leg as he continued to stroke his own shaft. His lightning worked over his skin and through the spots along his torso and thighs as he took in the sight of Samantha's naked body.

She slid between them, licking her lips as she ran her hands down the front of their bodies, her blunt nails digging into the flesh on their torsos. "How did a girl like me get so lucky?"

"Luck had nothing to do with it." Olan chuckled. "It was the stubbornness of a certain hunter who refused to kill the alluring little Star Born."

Olan picked his mate up, gently depositing her on the bed as he licked over the place he had marked her the first time they had taken her. A soft, swirling aqua pattern had replaced the wounds, a result of the venom the Seyton produced during a claiming. It looked as if someone had cast a stone into water. Zuran's mark on the other side was its twin in every way except color. His was the same deep inky black as his skin, and Olan ran his tongue over it as well.

"I really cannot properly express to you how sexy it is to see that you carry our marks, that they will be on you forever." Her cheeks turned a deep shade of red as she moved her right hand up to gently touch the raised skin. It would never lay completely flat again, and would never lose its color. Something about that awakened a primal instinct in Olan. "*Mine.*" The word sent a thrill through his female, and the scent of her arousal permeated the air.

"Forever," she breathed.

"Spread your legs." The command came from Zuran, and Olan

watched as she hooked her fingers into the sides of her undergarments, lifting her hips so she could work the fabric down her legs until they hung off of one tiny foot. Seduction shimmering in the blue depths of her eyes, she kicked her foot, giggling as they hit the wood floor of their hut. She arched her back, grasping the band of her chest covering and unclasped it. The material slid down over her arms, and it too joined the pile on the floor.

She lay bare before them, her stomach moving with each bated breath as her heart beat like a drum in his ears. He felt her gaze trail over him as if it were a physical touch. With her teeth sunk into her lower lip, Samantha slowly parted her thighs, exposing her slick folds to them both.

Olan dipped his head to capture her skin between his teeth, nipping her here and there as he trailed his way down her body. Each nip released a breathy moan as she arched beneath the pain, clearly enjoying the way the points of his teeth felt against her. Olan swirled his tongue over each mark he made on her pale skin.

"Gods, yes," Samantha moaned, pressing her body to his as her back lifted off the furs.

"What do you desire, Fanahala?" he growled, his tongue tracing the curve just above her hip.

The sounds she made affected him deeply, in a way that he didn't understand, more than anyone ever had before her. She was meant for both of them. She was the one who had called to his hunter's soul. *The one who brought him back to me.* Overwhelming need clawed at his belly.

"Olan."

"Tell me," he demanded. "Tell me what you need."

His mouth moved lower, nipping her mound before his fingers spread her sex. His tongue slipped into her folds, sliding over her clit and exploring the flesh around it. He stroked the bundle of nerves with short, slow passes of his tongue, drawing out his bride's need. The pleasure he built was slow, on the verge of exquisite torture that had her hips moving desperately in an attempt to grind herself against his mouth.

Olan caged her hips between his arms, holding her firmly in place for the torment as he moved his tongue on the center of her pleasure, hastening his strokes over the bud that pulsed with a rhythm of its own. Zuran's hands slid to her breasts, teasing and pinching her nipples, careful to avoid cutting her with the tips of his clawed fingers.

"I need you... I need *both* of you..." she cried out as she writhed on the furs. "Please. Come inside me together. Take me together."

All Mother, save him, he might die of pleasure tonight. They hadn't tried mating with her together yet. He and Zuran had been so concerned about hurting her that they hadn't even brought it up.

If their mate wanted them both, then that's what she would have.

Olan ripped his mouth away from her, moving up so that his hips were in line with hers, meeting her blazing eyes with a wicked grin.

He pressed the tip of his cock into her tight heat, shivering at the new sensation of the beads of his piercing rubbing along her walls, stimulating his flesh as he slid deep into her welcoming body. The current of his lightning pulsed over the skin of his cock, pulling cries of pleasure from his mate as he pumped in and out of her.

She reached for Zuran, pulling his mouth to hers so that she could moan her pleasure into him as Olan prepared her cunt to take them both. He pulled out, slipping first one, then two, and three fingers along his length and back inside her, stretching her slick walls as he thrust into her. When he worked the fourth digit into her, she came, jerking hard against him as she pulsed around him, her slick coating her thighs as she gasped.

She was ready for them.

Olan pulled out of her before he could lose himself within her body, watching as she broke free from the kiss to stare daggers at him. Zuran gently grasped her arms, lifting her body so that he could slide underneath her.

Once he was in a comfortable position, Olan grabbed his bondmate's cock, sliding his own against the jerking length. A surprised groan fell from his lips when the tendrils of Zuran's cock wrapped around his, making them as close to one as they would ever get. His eyes met Zuran's, and they moved in tandem to Samantha's entrance, pushing only the tips inside of her, testing her flesh to assure themselves she could take their combined girth.

"Accept us before the All Mother, little one" Zuran whispered to her.

Her cheeks reddened and she nodded as she spread her legs wider for their entrance. He knew the All Mother watched them, giving them her blessing as she did for each of her children. The feeling of having her in this—the knowledge that they were being watched—was almost shockingly seductive. His body blazed with need as Zuran's tendrils clutched him tighter, little sparks moving along his length as his piercings rubbed against the other male.

He could do nothing but watch as his mate panted and writhed, welcoming them both into her in the same way she welcomed the All Mother. Zuran's hands squeezed her breasts, making her mouth drop open, and her hips rocked to take more of them inside. She took and took, until they were seated fully within her pulsing channel.

The hunger he had for her shouted, screamed, and demanded for him to take all of her. It begged him to show the world who she belonged to—to show everyone that she would always be theirs. Normally the claiming for the All Mother would be done in the village center with all of the other couples who were a part of the festival, but he wanted her to do that with time, when she was comfortable with it.

For now, he would proclaim her as theirs before the All Mother here; in the safety of the home they had created together.

He needed them, needed more, and when he and Zuran began to rock inside of their female with slow strokes, delving inside of her slick heat, she cried out. She was bared and stretched tightly over their girth, demonstrating a need for more as she clung to Olan's shoulders, digging her nails into him.

The world around them disappeared, and all that existed were his mates and their combined pleasure. He could feel the wisps of the All Mother's love driving them forward, urging them on to bring their female to her peak again. Her body was slick with her sweat, and he bent his head, trailing his tongue between the mounds of her breasts, moaning at the salty taste of her skin.

"Yield to the All Mother, Fanahala. Give your body and your heart as we have given ours. Give us all you have to offer."

"Yes!" she cried, falling apart beneath him.

He felt himself being sucked into her pleasure as they worked each other into a mindless frenzy. Samantha clung to him with frantically clutching fingers. When he felt her nails break his skin, he hissed, relishing in the sting. His own hands grasped onto Zuran's hips, digging his claws into the male's skin, until Zuran groaned in pleasure and guided him in the thrusts so they moved in unison.

"You belong to us," Zuran panted.

"Yes!"

All at once, their individual releases crashed through them. Zuran's tendrils milked Olan's cock until their combined seed filled her body. He was desperate to leave their scent on Samantha, to let anyone who dared to go near her knew who she belonged to. His howl joined theirs as it rose in the throes of his pleasure. Their bodies and souls intertwined, solidifying the bond that was already there for so long.

When they finally collapsed onto the furs together, Olan could hardly string any thoughts together. Exhausted, Zuran and Olan wrapped themselves around their female, taking turns kissing her as their slick chests heaved with pride.

She would always belong to them.

Olan moved his hand to gently squeeze the sides of her neck as he twinned his tongue around hers before pulling back. His hand gently eased on her throat as he moved the tips of his fingers over their marks.

"You have given us more than we ever imagined, but I offer all that I have to you."

"And I accept," she whispered.

"You will have all that I am," Zuran murmured as his hand trailed over his stomach. "Even if I can never give you a kit of my blood, I will love every single one you bring into this world."

"You're all that I need, Z. Any child we have will be just as much yours as mine or Olan's."

Tears welled in the male's eyes as he pressed his face into her neck, nuzzling her soft skin.

"You will be a worthy papa to our kits, Zuran." Olan moved his hand to cup the other male's cheek, pulling him into a deep kiss.

"Thank you," Zuran whispered before they lost themselves in the kiss.

It didn't matter if he fathered their kits or not; in his eyes, they would belong to all of them equally. Olan couldn't wait to see what their mating brought them in the future and just how many kits they would welcome into their home.

CHAPTER 35

ZURAN

"*T*his is beautiful." Samantha ran a gentle finger over the hard surface of the vilebloom. The crystal-like surface pulsed red beneath her touch. "I remember holding it in my hands the day Zuran brought me into the village, but my translator hadn't caught up yet, so I had no idea what it was about."

"It's a tool used to test fertility," Olan told her as he looked at him. "Infertile females become hunters. Unlike males, females have no physical signs. If the vilebloom glows in their hands, the way it did when you held it, then they become breeders."

"And that's why I was given to you?"

"Correct." Olan nodded.

"Do you think it would be ok if I held it again?" she asked, glancing around the central hut. They were the only ones inside at that moment.

He shrugged his shoulders. "I don't see why not."

Samantha's face lit up as she carefully lifted the bloom from its nook, eyes widening when it glowed warmly. "I wish we had a functioning lab here. I'd love to understand how this works. Maybe one day when I figure out how to get my equipment up and running, we can run a few tests."

"Some things are not meant to be understood," Zuran said softly, his eyes trailing over her face, the red glow making her skin appear to be a shade close to Olan's.

"Z…" She took a step toward him, but her foot caught on one of the soft rugs spread across the floor, and she gasped as the precious stone slipped from her grasp. The light from within winked out the moment it left her hand, and Olan rushed forward, grabbing Samantha's arm before she could hit the floor. "Shit!"

Zuran caught the bloom just before it would have smashed against the floor, sighing heavily. He had to face it: their female was incredibly clumsy at times. They all paused for a moment before the hut filled with laughter.

"Nice catch. I'm so sorry, guys."

"No harm done." Zuran smiled before setting the stone back on its display.

Olan's eyes widened. "Pick that back up."

"What? Why?"

"Stop asking questions and pick the vacking thing up," Olan demanded.

Zuran raised a brow but reached out to cup the vilebloom in his palms. It immediately lit up brighter than he had ever seen it. His heart began to race in his chest as his stomach dropped to his feet. This couldn't mean what he thought it did… It couldn't.

"There is something wrong with it," he murmured in confusion.

"What's going on?" Samantha asked, her eyes darting between them. "Explain it to the human in the room."

"It only glows when held by fertile Seyton," Olan whispered.

"Oh. Oh!" Her hand went to her mouth when she finally understood. "But that would mean—"

"That I'm fertile." Awe filled him as he turned to Olan, watching the emotions play over his face. His bondmate looked up, and a shaky breath shuddered from between his lips. Would he be mad? Would Olan hate him for this affront?

"We will visit the healer. She can confirm it." Olan grasped the back of Zuran's head, drawing him close and pressing a firm kiss to his lips.

Samantha wiggled herself in between them, wrapping her arms around Zuran. "Let's move it!"

Zuran set the stone back in its nook before they stepped out into the village, Samantha's hand slipping into his. He wasn't sure how to feel. Surely this couldn't be true. Could it? Before they even entered the hut, he paused, addressing both of his mates. "Stay here near the door. Please," he added when Samantha tried to protest. "Make sure no one interrupts Vasana during the exam?"

"But, Z, I want to be there for you..."

Zuran cupped her face in his hands before he gave her a soft kiss. "I have to do this alone."

"Okay," she whispered before he disappeared into the hut.

"Sit down and let me have a look at you," Vasana, the healer spoke softly.

Zuran took a hesitant step forward before lowering himself onto the soft seat on the floor in front of the female. His mates stood outside the door of the hut and he was sure they had their ears pressed to the wood. This was something he had wanted to do alone. If the vilebloom was wrong, he was going to need time to prepare how to deliver the news.

"Can you be sure?" His voice came out harsher than he meant it to, and he winced when Vasana arched her brow. "Forgive me. This is incredibly important for my family and I."

"I understand, hunter. Turn so that you can place your head in my lap." He did as she asked, spinning around and lying back, his head resting against her crossed legs. The healer leaned over him, placing her hands over his chest before sliding them up his shoulders and neck, stopping on the sides of his head. "Close your eyes, Zuran. Let me communicate with you."

His body tingled all over, and he swore he heard soft whispers in his mind. It seemed like hours passed while he lay there on the floor, listening to the soft but indistinguishable voices. Vasana shifted under his head as the tingle along his skin stopped and his mind quieted once more.

"You may sit up now," she said gently.

Voices outside the hut caught his attention. He frowned up at the healer just before the door was thrown open.

"You cannot go in there!" Olan's voice boomed.

"I am his mother, and he happens to be my only son! You cannot keep me away from him forever. I have let you put me off for days, but You will not continue to stop me from seeing him, *male*," a familiar voice hissed.

Zuran sighed. He had known coming here meant he would have to deal with this sometime. He couldn't avoid it any longer, and if he wanted to move on with his life, he needed to make peace with the female. The last thing he needed was for her to corner Samantha when she was out alone.

"Let her in," he called. Zuran sat up, his eyes going directly to his mama's face as she burst into the room, looking as dramatic and over the top as she had always been.

"Oh, Zuran!" she exclaimed, rushing in and dropping to his side. "What's happened to you?"

His eyes narrowed on the older female. "What are you doing here?"

"Your sister told me that she saw you come to Vasana's hut. My only son visiting the healer? I had to come and make sure you were all right." Vura had been a small kit the last time he had seen her, barely even walking when he had gone through his

Choosing Ceremony. She was not far off from her own ceremony now.

Zuran snorted. "I haven't been your son since the day I stepped out of the agmari bloom and was proclaimed a hunter."

"I didn't stop loving you simply because you became a hunter, Zuran," she protested. "You knew we couldn't follow you to the other village, not with your sister."

He knew she was up to something. Her eyes were practically swirling with deviousness. She was playing a game here, calculating her odds. Zuran had no doubt she had heard about his triad and their acceptance. Not only had Ama publicly blessed them, but they received the private approval of the All Mother. Perhaps she sought to raise her status as the mother of the first hunter to be taken in such a way.

"You never even took the time to seek me out."

His mama huffed. "Well, you were constantly on the go. How were we to know where you would be from one day to the next?"

"I meant here," he growled. "I have been living in this village long enough for you to have come to see me, to visit my mates and make up for lost time."

The stunned look she gave him told him everything he needed to know. She didn't care about him, and he doubted she ever had.

"Get out," Olan growled.

"You cannot command me, breeder," his mama snapped.

"You never even wanted a son, remember? That is what you told him the day he emerged from his bloom. So why are you here? Are you looking for recognition? Do you think coming here and playing at being a doting and caring mother will make up for the poison you spewed when you saw him as a hunter for the first and only vacking time?" Olan seethed.

"How dare you!" she gasped, her face morphing into a snarl.

"How dare *you* come here?" Vasana snapped, slamming her hand down on the floor. "The All Mother will never accept you again. This poison within you is why she has not blessed you with more kits. This is why she has taken your fertility," the healer growled, her annoyance palpable.

A sigh escaped his lips and he turned to Vasana. "The results?"

The healer pulled her gaze away from where Olan and his mama nipped at one another. "Your extended breeding heat is a consequence of your hormones building up. Each year you went without breeding, it became worse, yes?" He nodded. "Your heat will eventually cease once your hormones have leveled out or once your body senses the change within your mate during pregnancy."

"And what about his fertility?" Samantha asked from the doorway. The talking in the room ceased as they turned to look at Vasana.

The healer placed a gentle hand on his and smiled. "Everything I saw within you tells me that there should be nothing to keep you from producing a kit with your mate."

"I'm fertile?" he heard himself ask.

"That's it. Out! You need to leave," Samantha said, glaring at his mama and for once in her life, the older female didn't argue. With one last glance at him, she disappeared through the door of the hut, but he knew from the firm set of her lips that it wouldn't be the last he saw of her.

"Are you upset?" Zuran whispered as Olan crouched down in front of him.

"Upset?" His bondmate's face screwed into a frown. "Why would this upset me?"

"You are Samantha's breeder. It was one thing when we thought I was unable to father a kit, but now..." The thought that Samantha could grow and birth a life that he helped to create left him speechless.

"Zuran." His little female wrapped her arms around him, pressing soft kisses along his jaw.

Olan's hand slipped into his, and he dropped his forehead down to Zuran's. "There has never been another male more worthy than you."

CHAPTER 36

SAMANTHA

*M*aybe it was the fact that life on the ship had always been hectic, a constant flow of movement and the never-ending hum of the machines, but she loved these quiet, lazy days with her guys. Olan was busy at his desk, sewing and creating patterns for the next festival, while Zuran worked on a steadily growing pile of wooden toys for the new human children. She might have thrown in a few requests of her own for their future babies, but they were at the bottom of his very long list.

In front of her sat a beaker containing the pink seawater she had collected earlier that morning. She had brought a few of her things in to see what all might work for her, but a knock on their door made her jump, and she cursed as the beaker toppled over, spilling the water across her table. She arched a brow, glancing back at her mates before she pushed away from her makeshift lab.

A young Seyton female stood on the doorstep. Her lack of wings and the small nubs on her head where horns would soon be told Samantha that this little one hadn't gone through her ceremony yet. Her yellow eyes took Samantha in before she took a deep breath, her tail wrapping around her leg nervously as she pushed her white hair back from her face.

"Is Zuran here?"

She heard movement behind her before hands dropped down to her shoulders, gently smoothing over the expanse of them before he spoke up.

"Has anyone ever told you that you look exactly like your mama?" Zuran asked over the top of her head. "What do you want?"

A shiver worked its way through the female, but to her credit, the girl lifted her chin and didn't back away. "Please don't compare me to her. I know what it is like to live with our mama. I'm not here on her behalf."

Zuran inclined his head. "I apologize. It isn't fair to pin her behavior on you. Is there something you need from me, Vura?"

"I know I cannot make up for the time lost, or the treatment you received from our parents, but I would like to build a bond between us, separate from them." Her eyes grew wet with unshed tears as she looked up at him. "I know I should have come sooner, but I didn't want to interrupt. I wasn't sure how much time to allow for you to bond with your new mates. I'm happy for you, brother, but I understand if you wish to have nothing to do with me. I just want... I need my brother back."

"You would want a hunter for a brother? What would you get out of this? Status?"

"No, you don't even have to claim me around others. I don't care about that. I just want back what was taken from me before I even got the chance to have it. I don't care about what you are. There was never anything wrong with you, and I'm sorry I never got to tell you that."

Zuran gently moved Samantha aside before he stepped

through the doorway to wrap his arms around his sister. Her heart ached for them, and she wanted to say something, but she knew they didn't need to hear anything from her right then. They needed each other. Zuran pulled back with a smile.

"When is your ceremony?"

"I'm actually heading there now, but I wanted you to know how I felt before I go in. I was afraid the agmari bloom would make me like *her*." She shook her head. "I know that isn't how it works, but still…"

"We will come with you."

"Really?" Vura's eyes lit up.

"I've already missed so much with you. I want to be there for the next stage of your life." Zuran turned back into the house, but Samantha and Olan were already waiting. If this was important to him, it was important to them.

⁂

"*H*ow much farther?" Samantha asked, running her fingers over the pretty blue leaves of the tree as she walked by.

"Nearly there," Zuran called back to her from his position up ahead.

Olan grinned when he turned back to look at her. Her short-leg-people struggles were a never-ending source of amusement for them. She had lived here long enough to know she didn't want to be too far away from her mates in the misty forest.

"Come on, Fanahala!" Olan called.

"Stupid aliens with their stupid long legs," she mumbled, picking up her pace.

It was nice to get to know Zuran's sister, but she kind of wished that they hadn't forgotten that she was human and not nearly as fast. By the time they reached the blooms, the same ones that they had placed Vane's body into, Samantha was panting and nearly gasping for breath.

The plants were massive, sporting long, flat leaves that spread across the ground. The area between the thigh stalk and the leaves was flattened almost like a platform. With her bottom lip clamped tightly between her teeth, Samantha drew closer. If she hadn't known better, she would have sworn the plant was calling to her, inviting her over.

Come, daughter, it called.

She crouched down and ran her fingers along the leaves that spread across the ground, marveling at the fuzzy feel. As long as she didn't climb inside the plant, it seemed safe. The bloom they had put Vane in was still closed and puffed up. The stalks looked to be the same, but as she stood to investigate, something caught the toe of her boot, causing her to lurch forward and land in the middle on top of the flattened center.

Within seconds the leaves began to rise, quickly closing in on her. "Guys! Help me! This plant's trying to eat me!"

"Samantha!" She caught a glimpse of her males and Vura running toward her, but the leaves enveloped her moments before they reached her.

Great, she was being eaten by a plant. Samantha pounded her fists against the inside of her organic prison.

"Don't struggle, Fanahala." she could hear Zuran telling her.

"Don't struggle? Seriously, Z, that's your advice?"

"It's the agmari bloom. Every Seyton will step inside one of these in their lifetime."

"That's super cool and interesting, but I'm not Seyton!"

"It's okay, Samantha. We will do this together," Vura said. "The All Mother will protect you, sister."

Her anxiety began to peak just as a strange fog filled the enclosed space. Well, this was it. She'd had a good run. Darkness overwhelmed her, and she felt her body go slack.

It seemed like only moments later when the leaves around her gave a massive shudder, falling open like they hadn't just tried to digest her. "What the hell was that all about?" she asked in annoyance as she stumbled away from the plant. "I can't believe you all willingly jump into those things." Samantha turned to glare at Zuran and saw he watched her from where he sat at the base of a tree, his mouth hanging open and his bright white eyes wide. "What? Is there something on me? Where's Olan?"

"I'm here, Fanahala." Her other mate stepped quietly through the trees, the same look of shock that Zuran wore plastered across his face.

Something soft brushed the backs of her legs, causing her to screech. Jumping forward, she spun around to see what had touched her, but again, the soft brush followed her. "What the hell?" Her whole body lurched back, and she suddenly found herself off balance. She stumbled, her arms flailing, just before Zuran steadied her. From the corner of her eye, a large black mass appeared and she turned her head. *Wings?* Who did they belong to? She spun around, but they only followed her.

"Stop!" Zuran snapped, grabbing her shoulders. "You are going to damage them."

"Damage what?"

"Your wings."

Her what? Samantha grabbed at a few of the feathers, tugging sharply. A screech escaped her at the zing of pain. "Holy shit. *Holy shit*, I have wings!"

"Perhaps this is a gift from the All Mother, a sign to show you that she has welcomed you and your people," Olan suggested.

"Ama needs to see this."

"Did it change anything else?" Samantha ran her hands over her face, hair, and body. There were no horns on her head and, from the parts of her body that she could see, everything else looked unchanged. The only difference in her appearance were the wings. Massive black feathered wings.

In comparison, Zuran's little sister had changed a lot to resemble the fully grown Seyton females. Her horns now stood tall above her head, her teeth sharp, and her nails were now claws. The only thing they shared were the wings.

"What now?" Samantha asked, afraid of the answer.

"Now we go to the cliffs," his sister said excitedly.

But as they traveled back to the village, Samantha wasn't so sure she was so excited about the cliffs. There were vids from old Earth of mother birds throwing their babies from trees to teach them to fly, and she had a sinking suspicion she was about to be the baby bird in this scenario.

"Ama, I like you, really, but I'm not doing this."

The chieftess's laughter rang out over the cliffs, the same ones Zuran had brought her to after their escape from the ship. "It is not as bad as you think."

"You can do it, Fanahala. Every female does."

Samantha looked over the edge and her stomach dropped. The pink waters of the ocean lapped at the exposed rocks below. She wasn't too keen on ending up spattered against them. She shook her head. "No. Not gonna happen."

"Your wings will carry you," Ama spoke, her voice full of amusement.

"Look, I've only had them for a couple of hours. I've flapped them around; I know they can move, but how am I supposed to know if they will actually work?"

"Like this." The chieftess pressed her hand between Samantha's wings and shoved her forward.

A scream was ripped from her throat as she fell toward the rocks, her stomach twisting and flipping.

"Open your wings, Samantha!" She turned to see Ama in a freefall beside her.

The massive wings at her back twitched, catching on the wind and making her wobble some. *Open up!* Her mind screamed frantically, and suddenly she felt her new muscles respond to the command, going wide and sending her shooting up into the air in a motion that nearly had her losing her lunch.

"That's it! You've got it!" Ama encouraged, showing her how to push herself up farther.

Holy shit, she was flying. Samantha followed Ama through her paces, learning how to use her gifts. As the twin suns began to set on one of the most amazing and confusing days of her life, Samantha swooped down toward the ocean, her fingers trailing through the pink waters before she ascended to the cliff where her mates were standing, watching her with proud smiles.

She had never in her wildest dreams thought she would have a life like this; here she was with wings, two mates that adored her, and the fledgling beginnings of a new future for her people.

She was going to get to do more than experience her life. She was going to live it.

EPILOGUE

SAMANTHA

ONE YEAR LATER...

*T*he dream wrapped around her, and Samantha found herself lost to the memory as the hunter spoke to the Venium male in front of him.

"I have a family. All I want to do is get back to them," the Venium pleaded, raising his hands in a show of submission.

The hunter tilted his head as if he didn't understand him, and as time moved forward, skipping through days, she realized he hadn't understood the other male at all, but he learned. The All Mother had her hands on the hunter, helping him to decipher the foreign tongue.

"...I just need to fix my ship and then I can get home."

The hunter's head shot up in surprise when the words finally came through. "You will not be staying with us?"

"I have a family waiting for me. I need to get home."

Again, Samantha saw the days as they passed. She saw the images of the hunter helping the Venium warrior, saw the heartbreaking death of the breeder again, but this time she could hear the words the hunter spoke to the other male.

"You killed my bondmate!"

"It was in self-defense! I tried to make him listen and he attacked me. If I had done nothing, he would have killed me."

"Go! Get away from our home and never come back. None of your kind will be welcome."

"I am sorry. I never meant for any harm to come to him—"

"Leave!" the hunter roared.

Samantha could see the pain in the Venium's eyes as he watched the hunter lean over the body of his mate. "I promise to do all I can to prevent this in the future. I swear to you."

Samantha shot up in bed, her brow covered in sweat as her hand moved down to caress her abdomen. It was like this every time she had these dreams. Since getting pregnant, she had some of the most lucid and utterly strange dreams she'd ever had in her entire life; dreams of the All Mother speaking to her, dreams of memories that weren't her own.

She didn't know if the events in them were true, but Ama told her to listen and to avoid shutting out the All Mother again. Her wings fluttered behind her, and both of her males sat up in bed.

"Another one?" Olan asked.

"It's getting harder to tell what is real and what is not when I'm in them."

"You are here in our home, pregnant with our kit, and loved beyond measure." Zuran nuzzled her neck. "That is what is real."

"I know," she turned to Zuran with a seductive smile playing over her lips. "Maybe I just need to be shown that love again. I think I might have forgotten who I belong to with all of these memories bombarding me."

Her males growled in unison, laying her back on the warm furs. Olan slowly pulled her underwear off before Zuran pushed her legs open. He was bending down, leaning close to her when she felt a pinch and then a rush of fluid gush from her body.

The hunter jumped back, his tail flailing wildly as he looked down at her in horrified fascination. "How did you already find your release? I haven't even touched you. What type of dream did you have, little one?"

She gasped when the contraction hit her. "It's not release, Z. I think that was my water. The baby... the baby is coming."

"*Fuck*," Zuran mumbled. Samantha took a moment to bask in her pride. Zuran had picked up some of her favorite Earth words over the last year. She was corrupting him, one bad word at a time.

Olan was a flurry of activity, grabbing water before heating it up in a basin with his lightning, gathering the fabrics he had been busy making for their child, and assuring himself that she was as comfortable as he could make her. All the while Zuran paced, his fingers twisting his braids as he took in everything happening around him.

Hours passed by slowly as Samantha walked and bounced the pain into submission. She let her mates hold her, taking the comfort they offered. She closed her eyes as they spoke in hushed voices, encouraging her, telling her all the things they loved about her. Her body absorbed their gentle caresses, relaxing in between the painful contractions.

Samantha's mother had once told her about how she had experienced a horrible labor. It had lasted seventy-two long hours, and two of those were spent pushing. So when Samantha felt the urge to push on the third hour, she felt the panic begin to rise.

She wasn't completely unprepared though. They had spoken

with the healer about what to expect during the labor, and she knew that most Seyton women delivered quickly and assisted only by their mates. It was something breeders were trained for.

When it finally came time to push, Olan got to his knees like she asked and she squatted in front of him, her hands gripping his shoulders for support as the next contraction slammed into her.

Olan ran his hands down her back. "Fanahala, wait! I cannot catch the kit if—"

"Just shut up and stay still!" She gritted between clenched teeth as she bore down against the pain. Her whole body shook with her effort and she couldn't think straight.

"Zuran!" Olan snapped. "Come and catch your kit before they are born on the floor of the hut."

"I don't know what I'm doing! I wasn't trained for this!"

"Hands between her legs and catch whatever comes out!" he commanded.

Samantha felt him kneel down behind her, and just as she started to push again, the door to the hut was thrown open and a very frazzled Ama stumbled inside. Her hair was disheveled, and her eyes were sleepy, but Samantha had run out of time.

A sharp burning sensation rushed through her lower half, and she bore down against it again, grunting as and crying out as she felt her baby slip free of her body. The tiny, helpless first cry of their baby brought tears of relief to her eyes, and she dropped her forehead to Olan's chest, laughing as she let the sound wash over her.

She twisted in Olan's arms, smiling as she turned to face Zuran. He had their baby cradled in his big hands, staring down at them in disbelief. "What is it? What's wrong?" When she looked closer, Samantha gasped. Little black wings sprouted from their baby's back. *A daughter.* She had a daughter now.

"Ama..." Zuran whispered.

"What?" Samantha looked up, noting the awe on each of their

faces. Ama's eyes filled with tears as she stepped closer and her lightning sparked along her skin, jumping in excitement as she reached out her hand to brush across the baby's forehead. The chieftess dropped to her knees when Samantha's daughter began to cry.

"Thank you, All Mother, for your continued blessing. May she bring us wisdom, understanding, acceptance, and the will to right our wrongs."

Olan reached out to touch the baby's wings as Zuran slowly placed in Samantha's waiting arms. She looked down at her child, into her beautiful yellow eyes as she stared up at her with intelligence beyond years.

"Thank you," Ama said as she touched Samantha's face.

"I'm not sure I understand," she replied.

"An Ama is not chosen. She is born," Ama explained. "Every Ama who ever existed came into the world just like your daughter, with tiny black wings, ready to face each challenge that stands before her." Samantha watched as her little girl gripped the chieftess's finger, as if she was already communicating with the female. "As she grows, so too will her power. I believe this is why you have been suffering from your dreams."

"How did you know to come?"

"The All Mother woke me, as she has done before the birth of every Ama." She sat back, watching as the baby nuzzled against Samantha's chest. "One day, your little blessing will be called Ama, but for now, she waits for you to give her a name."

Life is going to be so wonderful with you in it. She thought as she stared down at the little miracle she and her mates had created. There was so much she would have to learn about raising the next leader of their tribe, but with her mates by her side, Samantha knew she could take on anything. She couldn't wait to watch her little girl and her family grow.

"Nari," she said with a smile, as she glanced up at her males.

"Her name is Nari." When she looked back down, she saw all of the love she felt reflected back in those pretty yellow eyes.

ALSO BY OCTAVIA KORE

Venora Mates:

Ecstasy from the Deep (Short Story)

Ecstasy from the Deep (Extended Edition)

Dauur Mates:

Queen Of Twilight

Seyton Mates:

Breaths of Desire (Short Story)

WORKS COMING SOON BY OCTAVIA KORE

Venora Mates:

Kept from the Deep

Awoken From the Deep

Kidnapped from the Deep

TO KEEP UPDATED VISIT OUR GROUP ON FACEBOOK:

https://www.facebook.com/groups/MatesAmongUs/

ABOUT THE AUTHORS

Born in the Sunshine State, Hayley Benitez and Amanda Crawford are cousins who have come together to write under the name Octavia Kore. Both women share a love for reading, a passion for writing, and the inclination toward word vomiting when meeting new people. *Ecstasy from the Deep* (*From the Depths* anthology version) was their very first published work. Hayley and Amanda are both stay-at-home moms who squeeze in time to write when they aren't being used as jungle gyms or snack dispensers. They are both inspired by their love for mythology, science fiction, and all things extraordinary. Amanda has an unhealthy obsession with house plants, and Hayley can often be found gaming in her downtime.

FACEBOOK:
https://www.facebook.com/groups/MatesAmongUs/
SIGN UP FOR OUR NEWSLETTER:
https://mailchi.mp/27d09665e243/matesamongusnewsletter
INSTAGRAM:
https://www.instagram.com/octaviakore/?igshid=1bxhtr1snonz4
GOODREADS:
https://www.goodreads.com/octaviakore
BOOKBUB:
https://www.bookbub.com/profile/octavia-kore
AMAZON:
https://www.amazon.com/Octavia-Kore/e/B0845YHRVS

Printed in Great Britain
by Amazon